BOOKS BY
ALEX BLEDSOE

Blood Groove
The Girls with Games of Blood

The Sword-Edged Blonde
Burn Me Deadly
Dark Jenny
*Wake of the Bloody Angel**

The Hum and the Shiver

*Forthcoming

ALEX BLEDSOE

Dark Jenny

AN EDDIE LaCROSSE NOVEL

TOR®
fantasy

A Tom Doherty and Associates Book
New York

DARK JENNY: AN EDDIE LACROSSE NOVEL

Copyright © 2011 by Alex Bledsoe

All rights reserved.

A Tor Book
Published by Tom Doherty Associates, LLC
175 Fifth Avenue
New York, NY 10010

www.tor-forge.com

Tor® is a registered trademark of Tom Doherty Associates, LLC.

ISBN 978-0-7653-6589-7

First Edition: April 2011
First Mass Market Edition: June 2012

Printed in the United States of America

0 9 8 7 6 5 4 3 2 1

To the memory of
Lucy Mogensen
(1964–2010)

ACKNOWLEDGMENTS

Special thanks to Marlene Stringer, Paul Stevens,
Craig Merlin Broers aka Craig of Farrington,
Krystyna Kostecka, Sjolind's Chocolate House,
Caroline Aumann, my mother Grace West,
and Valette, Jake, and Charlie.

REPORTER: What would you call that hairstyle you're wearing?

GEORGE: Arthur.

—from A Hard Day's Night (1964)

Dark Jenny

6 ary Bunson, Neceda's slightly-honest-but-mostly-not magistrate, came into Angelina's Tavern accompanied by a blast of winter air. Immediately an irate chorus erupted, some with language that implied Gary had carnal relations with livestock. Gary was used to that sort of response so he paid it no mind, and it stopped when he closed the door behind him. He shook snow from his long coat and looked around until he spotted me sitting with Liz at the bar.

"LaCrosse," he said. "There's somebody outside looking for you."

"Me? Must be a mistake."

"No mistake. He knew your name, and knew to find you here."

As a private sword jockey who either helped find the skeletons or made sure they stayed in the closet, I got my share of visitors, but not on a day like this. It was the worst winter in Muscodian history, and Neceda had it harder than most, being right on the frozen Gusay River where the wind had room for a running start.

Liz Dumont, my girlfriend, said, "Expecting someone?"

I shook my head and asked Gary, "Who is it?"

"What am I, your secretary?" Gary snapped. He straddled the empty barstool on the other side of Liz. "He's outside, go find out for yourself. Angie, get me something hot to drink, will you?"

Angelina, the tavern's owner as well as its main hostess, said to me, "You must owe someone a lot of money if they'd come out in this weather."

"I owe you more than I do anyone," I pointed out.

"That's true. But I always know where to find you."

"Maybe it's someone coming to hire you," Callie the waitress said. Even dressed in winter clothes that covered her from chin to ankle, Callie's beauty could melt icicles at ten paces. It was a shame those same icicles could probably outthink her.

Gary put both hands around the mug of hot tea Angelina placed in front of him. I watched the door expectantly. When nothing happened, I asked Gary, "So is he coming in?"

"Hell, I don't know, the snow's blowing so hard I could barely see him. He's got some kind of box with him."

"Box?"

"Yeah, you know, a box. Like a coffin or something."

He was wrong, though. It wasn't "like" a coffin, it *was* a coffin. It rested in the middle of the snowbound street. The horse that pulled it stood knee-deep in a drift. The animal had a thick winter coat and a heavy blanket draped over it from neck to tail, but still looked pretty put-out.

The blizzard had subsided to a steady flurry of flakes by the time I went outside. The figure seated expectantly atop the coffin was a small old man with a white beard, huddled beneath a cloak and heavy cap. His bright eyes peered from under the brim. He seemed unconcerned with the weather, puffing serenely on a long-stemmed pipe. The smoke vanished in the wind as soon as it appeared.

"You looking for me?" I said.

The old man looked me up and down. "Depends. Eddie LaCrosse?"

"Yeah."

He hopped to his feet, slogged to me, and reached inside his clothes. Beneath my own coat I closed my hand around my sword's hilt; a single twist would make a hidden dagger spring into my hand. To any opponent, I'd look as if I were idly scratching myself.

But the old man withdrew only a folded document with a red wax seal. "This is the paperwork." His voice was high-pitched, almost girlish, and this close his eyes looked a lot younger than his white beard implied. He gestured at the coffin. "And this is the delivery."

I tucked the document inside my coat. "Who's in there?"

He shrugged. "Beats me, pal. I was just told to deliver it."

Skids were nailed to the bottom of the coffin to ease its passage through the snow. As the man unhitched this sled of the dead from his horse, I examined it for a sign of its origin.

The first clue was its size: whoever was inside would be well over six feet tall. I'd crossed paths with a lot of big men over the years and mentally went down the list. I couldn't imagine any of them sending me their mortal remains.

When the old man finished, I dug out what seemed like a respectable tip, but he declined. "I got paid enough already. Keep your money." He swung easily into the saddle, looking even tinier on the huge horse. "Tell me, is there a whorehouse in this town?"

"Closed until the blizzard passes. Being seductive in this weather is heavy going."

"Being horny in this weather ain't that easy, either, but I'm doing my part." He looked around as if determining which way to proceed. "Oh, well. Best of luck to you, Mr. LaCrosse."

I watched him disappear into the snow. A few Necedans, bundled up so that only their eyes showed, had emerged to see what the commotion was about. It only then occurred to me that the old man had left the coffin in the middle of the street. I got behind it and, once I broke it free of the latest snow, pushed it with surprising ease over to the tavern. I left it outside the door and went back in.

"A coffin?" Callie said as I waited for my fingers to warm up. "Who would send you a coffin?"

"I think the point is who's inside it," Liz said.

"So who is it?" Gary asked.

I withdrew the document. "Don't know. Supposedly this will tell me."

Liz, Angelina, Callie, Gary, and at least half a dozen other people gathered around as I broke the seal. I glared at them until they backed off enough for me to read the message in private. It was brief, explained the coffin's contents, and made it perfectly clear why it had come to me.

It also opened a pit in my stomach big enough to swallow the coffin, the tavern, and most of the town.

I put away the document and took a long drink of my ale. Everyone watched me expectantly. At last I said, "I'm not reading it to you."

The air filled with their moans and complaints.

I held up one hand. "*But* I will tell you about it. I just need to go up to my office for a minute."

"Why?" Angelina asked.

"I need to find a file. Refresh my memory on some things. I'll be right back." I kissed Liz on the cheek and went up the short flight of stairs.

My office was in the attic above the tavern's kitchen. I hadn't used it in a month because it had no independent source of heat and the kitchen's warmth didn't rise that far in this kind of weather. The shutters were closed, and ice around the edges assured me they'd stay that way until spring.

I lit a lamp, then bolted the door behind me. It felt a little weird locking Liz out with everyone else, but this had nothing to do with her. It started long before she and I met.

My "files" consisted of rolled-up vellum sheets kept in a large freestanding cupboard beside my sword rack. They contained details about cases that I suspected might one day come back to bite me. They weren't the kind of notes the Society of Scribes kept; these were brief accounts designed to jog my memory. To anyone else they'd be mostly gibberish.

I opened the cabinet and searched through the scrolls.

They were organized, but not so anyone else could tell it. I knew the pattern and quickly retrieved what I sought. I took it to my desk, untied the ribbon, and unrolled it. I used four rocks to hold down the corners.

There they were, the names I hadn't thought about in months, in some cases years. I'd sketched a map of my travels as well, since geography had been so crucial to this case. But none of the words or drawings captured the *scale* of what happened during those long-ago days. In the blink of an eye the mightiest king in the world had lost everything. And I was there.

I didn't need the scroll to remind me about it, though. What I needed was time to choke down the emotions it brought up. I knew I'd have to tell the folks downstairs something, and it might as well be the truth. There was no one left to benefit from secrecy now. But some things always felt immediate, and some wounds, while they healed, nevertheless always ached.

At last I replaced the scroll, relocked my office, and returned to the tavern. By then even more people waited for me. Not much happened in Neceda on its best day, and there had been little entertainment during this brutal winter. The coffin made me the main attraction.

As I settled back onto my stool, Liz leaned close and said, "You don't have to tell anyone, you know. Not even me."

"I know. But what the hell, it beats more talk about the weather." To Angelina I said loudly, "A round for the house first, Angie. On me."

A grateful cheer went up. Angelina scowled, knowing she'd have to add it to my already-lengthy tab. But she poured the drinks, and Callie distributed them.

I faced the room with my back against the bar. I said, "This all happened seven years ago, before I came to Neceda. Before," I said to Liz, "I met you."

"Oho," Angelina said knowingly. "So there's a *girl* in this story."

"I knew *somebody* had to teach him what he knows," Liz said teasingly. "He's not a natural talent."

I winked at her, then continued, "I hadn't officially been a sword jockey for very long, so I was still building my reputation. I'd go somewhere for a client, and when I finished, I'd look around for another one that would take me somewhere else. That's how I got word that my services were needed in Grand Bruan."

My listeners exchanged looks. These days the island kingdom of Grand Bruan was primarily known as the site of the most vicious ongoing civil war in the world. Unofficial estimates said more than half its population had fled or been killed, and the land was overrun with invaders, mercenaries, and pirates. But it hadn't always been that way, and they knew the story behind that, too. Hell, everyone did.

The tale of King Marcus Drake and the Knights of the Double Tarn had passed into legend almost before the great ruler's corpse was cold. Thirty years earlier the island of Grand Bruan, a chaotic place of warring petty kingdoms, was on the verge of total chaos when a young boy did something no grown man had ever been able to do: he withdrew the magical sword Belacrux from the ancient tree where it was embedded. This signified that he was the true, rightful ruler of all the land.

Naturally there were those who disagreed, but they hadn't

reckoned with young Marcus's determination, and his core allies: the wise adviser Cameron Kern, the great knight Elliot Spears, and the brotherhood of warriors known as the Knights of the Double Tarn. Every child could recite their great deeds of arms in unifying the island.

Then came the golden time, when Drake and his queen, Jennifer, naturally the most beautiful woman who ever lived, ruled in fairness and grace. Laws were passed to protect the common folk, and peace reigned for a generation.

But the brightest light casts the darkest shadow, and in that shade dwelled Ted Medraft, bitter knight and jealous nephew of the king. He fomented a rebellion and forced a final great battle. Drake killed him, but Medraft mortally wounded the king. Drake died, the land returned to chaos, and the great sword Belacrux disappeared, awaiting the hand of the next destined ruler, who had so far not appeared.

The ballads and broadsheets kept coming, though, embellishing the tale until it was an epic of how hubris and fate brought down even the loftiest men. In the seven years since Drake's death, he'd become such a literary figure that some people believed he'd never existed. In another ten years, he'd be a full-fledged myth.

But he *had* existed, and the truth was a little different from how the ballads told it. I might be the last man living who knew it.

I continued, "My client was a Grand Bruan noblewoman named Fiona, and she had connections. As a result I found myself at a party given by Queen Jennifer Drake at Nodlon Castle on the island's west coast."

I paused long enough to take a long draft of my own ale. A

lot of things in my past had grown hazy with the passage of time, but not this. The details all came back in a rush, from the odor of the banquet hall to the unmistakable coppery smell of blood thick on the wind. And the look on a king's face as a woman rose from the dead before him. . . .

odlon Castle was built so close to the edge of the cliff overlooking the western ocean that first-time observers always wondered why it didn't just fall off. Most assumed this precarious-looking position was due to erosion, but in truth it was entirely on purpose: the king's former adviser Cameron Kern had designed it as a psychological ploy to prevent enemy troops from trying to scale those same cliffs in an attack.

That had been in the old days, during the wars of unification. And by *old*, I meant twenty years from the summer I arrived. That might not sound like much time, but the changes in Grand Bruan were so significant that its prior incarnation might as well have been a century ago.

Nodlon Castle's big central hall was freshly and thoroughly scrubbed. Flowers, banners, and tablecloths tarted it up in anticipation of its royal guest, Queen Jennifer Drake. Chauncey DeGrandis, the castle's current lord, lumbered about greeting people as if he were doing the queen a favor by allowing her to visit. I moved away whenever I saw his three-hundred-pound bulk approach, which was easy since his outfit was done entirely in shades of yellow.

At that moment I hid among a group of puffy-sleeved lords and ladies in pointy hats, all of us laughing at some story whose beginning I'd already forgotten. I hoped they didn't laugh too hard: they had on so much makeup that if they cried, they might erode. And that included some of the men.

I wore no makeup, but in my new suit, fresh haircut, neatly trimmed beard, and expensive manicure, I blended right in; that was the point of a disguise, after all. Since I had no visible female escort, I was set upon like a ham bone tossed among starving dogs. There wasn't a woman present who didn't look me over as thoroughly as the weight guesser at a fair, as either a potential son-in-law or possible bedmate when her husband was away. This wasn't because I was particularly handsome or noticeably wealthy; all that counted was that I was new meat. For those who never suffer from hunger, the only variety comes from taste.

And that was the source of the delicious irony. Long before I decided to become a private sword jockey, I'd grown up in an atmosphere identical to this. The court politics in far-off Arentia might be different in detail, but ass-kissers and sycophants were the same all over. Although I'd left behind that world of pomp and suck-uppery, I now relied on my memories of it to complete my current job. Oh, the delightful paradox.

It was hard not to tease these soft-bellied, overpainted

glowworms. Heck, even the men wore too much eye shadow. A lot of them weren't native to the island; they'd swarmed here from other kingdoms after the end of the wars, bringing gold to shore up the economy in return for status they could never achieve in their home countries. They taught the Grand Bruan nobles all the arts of courtliness, as well as its subdisciplines of gossip, polite treachery, and smiling through your fangs.

I took another drink of the free wine, top-barrel stuff only kings and high priests could afford. My head felt it a bit, and I knew I should slow down, but this wasn't a dangerous assignment, or a complex one.

"So, Baron Rosselac, what do you think?"

I blinked. I had picked my alias, an anagram of my real name, without too much forethought and kept forgetting to respond to it. I used the arch, proper tone of someone showing off his education and said to the matronly woman, "Oh, I'm sorry, my lady. My thoughts must have been distracted by your overwhelming beauty. What were we discussing?"

In response, she made a noise I assumed was laughter. It sounded more like the defensive chatter of some small rodent. "Oh, Baron Rosselac, you're making me blush."

It was hard to tell; she wore enough white face powder to ballast a frigate. "More color to those cheeks will only add to your loveliness," I said with a slight bow. "Were we still debating the necessity of adequate leisure time for serfs and vassals?"

"Why, no, we finished that discussion ages ago. I asked if you thought Queen Jennifer would wear her crown jewels tonight."

"Oh, of course she will," I responded with faux certainty. "Why, just today I heard from my friend Lord Huckleberry— you all know *him,* don't you?"

They quickly affirmed they, too, were intimately acquainted with my oddly named and entirely fictional best pal.

"Well, he told me in confidence that the queen would be wearing a whole new set of jewelry tonight, some . . ." I stopped, looked around in mock discretion, and motioned them all in close. The tips of the women's tall hats tapped against each other above me. "Some of the jewels worn in places where they can't even be seen by anyone other than the king!"

Handkerchiefs flew to cover heavily painted mouths, and eyes widened beneath eyebrows plucked away and redrawn as thin arches. The men couldn't repress lascivious grins and brow waggles. "Now, don't spread it around," I cautioned. "I wouldn't want dear Huckleberry to think I'd broken confidence with him."

"Oh, of course not," a thin woman assured me.

"Won't breathe a word," added a corpulent fellow with bulbous, lavender trousers. Naturally, I knew my little rumor would be spread all over the hall before they tapped the next wine cask. Eventually someone would point out that there *was* no Lord Huckleberry, and a reverse wave of social reprisal would travel back along the gossip channel, with any luck crashing down on the very powder puffs around me. I'd be off the island by then, so I'd miss the ultimate punch line, but I got a warm feeling from setting it in motion.

My eye fell on the big Drake family banner stretched across the wall behind the throne Queen Jennifer would soon occupy. The red dragon emblazoned on it was not snarling or breathing fire, but instead held the island of Grand Bruan protectively in one claw and looked over the room with the steady, even gaze of a concerned but supremely self-confident nanny. The other claw held a sword with distinctive dragon designs along the blade: this was Belacrux, King Marcus Drake's royal talisman, supposedly unbreakable and invincible. It was probably the best-known single weapon in the world.

Fame had come hard and sudden to Marcus Drake. He'd claimed the crown at fifteen, winning over the other warlords with both charm and force, and used this alliance to drive the mainland invaders back across (or into) the sea. Now Grand Bruan stood as a shining example of the way a kingdom ought to be run, and rulers the world over were being held to Drake's considerable standard. He'd set the bar pretty high, especially with his insistence on a rule of law that applied to nobles as well as citizens, a clear path to justice for the peasantry, and over a decade of peaceful relationships with the island's offshore neighbors. Even when they fought each other, they left Grand Bruan alone, because no one wanted Drake breathing fire down his neck.

That titter that made my teeth gnash broke my train of thought as someone else amused my rotund lady friend. It reminded me of the ways Grand Bruan was exactly like every other kingdom: no matter how noble the man at the top or how loyal the citizens at the bottom, those in the middle would always serve their own interests first. Every king learned that truth eventually, even Marcus Drake; and that same truth kept guys like me in business.

It was also the reason for the party I'd crashed. Given that

Drake's reign depended on a network of internal alliances, it made sense that he occasionally gathered his landed-gentry supporters for some free booze and a pep talk. With no legitimate complaint against him, any rebellion would be driven by purely personal malice, and he knew that no one stayed mad at a guy who regularly fed them and got them drunk. The pageantry on such occasions also let him show off his power and warned any potential insurgents that they'd have quite a fight.

Even the great King Marc couldn't be everywhere at once, though, so today Queen Jennifer would take up the slack. Her grand entrance would mark the beginning of the festivities and mean we could finally get something to eat. I looked forward to her arrival not just because I needed something in my stomach to pad out the wine, but because Jennifer Drake was, by conservative estimate, one of the two or three most beautiful women in the world. I wanted to verify that for myself.

I also kept my eye on the far side of the room, tracking the skulking form of the man who'd brought me here. Kenneth Spinkley, aka the Lord Astamore, leaned against the stone wall. His gaze flitted around the room. Astamore was a skinny, pasty-faced guy with the twitchy demeanor of a ferret. He wore ritzy clothes in the latest Bruanian style, something that did not accent his best qualities. A huge tapestry hung beside him, its life-size depiction of warriors in battle making him look as if he were fleeing the carnage. I could've quietly confronted him at any time and done what I was hired to do, but I held off to see who approached him. My client would definitely want to know.

"I heard," said the spindly man beside me, "that dear Marc

never lets Jennifer take her real jewels on these jaunts. He doesn't trust his subjects in these outlying castles, even this one, which trains all his knights."

"Does your friend Huckleberry have any insight on that?" the blushing woman asked me.

"I imagine Jennifer does what Jennifer wants," I pooh-poohed, and batted my eyes for emphasis. When I turned away from the smug chuckles, Astamore had vanished. That figured; the instant I take my eye off the little dung beetle, he finally makes his move. "You'll excuse me," I said with a bow, "but I must find the nearest water closet."

"Do return," the matron said. "We have so much more to discuss."

"And you must tell us more about that old rascal Huckleberry!" the man beside her called after me. "I'm dying to know what he's been up to of late."

It may have been the "great hall," but it wasn't that big a room; where the hell did Astamore go? The main doors were barred and guarded; along the walls were discreet service entrances, and behind the raised throne platform a guarded door led to the private chambers. I trusted that my peripheral vision would've alerted me if Astamore had moved toward any visible exit, but it was as if he'd just melted away where he stood.

Trailing muttered *Pardon me*'s, I went to the last spot I'd seen him. I confirmed that he couldn't have reached any door without my noticing. Finally the obvious occurred to me and I peeked behind the tapestry. Sure enough, there was yet another service doorway.

I slipped behind the cloth, opened the door, and entered the small room. Although not stocked for this particular banquet, it was getting plenty of use. A young lady was bent forward over a table with her huge dress pushed up to her waist. Astamore stood behind her, his frilly pants down around his knees. They had their backs to me—not an appetizing sight—and were so single-minded they didn't hear me enter.

"Oh, yes!" the girl cried in that fake, ego-stroking way some women use in a clinch. "Lance me, sir! *Lance me!*"

Now I *did* need that water closet. I said, "Let's hope they wash that table before they use it again."

It's always fun interrupting an illicit tryst. Astamore had such a firm grip on the young lady's waist that when he turned toward me, he inadvertently dragged her off the table, toppling a neat stack of ale mugs onto the stone floor. The lovers fell in a loud tangle of expensive silk, pasty flesh, and shattered crockery.

"Who the hell are you?" Astamore demanded as he struggled to fasten his trousers.

"The name's LaCrosse, Eddie LaCrosse. I was hired to keep an eye on you, Lord Astamore."

"Hired?" he exclaimed. He got to his feet and, ignoring the disheveled girl, tried to salvage his dignity. "By whom?"

As if he didn't know. "Fiona. The *Lady* Astamore."

He bit back whatever else he was about to say. The girl finally got to her feet, turned to me, and cried, "Oh, thank you, sir! He was compromising my honor!"

"Compromising the hell out of it, from what I saw," I said. "What's your name?"

"Deborah," she said, managing a curtsy despite the unmentionables around her ankles. "My father is—"

I nodded toward the door. "Save the damsel act, sweetheart, this has nothing do with you. Hit the flagstones."

She scurried for the opposite door that led into the kitchens. "Keep your mouth shut, whore!" Astamore cried after her, but his voice cracked on the last word.

We stood quietly for a long moment, the noise of the party audible outside. Finally he said with a gulp, "So did Fiona send you to . . . kill me?"

He really *was* a weasel, and I thought about tormenting him a little. But that would just keep me here longer, and the fun had gone out of the game. "No, I'm just supposed to confirm her suspicions about you. I'd say I have."

"You don't have any proof," he protested, but there was no juice in it.

"This isn't one of your king's law courts, Ken. *Your* money is actually *her* money, and we both know it's the reason you married her. And if she wants to, she can take it all away. That would put a crimp in the ol' lifestyle, now, wouldn't it?"

He nodded, his eyes freshly wet. "What *does* she want?"

"You on a shorter leash." I recalled homely, tearful Lady Fiona as she told me of her suspicions about him. This jackass's infidelity had damn near broken her naïve heart. "So go home, Ken. Be nice to your wife. Be grateful for her, in fact: she's rich enough that she *could* have had you killed. You're a lucky man."

He was about to reply when we heard the horns announcing the imminent arrival of Queen Jennifer Drake. "May I stay for dinner?" he implored in a tiny voice.

I shrugged. "Sure, why not? But keep it in your pants,

Ken, or I might just have to cut it off so your wife can lock it up somewhere."

I followed him back into the great hall. We joined the neat rows of revelers standing on either side of the long table to watch the pageant of arrival.

A dozen tough-looking men in shiny show armor bracketed the royal table. This was a contingent of the famous Knights of the Double Tarn, trained in this very castle and trusted with accompanying the king's most valuable property. But these were no raw recruits; they were veterans of Drake's campaigns, old enough to have fought under the king in the wars of unification. They now served as overqualified bodyguards.

The big main doors faced directly west, so the evening sky provided a glorious backdrop. To the cadence of a fresh fanfare, two small girls spread flower petals along the path the queen would take. Next came a dozen fresh graduates of the knight training school, who flanked either side of the flowered walkway.

Four exceptionally beautiful young women appeared next, daughters of Drake's allies sent to serve his court and perhaps snag a suitable husband. They kept their heads demurely lowered as they stepped in pairs to either side of the door.

At last, accompanied by a longer, fuller blast of horns, Queen Jennifer Drake strode into the room.

It was worth the buildup.

She had wavy brown hair loose around her shoulders and enormous green eyes above a delicate nose and full, wide lips. Her emerald-green dress clung exquisitely in all the right spots. From the sparkle, I guessed that just one tasteful earring probably cost more than I made in a year. She was only in her thirties but radiated the power and assurance that always shone from rich, beautiful women. She'd been queen for her entire adult life and had settled gracefully into the part.

After pausing to be admired, she proceeded at that slow, measured royal pace down the length of the room. She made eye contact and nodded to various attendees as she proceeded. If it was insincere, it was a good act, because she kept up an almost constant murmur, greeting people by name and acknowledging bows and curtsies. Part of any queen's job is to keep the people on her husband's side, and Jennifer Drake had mastered it.

When she reached the royal table, two of her maids pulled out the chair, another took the queen's trailing cape from her shoulders, and a third tapped the goblet with a silver knife to get everyone's attention. As if anyone in the room watched anything else.

Queen Jennifer smiled. It wasn't quite as bright as the summer sun. In a rich, commanding voice she said, "Lord and Lady DeGrandis, my friends of Nodlon Castle, Marc and I thank you for hosting this event. As you know, this special dinner is being held in honor of the brave men dedicated to our country's service who learn the skill of arms inside these very walls. We owe our peace and prosperity to the soldiers trained at Nodlon, and we wish to show our gratitude."

The polite applause grew more intense wherever the queen's eye happened to fall. She waited patiently until it faded.

"To continue, I'd also like to introduce my escorts for the evening, who have accompanied me all the way from our main court at Motlace for this occasion. They are the country's champions, and my personal friends. They have proven their valor more times and in more ways than I can say. And someday, the men trained at this very spot will fill their ranks. So lords and ladies, gentlefolk all, I give you the heroes of Grand Bruan, the Knights of the Double Tarn."

To another blast of horns, the men snapped ramrod straight, hands clasped behind their backs, eyes fixed on a spot slightly above the heads of the crowd. The sound of their boots striking the stone floor in unison rang out.

I noticed a couple of the knights cast decidedly uncomfortable glances toward the queen, as if something in the ceremony bothered them. But before I could pursue the thought, something else caught my eye.

Yet another beautiful young woman stood outside a serving door. She held a silver tray loaded with apples, and as I watched, a newly minted knight at the end of the line surreptitiously snatched one from it. He grinned at the girl, who blushed and returned the smile. No one else seemed to notice.

And that's how it starts, I mused. In a year's time this girl was likely to be a disgraced single parent living in squalor and supporting herself and the knight's bastard child with the very physical beauty that led to her downfall. Within five years she'd be reduced to simply begging, and by the time her illegitimate offspring was ten, she'd be dead. And all because she caught the eye of some handsome knight at a banquet.

I shook my head. Wow. When did I become so completely cynical? No wonder I didn't have many friends.

"And I have a special gift for one of our most notable knights," Jennifer continued. "Sir Thomas Gillian is my husband's cousin and was knighted on our wedding day. Since then, he has proved himself in both combat and kinship as a worthy knight indeed." She gestured with one delicate hand, and the girl carrying the fruit started toward her at a slow, ceremonial pace.

"As anyone who's ever hosted him knows, Tommy has a taste for apples," Jennifer said with a smile. "The first thing he always asks is, 'How may I serve you, Your Majesty?' followed almost immediately by, 'Are there any apples about?'"

There was polite laughter at this.

"Tonight, in his honor we have apples that I picked myself in the royal orchard and brought personally from the palace, so that everyone, including Thomas, might truly know the esteem in which he's held." The girl knelt before the queen, who selected an apple and motioned for the honored knight to step forward.

Gillian was roughly the same age as the queen, with long black hair pulled back in a ponytail and the kind of solid, square build that served well in battle. As she handed him the apple, there was a moment of grim, serious eye contact completely at odds with the frivolous situation. It reminded me of the uneasiness I'd noticed earlier in the other knights. Then he lifted the apple to his mouth.

Just before he bit into it, a ragged cry of pain filled the room. The young knight who'd earlier snatched the apple from the tray fell forward onto the stone floor with a wet, painful smack. He immediately went into violent convulsions.

With cries of horror, the demure lords and ladies bravely scurried away from him. The veteran knights, as such men will, immediately drew their weapons and looked for the next threat rather than aiding the victim of the last one. Most of the new soldiers followed suit, although several just froze.

I pushed through the crowd in time to see the young knight stop thrashing and lie completely still in that final, unmistakable way. His eyes were wide-open, and his tongue stuck out between his teeth.

I knelt beside the man—hell, a *boy*, with a beard that was no more than a few ambitious wisps and a neck still dotted with pimples. Black foam oozed from between his clenched teeth, and his body had already so swelled so much that his thin show armor could barely contain him. His hand still clutched the apple.

I pried the piece of fruit from his fingers, careful to use a handkerchief so I wouldn't touch it, and sniffed. Under the normal juice smell was the distinctive pungent odor I expected. *Poison.*

In the silence, a voice I instantly recognized called out, "That man killed a knight!"

I looked up sharply. Between the pale faces at the front of the crowd, Lord Astamore glared at me with a mean, triumphal grin. "He slipped him some poison! I saw it! Don't let him get away!"

"He's a murderer!" another man cried.

"Yes, I saw it, too!" chimed in a third voice

"Now, wait a—," I started to protest, but suddenly strong hands grabbed my arms and yanked me to my feet. Two Knights of the Double Tarn held me between them, and from the looks on their faces I knew I wasn't going anywhere. I wore no sword, and the knife I always carried in my boot might as well have been on the moon for all the good it could do me.

Then a third knight, bigger and older than the rest, approached me. I decided he deserved all my attention. He held out his hand for the apple. "I'll take that." He wrapped the handkerchief around it and put it in a pocket. "And who are you?"

Murder was too serious for aliases. "I'm Edward LaCrosse."

"There's no LaCrosse on the guest list."

"You know every name by heart?"

"Yes." He said it with such certainty I couldn't doubt him. "So what are you doing here?"

"Being in the wrong place at the wrong time, apparently."

"I'll decide that."

Lord DeGrandis lumbered out of the crowd. His red face contrasted sharply with the yellow frills at his neck. "Why are you standing there? *Execute* this man!"

"No one's getting executed," the older knight said, "until I get answers."

"This is *my* castle, Sir Robert," DeGrandis boomed.

Sir Robert faced him steadily. "Then give some orders."

With a wave of his hand, DeGrandis said, "Execute this man!"

The knights holding me neither moved nor responded.

"Did you hear me?" DeGrandis said. It came out high, whiny, and desperate. "I'm the chancellor of this training school, the lord of this castle, and I gave you an order!"

"Did you hear anything?" the man holding my right arm said.

"Just a big yellow fly buzzing around," the other responded. Neither smiled.

To my handlers Robert said, "Secure this gentleman in one of the serving rooms. I'll speak to him in more detail shortly."

"Hey, wait a minute," I said as they pulled me away. "You know this kid was already dead when I got to him, right?"

"I know he's dead *now*," Robert said, then turned to the crowd. "Ladies and gentlemen, I ask that you remain calm. No one's leaving the hall until we know more about what happened, so I suggest you take advantage of the free food and drink."

Trying to take on a roomful of Knights of the Double Tarn would be efficiently fatal, so I let them drag me away without a fight. The knights handed me over to a pair of the newly minted soldiers, whose grip was no less formidable. "Take him into a side room and sit on him," one veteran said. "Sir Robert will be along shortly to question him."

"Yes, sir," the first soldier replied, and they quickly hustled me out of the hall. Great, I thought, a whole new irony: in trying to help a stranger, I'd fallen into the middle of something deadly here in Grand Bruan, where I knew no one and had no resources at all. Who was laughing now?

My keepers slammed me down so hard the wooden chair cracked from the impact. "Sit there and be quiet," one of them snarled. He'd clearly perfected it in a mirror and would need a lot more practice before it had the desired effect. Given my circumstances, though, I didn't point that out.

They'd taken me to a tiny room outside the main hall. I was far enough away that I heard nothing except the breathing of my minders, the occasional pop from the torch outside the door, and my own thundering heart. It wasn't a cell, though; it was filled with wooden crates, box-laden shelves, and the distinctive odor of disuse. Most castles were full of forgotten rooms like this, and I was grateful it wasn't a fully equipped interrogation chamber. Maybe it was all there was: had the castle been so thoroughly decommissioned for peacetime training that no prison cells remained?

"Hold out your arms," the other one said. He produced a pair of elaborately engraved manacles. A few links of chain attached each wrist cuff to a thick metal disk the size of a saucer. He snapped the manacles around my wrists.

My guards seemed to think pitching me into the chair and cuffing me meant I could no longer hear them talk. "Did you see the look on his face?" the taller man asked his friend. "He was spitting up black foam. *Black foam*."

"I know," his compatriot agreed. He had short sandy hair and was missing half his left earlobe. His voice shook a little.

"And did you see the look on the *queen's* face?" the other said. He had one of those high, insinuating voices that seemed naturally suited to gossip. "She was aiming for Gillian."

"No, man, I don't believe that. She's the queen."

"She's also a woman, and they're a hell of a lot meaner than men. That fancy headband doesn't make her any less female."

"Don't let Kay hear you say that," the first soldier whispered urgently. "You'll have us both peeling potatoes for a week."

"Look, you stand guard here. I'm going back upstairs."

"Me? Why do I have to stay?"

"Because I have seniority."

"A week and a half is not seniority."

"I was commissioned before you, soldier," the taller man said with a quavering attempt to pull rank. "That's a fact. So you stay here and wait until someone relieves you."

The taller man departed. The remaining guard stood with his back to the door, hand on his sword hilt, and watched me with what he assumed was an ass-puckering glare. I smiled, closed my eyes, and settled in to wait, a skill I'd mastered long ago.

Finally big Robert, who knew the names of all the guests, came into the room. His expression was grim, and he loomed over me with practiced intimidation. His muscles bulged under clothes about half a size too small. I got the feeling that, if he grew angry enough, arrows would bounce off his bare skin.

He slapped my foot off my knee and said, "If you're looking for trouble, wise guy, I come from where they put the edge on it. So your best choice would be to answer my questions truthfully and completely."

"I agree." I deliberately crossed my leg again. He was using a standard tactic: make the suspect think only the interrogator stands between him and certain death. It worked, unless the suspect was someone like me.

"So who are you?" he demanded.

"Like I already told you, my name is Edward LaCrosse. I'm on your guest list as Edward, the Baron Rosselac."

His eyes narrowed. "Why the alias?"

"I'm here on business."

"What kind of business?"

"A tail job. There was a slight chance the man I was hired to follow might have heard my real name, and I didn't want him to see it on the list. Seemed harmless enough at the time."

"A sword jockey," Sir Robert said disdainfully. The reaction didn't surprise me. Soldiers who'd bought into the system had little use for people like me, who knew the system but worked outside it. It annoyed them that we used our job skills in our own service, not that of the local monarch. The argument that the skills belonged to the soldier, not to the king or commander, generally fell on unsympathetic ears.

"A man's gotta eat," I said.

"Who were you following?"

I shook my head. "That's confidential."

"Somebody's been killed here, pal. Don't get cute."

"I can't help that," I deadpanned. "But my guy had no more to do with it than I did."

Sir Robert didn't smile. "How'd you get an invitation?"

"My client arranged it."

"And who's your client?"

"Like I said, that's my business."

He grabbed the manacle chain and pulled it until I was forced to lean forward. "I could make your business my business."

"You wouldn't like it, the hours are awful."

He was silent, but his face flushed red, revealing the white lines of old scars. He released the chain, and I put my hands nonchalantly behind my head. The hanging metal disk tapped the chair back. "Harrigan," he said to the young man guarding me, "step outside."

Harrigan blinked uncertainly at this breach of procedure. "Uh . . . you know, maybe I shouldn't—"

"Maybe you shouldn't question a direct order!" the big man roared. "Don't they teach you that here?"

"Yes, sir," the youngster said, and went into the hall. His last glance did not bode well for my immediate future.

My interrogator kicked the door shut without turning away from me. "It's just you and me now, sport. So why did you kill Sam Patrice?"

"I didn't kill anybody and you know it. And you can lay off the psychotic-troll act, I'll cooperate as much as I can without compromising my client."

He smiled, an expression about as friendly as a bone saw. "A sword jockey with a conscience. I should tell you that the Bodice Brigade in the banquet hall is already howling for your hide. Maybe I should just hand you over to them. Under all that lace and powder they're vicious little bastards, especially in a mob."

"So if I cooperate, what then? Do you plan to just keep me in this closet until they all go home, then send me on my way?"

"Depends on what you tell me. Give me the truth, and then I'll decide what to do."

I put my manacled hands back in my lap and thought this over. I felt bad for betraying my client, but under the circumstances protecting a cow pie like her husband seemed pointless. Plus I got a good vibe from Sir Robert, who seemed decent enough under the gruff: he hadn't hit me with an iron bar or heated up any metal tongs. "Okay," I said at last. "I was hired by Fiona, the Lady Astamore, to follow her husband around and catch him dipping his ladle in the wrong vat. It wasn't difficult. I delivered his wife's warning, planned to grab some free food courtesy of Queen Jennifer, and then leave to report to my client."

"Anyone here who can confirm that?"

"Sure. Lord Astamore. But he probably won't. He was the soloist in the choir singing for my blood."

Sir Robert cocked his head and narrowed his eyes. "So why should I believe you?"

"My angelic smile. Or because I had no motive to kill the dead guy. I didn't even know his name until you told me just now."

"You say."

"Yeah, I say."

He scowled thoughtfully, and a long moment hung silently between us. Finally he said, "The 'dead guy' was Samuel Herbert Patrice. He'd only been a knight for a few weeks. Graduated from the previous class here, so it was a big deal for him to come back for this ceremony. He got to show off for all his underclassman friends."

"Did you know him?"

"I know them all. Wiped most of their noses at one point or another. Sam was no better or worse than any of them." Sir Robert leaned back against the wall. "Okay, if you're who you say you are, then you had no motive."

"Or opportunity," I said, pressing my advantage. "He ate a poisoned apple that, according to your own queen, hadn't been out of her sight since it left the tree. When could I have tampered with it?"

He chewed his lip thoughtfully. "There is that," he quietly agreed.

"Yeah. So now that I've told you everything I know, if it's all the same to you, I'll just quietly slip out the back door and get out of here." I held up my wrists. "You've got an internal crime here, and I'm glad to be an outsider."

He frowned and made no move to unlock the manacles. "Why do you say it's 'internal'?"

"It's pretty clear that someone wanted to kill the famous Thomas Gillian. He's the one with the fruit fetish, and he'd also be the *dead* one if Patrice hadn't snatched that apple at the last minute. And I'll tell you something you missed: poisoning takes both cowardice and a certain level of intelligence. They say it's a woman's weapon, but in my experience men are just as fond of it. If I were you, I'd look over your guest list for a well-educated minor official who might have once crossed paths with Gillian and still holds a grudge."

I shook the manacle chain slightly to get his attention. He ignored it and said, "What makes you think the killer's here? Why not just poison the apple back at Motlace and send it on its way with the queen?"

"Human nature. Someone who goes to all this trouble would want to be on hand to see it play out."

Sir Robert looked impressed. "You're right, I hadn't thought of that."

"I make my living understanding people's worst tendencies. Now will you please take these bracelets off me?"

"Maybe." Again his eyes grew narrow. "Or maybe you're the kind of guy who poisons people and then acts like the kind of guy who *doesn't* poison people."

I laughed. He got bonus points for tenacity. "Yeah, I could be. And I bet you didn't get to such a high rank by being a bad judge of people, Sir . . . Robert, is it?"

He smiled sadly, wearily at me. "Robert Kay, King Marcus's seneschal."

A seneschal, I knew, was an administrative second-in-command in charge of making sure the day-to-day affairs of state ran smoothly. "Tough job," I said.

"Nah, not usually. But definitely today."

I was about to mention the cuffs again when a sharp knock

rang on the door. Kay opened it, and Harrigan, almost white with apprehension, crisply saluted. "Uh, excuse me, Sir Robert," he said with a dubious glance at me. "I'm sorry to interrupt you, but there's a problem."

"Oh, good," Kay muttered, and stepped outside to hear the report. He didn't close the door all the way, which meant I was probably off the suspect list, but he also didn't leave it open as an invitation to depart. When he returned, he was even grimmer. "We've got *three* problems now," he said as he closed the door again. "First is the dead man, of course. Second, those damn courtiers expect to see *your* head on a pike by the gate before dawn. You've embarrassed Lord DeGrandis, and to them that's far worse than any lowly knight's murder."

"What's the third problem?"

Kay paced to the nearest shelves. "The rest of the Double Tarn knights. *They* don't believe you had anything to do with it, at least. Most of them saw Sam fall before you were anywhere near him."

"And that's a problem why?"

He met my eyes and said, "Because they think it was Queen Jennifer."

"Really? I thought everybody loved her."

He shook his head. "Everybody loves Marc. They tolerate her."

I recalled the beautiful, regal figure I'd seen and wondered if the kindness and consideration in her demeanor really *had* all been an act. It wasn't unheard of for public and private faces to be completely at odds, but I hoped I'd learned enough to see through it. "Is she that bad?"

"Not at all. I've spent a fair bit of time with her, and she's generally a decent person. She had her rough times at first, learning to rule while Marc was off fighting, but she made it through." Kay shook his head. "Some lines, though, even the nicest people shouldn't cross."

I waited, but he offered no additional explanation. Finally I said, "You're not going to take these off me, are you?"

"I'm deciding. You make a better culprit than the queen, at least for public consumption."

"I can see that. But why would the queen even *want* to kill one of her own bodyguards? Especially at a banquet where everyone was watching?"

He gnawed his lip again before finally saying, "You broke professional silence for me, guess I can do the same for you. You ever heard of Elliot Spears?"

He was the best of the Double Tarn knights, legendary for both his battle skills and chiseled good looks. He wasn't a native of Grand Bruan, but had come to the island to join Drake's campaign back when the young king was first crowned and became, by all accounts, Drake's closest friend. "Sure. Who hasn't?"

"That's true. He's our best and bravest. And he's the king's best friend." He fell silent and looked at the floor.

"But?" I prompted.

"Well, he hasn't been around much since peace broke out. Most of the knights believe the reason is that Elliot and Jennifer were . . . well, jousting in private behind Marc's back. Rumors that the queen made secret visits to his castle, and so on."

"Ah. So is Spears here?"

"Elliot? Nah. He spends most of his time at his own place. They say it's because the queen broke his heart when she wouldn't leave Marc for him." Kay scratched the back of his neck thoughtfully. "And that's a *kind* of motive, I suppose. I mean, if Jennifer wanted to assert herself, remind the knights that she as well as Marc held the power of life or death over them . . ." Kay spread his hands in a shrug.

When he offered nothing else, I asked, "So am I free to go?" Again I held up my wrists.

Kay's eyes narrowed. "You know . . . you seem to know a lot about this kind of thing. Motives, behavior, that stuff. As you can probably tell, I really don't. I just kill people trying to kill me and train other people to do the same thing."

I just looked at him.

He continued, "If you're as smart as you act like you are, you ought to be able to smoke out the real killer before dinner gets cold."

"So you think I'm innocent?"

He grinned, but only so a professional observer would notice it. "This is a small island; I went to school with Lady Astamore back when she was simply Fiona. Never met a sweeter soul. If she trusts you, that's a pretty good reference for me." Then the smile faded. "But of course, I've only got your word for it. So until I can verify it . . ."

He produced a key from a pocket. "I have a feeling you're innocent. Of course, I also had a feeling that my wife would keep her figure. I was wrong about that." He inserted the key not into the manacles, but into the flat disk between them. Instantly more chain unrolled, putting enough slack between the cuffs so that I could spread my arms wide. He locked the disk again, pocketed the key, and patted my cheek. "So until I'm more certain about you, those stay on."

"I'll keep my figure, I promise."

He laughed. "I'm sure someone somewhere is pleased to know that."

I looked down at my wrists. The weight of the chain and disk, which now hung past my knees, were not encouraging. "All right, then, let's get to work. A murder goes stale faster than a wife's good nature."

"True words indeed," Kay said, and opened the door.

I followed Kay back to the banquet hall. The disk in the middle of the manacle chain tapped my shins as I walked, so I held it in my left hand.

The Knights of the Double Tarn had sealed the room, allowing no one in or out without Kay's permission. They'd used the graduating class of Nodlon Grange as the muscle for this, so the newly minted soldiers, anxious to impress these legendary veterans, stood at rigid attention before all the exits and made no eye contact with their muttering, frilly charges.

It occurred to me that creating a new generation of Double Tarn knights might be one of Marcus Drake's few tactical errors. Train a man to do something, and he'll find a reason to do it, especially if you've trained him to kill. Peace meant these new warriors had no battles to fight, so what would they do with their new skills?

The rich folks, hemmed in and unaccustomed to hearing the word *no,* milled about in little knots concentrated around the big central table. Oblivious to the idea that something else might be poisoned, they'd made a serious dent in the victuals and a good start on the bar. When I entered the room behind Kay, though, the conversations trailed off and every well-painted eye fell on me.

Sam Patrice lay where he'd fallen, and the odor from his poisoned body had grown stronger. Chairs from the big table formed a respectful circle around him so no one could disturb the body. Someone had draped a lavish tablecloth over him, and only his rigid hand protruded from beneath it. The blueish fingers still marked the shape of the lethal apple. Where the fabric rested on his face, a stain from the bloody spittle had already soaked through.

Kay bellowed, *"Officers!"* as soon as we came through the door. Seven knights quickly appeared and formed a double-tiered circle around us, a practiced move designed for both protection and to prevent eavesdropping during battle briefings.

"This man is Edward LaCrosse," Kay said with a nod to me. "He'll be assisting me. If he asks you a question or gives you an order, it's the same as me doing it."

"If he's such an expert," one asked, "why is he in cuffs?"

"Insurance," Kay said. "His authority still stands."

"Exactly *what* is he an expert in?" Thomas Gillian asked. He had the kind of eyes that methodically swept over you, cataloging and analyzing as they went.

"Investigating murders," Kay said.

"The ones he committed?" a tall man with red hair snorted.

"We don't know that," Kay said. "He has an alibi, and as long as it holds up, I'm satisfied with it. But I haven't had time to check it out. That's why he's restrained."

A slender man with a long, drooping mustache said, "The guests sure think he's guilty."

"The guests also think they're the whole reason the world exists," Kay said. "Neither one is true. Mr. LaCrosse is a professional, just like we are. And hear this: Mr. LaCrosse better stay healthy, or I know some knights who won't. Is that understood?"

"Yes, *sir*!" they barked in unison.

Kay turned to me. "The show's all yours. What do we do?"

I was rarely the shortest man in any group, but I was here, and it felt odd, as if I were the new kid in a tough school. "Gentlemen, I appreciate that you've lost a friend here today. I wish there was more time to mourn him, but right now, the longer we let things sit, the better chance the real murderer has of getting away. Has anyone left the room since this happened?"

"The queen retired to her quarters with her women," the red-haired man said. "The only guest who's left the room is you, sir, and the soldiers involved in guarding you. The other guests and all the servants have been kept here. The perimeter is secure. Sir," he added, with a glance toward Kay.

"Well . . . ," began another knight, scarred from a burn across his chin.

"Well, what?" Kay demanded, then suddenly answered his own question. *"Agravaine,"* he spat.

"Yeah," the burned knight said. "He took it on himself to question the serving girl who delivered the apples."

"And he took Vince and Aidan with him," Gillian added.

"Of course he did," Kay snarled. "And none of you brave warriors stood up to him?" They all looked down or away, like guilty schoolboys, except for Gillian, whose expression remained neutral. "I ought to put the lot of you on report. You can be sure the king will hear about this."

"Well, what difference does that make, anyway?" one of the other knights said. "Has anyone talked to Perfect Jennifer? She brought the murder weapon, after all."

Kay was instantly nose to nose with the speaker; the younger man could not meet Kay's furious gaze. "Back that talk down, mister. You are a member of the Knights of the Double Tarn, and you *will* show respect to your queen."

"Yes, sir," the offending soldier said, as sincerely as a pimp says, "I love you."

"An investigation starts with the actual crime and works backwards," I said, trying to sound as authoritative as my handcuffs allowed. "We follow the trail where it leads, not where we assume it goes, no matter how certain we might be. A smart criminal knows how to use assumptions like that, and since your friend was murdered right under the noses of the country's best soldiers, I'd say the killer was pretty smart." To Kay I said, "We should talk to the serving girl ourselves. She can at least tell us where she got the apples."

Kay nodded. "Where are they?"

Gillian nodded at a door. "In there."

As Kay and I crossed the hall, I felt the eyes of every single banquet guest follow me. I knew they were concocting elaborate conspiracies that had the Knights of the Double Tarn protecting me from justice for murky, nefarious reasons. I could do nothing to change their minds except produce the actual murderer, so I tried not to worry about it. "So who's this Agravaine?" I asked Kay.

"Dave Agravaine," he said through his teeth. "He's a wild knife, and he's got two toadies, Vince Hoel and Aidan Cador, who ask 'How high?' when he says 'Jump.' They're all three worth their weight in gold in a battle, but they stink as human beings in peacetime."

"I've known a lot of soldiers like that." For a while, I'd even been one, but I kept that to myself.

Just as we reached the door to the indicated serving room, I glanced back and spotted Thomas Gillian, the intended murder victim, still watching me with that hawklike intensity. I couldn't read his expression. I wondered if anyone ever could.

"Agravaine!" Kay bellowed as we entered the small room. It was identical to the one in which I'd earlier cornered Astamore, except that the door leading into the kitchens was closed and bolted.

Three knights surrounded a stool, on which perched the unfortunate serving girl. She huddled like a frightened sparrow, head down and arms around herself. "Get out there with the rest of the men," Kay snarled, holding the door open. "We'll take over here."

One of them completely ignored Kay and glared solely at me. He was the first Double Tarn knight I'd met shorter than me, but he had wide shoulders and a white streak in his hair that indicated a serious battle scar on his scalp. He moved with a cocky shoulder roll that radiated arrogance, and his features seem to have adopted a disdainful sneer as their natural expression. I guessed he was about forty, old enough to have fought in the last of the unification wars. "You're the guy we pulled off Patrice's dead body."

"And you're this far from getting a boot enema, Agravaine," Kay snarled. "You had orders to stay in the hall. Were they too complicated, or have you just not washed your ears lately?"

"This skanky little wench gave Sam the poisoned apple," Agravaine said. "She might be dangerous. We can keep a better eye on her in here." Then, in an insolent, singsong taunt he added, "Isn't that what Marcus would want, big Sir Bob? And don't you *always* do what Marcus wants?"

The tension between Kay and Agravaine had an almost physical presence. Before Kay could throttle him, I said to him, "Thanks, we appreciate your initiative, but we need some time alone to ask the young lady some questions."

Agravaine's hateful gaze shifted back to me, and he smiled. It was the kind of smile that begged to be forcefully knocked down his throat. "Right. I always do what a man in chains tells me. Well, here she is." He snapped his fingers, and the other two knights stepped aside.

The girl had not moved or spoken during this exchange. She sat hunched with her hair down over her face and shook so violently the stool's legs tapped against the floor. I put my hand on her shoulder, careful not to let the manacle chain touch her. "Miss," I said gently, "I'd just like to ask you a couple of questions, and then you'll be free to go."

She looked up slowly, and her hair fell away from her face. I saw bruises and an eye swollen shut. Fresh tears made tracks through the dried blood around her puffy lips. She was so terrified her breath came in rapid, shallow whimpers.

Kay inhaled sharply behind me.

Her beautiful serving gown had been torn off one shoulder, and her fingers clutched the ripped fabric so tightly her nails dug into her palms.

"Please, sir," she said in a trembling, mechanical whisper.

My own hands began to shake. "I'm sorry," I said genuinely. "I wish we'd gotten here sooner."

Behind me, Kay stepped close to Agravaine. "You little pissbucket—"

His two pals stepped up behind him, their presence a looming threat that Kay ignored. "She insulted the queen," Agravaine said defensively. "We can't have the servants doing that, can we?"

"You just like smacking women around," Kay hissed. "Don't pretend otherwise."

Agravaine laughed. In the small, dim room it sounded especially malicious. "Sure, if a whore needs it, I'll knock some sense into her. Got to keep them in their place. Right, fellas?"

The two men chuckled in agreement.

The girl squeezed out fresh tears at Agravaine's description of her. "I'm not a whore," she whispered, so quietly only I heard it.

"Excuse me a moment," I said softly, and turned. Somewhere in that simple motion, I made a fist and swung it with all my weight and strength into Agravaine's round, smug face.

I hit him harder than I'd ever hit anything in my life. The weight of the manacle added that little extra grace note, and the chain slapped me in the cheek. Bones snapped, some in my hand, most in his nose, and he dropped like a bag of wet mud.

He sat up almost at once and clutched his nose as blood oozed between his fingers. *"Som ub a bid!"* he cried, his voice distorted.

His two pals drew their swords. The distinctive *shting* was especially loud in the small room, and the blades took up an awful lot of space.

"Cador! Hoel!" Kay yelled, and stepped in front of me. "Scabbard those swords *now!*"

For a moment everyone was silent and still. Then the two sidekicks put their weapons away.

"He broke my nose," Agravaine said as he stood. It came out as *He brode my node.* He pulled his hand away from his face and looked at the blood. "Hold him for me, boys. Oh, you are about to get *such* an ass-kicking."

The tip of Kay's sword touched the hollow in Agravaine's throat, then lifted his chin. He'd drawn it so fast and silently none of us noticed. "You're not doing anything, soldier. All three of you are on report. Get back out there, and if I see any sign of you anywhere else before we leave, I'll personally demote each of you back to assistant squire." Kay glared particularly at Agravaine. "And I promise you, that's a *lot* less than Marc would do if he were here."

Agravaine pointed a bloody finger at me. "Me and you, asshole. Soon." Then he looked at the girl, who curled up even tighter under his glare. "And you? Remember what I said."

Then they left, slamming the door behind them.

Kay turned to me. "That was smart," he muttered as he sheathed his sword. He opened the door and yelled, "Morholt! Find a doctor and send him over here. Now!"

He closed the door, then turned to the girl. His whole demeanor softened, and he spoke with a kindness that surprised me. "Miss? What's your name?"

"Mary," she said in a tiny voice.

"Mary, I'm Bob Kay, and this is Mr. LaCrosse. We're truly sorry those men hurt you. They did *not* have orders to do so and they *will* be punished for it. I know they probably threatened you as well, but I promise you they won't be in any shape to hurt anyone when I get done with them. You saw they were scared of me."

She made a low, whimpering sound that eventually became the words "All I said was that the queen gave me the apples. I never said she poisoned them. I swear, I'm a good citizen, I love Grand Bruan."

I found a basin with some water in it, dipped a napkin, and reached to wipe some of the blood from her face. She winced and drew back from my hand; I abandoned the idea. Instead I asked, "Mary, did Queen Jennifer give you the apples personally?"

She nodded slightly.

"Did you notice if they smelled funny?"

She shook her head. "We were in the kitchen; there was so much cooking, I couldn't smell anything."

"Did she arrange to give them to you before the banquet?" I pressed, as gently as possible.

"No. She brought them down to the kitchen, and I just happened to be the one picked to carry them. She said . . . she said I looked the prettiest."

She began to sob, and I glared over the top of her head at Kay. "That guy owes me more than a broken nose to settle this."

"Not while you're toting that hand," Kay said.

I looked and saw that the knuckles were already red and swollen. I'd been so angry I hadn't really registered the damage. When I tried to flex my fingers, pain shot up my forearm.

"Uh-huh," Kay said wryly. "A sword jockey with no sword hand; choice."

Someone knocked softly at the door. "It's Dr. Gladstone," a woman's voice said, and she entered without waiting for an invitation. She closed the door behind her, looked around, and said, "I can't work with romantic mood lighting. Turn up that lamp, will you?"

Kay adjusted the wick, the room grew brighter, and I got my first look at Iris Gladstone. She was about thirty, clad in a distinctive white coat and toting the little black satchel of her profession. Everything about her spoke of strength and elegance, from her short black hair to eyes so big and blue it was like looking into the sea itself. She seemed somehow too glamorous for such a down-and-dirty job as physician. Or maybe because she was such a knockout, I couldn't imagine her tending bloody injuries.

"That's better," she said as the lamp stopped flickering. "So I was told there'd been an accident in the kitchen," she said in a deep, take-charge voice. "Somebody slice open a finger?"

"Ah . . . no," Kay said, and stepped aside to reveal the girl.

The doctor's face darkened when she saw the injuries. Her hands quickly danced around the bruised eye and cut lip, brushing back the hair to check for other marks. She murmured soothingly to Mary, then turned and glared at us with the kind of fury only the morally righteous can have. "And which one of you chivalrous sons of bitches did this?" She glanced at my manacles. "You?"

"You'll probably get a visit later from a knight with a broken nose," I said. "His fist matches up with those bruises."

She stared at me for a moment as the words got through her fury. Then she noticed how I cradled my hand, and the tiniest smile I'd ever seen moved across her moist, voluptuous lips. "So does *your* fist match *his* broken nose?"

I shrugged. "I swatted a fly."

A flicker of appreciation, but no more than that, touched her face. Then the hard look clamped down again. "Amazing how often you armor-clad assholes manage to hurt the people you're supposed to defend, especially if they've got breasts." She opened her black bag and brought out a small jar of ointment. "Now, will one of you boys be genuinely useful and light a couple more lamps? I'd like to see what I'm doing."

I took down a pair from a shelf with my good hand. Kay took them from me, arranged them for best effect, and lit them. Gladstone ignored us, but that was okay. It gave me the chance to watch her slender form as she worked, attending to the wounds with efficient gentleness. She produced vials and powders from her bag and applied them sparsely, but with a feather-light touch. Mary obeyed the doctor's entreaties, and within moments she'd stopped crying and started to lose the red flush of panic.

"Will she be all right?" I asked softly, not wanting to startle the girl.

The doctor looked up and our eyes met. It was no more than an instant, but it was enough. Sometimes you meet someone and just *know*, instantly and without a doubt, that you're destined to cross all the boundaries that separate you. The process defies logic and common sense, but everyone's experienced it at least once. At that point in my life, it had happened twice before, and both those women were dead. It scared the hell out of me to feel it again for this no-nonsense doctor, and I was actually glad I had a murder to solve to help keep my mind off it.

"Yes," the doctor said. "Eventually."

"May I ask her one last question?" I said.

"Not on my watch," Dr. Gladstone snapped as she applied a bandage over the girl's split cheek.

"No, it's okay," Mary said. "I want to help." She looked up at me with the tiniest spark of renewed defiance in her battered eyes.

I asked gently, "What happened to the rest of the apples?"

She looked blank and thought for a moment. Finally she said, "I don't know."

"All right, that's enough," Dr. Gladstone snapped. She put her hands on her hips and gave us both a hard expression that would've done credit to a North Sea berserker. "This girl's coming back to the infirmary. If I even *smell* a knight in shining armor trying to get near her, I'll show you what an angry doctor can do to one of you walking meat sacks." She turned away to stow her gear back in her bag and added, "And you— come see me about that hand in about three hours. It should be nice and painful by then."

"Miss, I'm truly sorry," Kay repeated to Mary. "We'll make sure you get the best care, and those men *will* pay for what they did to you."

Mary nodded, but her eyes had gone glassy again and I had no idea if she really heard his words.

We went back into the main hall. Once the door shut behind us I asked Kay, "Do you know her? That doctor, I mean."

"Sure. Iris Gladstone. She was with us on a couple of campaigns back before Marripat Hill when she was still a girl apprentice. She stitched up a cut on my back once."

I nodded, resolved to seek out this Iris Gladstone later whether my hand hurt or not. Assuming, of course, I wasn't locked up awaiting execution. "She's tough."

If Kay knew what I meant from my overly appreciative tone, he let it pass with a shrug. "Field doctors have to be. Since peacetime, she's trained healers to go out into the country, opening their own practices."

"You don't use moon priestesses?" That altruistic but secretive sisterhood operated hospitals in most parts of the world.

"There are no moon priestesses on Grand Bruan," Kay muttered. "They're against the law."

I was about to ask why when I spotted Agravaine and his

pals huddled conspiratorially near the main door. When they saw us, they looked away, then at the ground, then slunk off into the crowd.

"Those guys really push it," Kay said. "Now what?"

"Let's go talk to the queen before Agravaine has a chance to get to her."

"The queen?" Kay said, and sounded startled. "Why do you think Agravaine would go to the queen about any of this?"

I looked at him in genuine surprise. "You're kidding, right?"

"Humor me." The suspicion in his voice added the unspoken, *Unless you're more involved than you've said.*

"It's simple. Who else would've sent him to intimidate a key witness whose testimony implicates the queen? That girl is the one link between the queen and the apples. Another couple of minutes and they would've had her convinced apples didn't even exist. And even if the queen didn't personally send them, they were surely doing it on her behalf."

Kay nodded. "Pretty simple when you explain it that way."

"My question is why? If all the other Knights of the Double Tarn are against the queen, why are those three on her side?"

Before Kay could answer, a new voice yelled, *"You!"*

DeGrandis, his cheeks reddened with wine beneath his face powder, waddled toward us. "That's close enough," Kay warned when he was about ten feet away.

He pointed one frilly yellow sleeve at me. "Why is that man running around loose? He's a murderer! We've heard all about him and his crimes, from a *very* reliable source!"

"This gentleman," Kay said in the voice he must've used

on the battlefield, "is not running around loose, as you can see." He rattled the chain between my manacles. "And he's under *my* sword at the moment."

"Well, I assure you we will *not* allow him to leave Nodlon Castle," DeGrandis snapped. His chins wobbled with outrage. Behind him, his fellow nobles muttered encouragement from a safe distance.

Kay wasn't impressed. "You'll do as you're told for the moment. Now please rejoin your friends and await an official announcement. *Sir.*"

DeGrandis gave me a look as if I'd snatched the last piece of pie from the table, then returned to his group. Among them, Lord Astamore resumed weaving the mendacious tapestry of my criminal exploits.

"Thanks," I said to Kay. "He might've rolled right over me if he got too excited."

Kay nodded. "Yeah." Then he frowned and, in the same difficult pleading tone he'd used when he asked me to help, said quietly, "So do we *really* have to go see the queen?"

I wanted to smack him in the forehead. "*Yes,* we have to see her. Come on, don't get dense on me now. She may be the queen, but she's also a legitimate suspect, and if you're going to have a real rule of law, it's got to apply to everyone. Isn't that what Drake's grand design is all about?"

"She'll take it personally."

"That's not our problem."

"And she isn't the best person to antagonize."

"In my experience, people only feel antagonized when they have something to hide. If she had nothing to do with the murder, she shouldn't get upset."

"Maybe that's true," Kay granted.

"And I'll be polite. I know how to behave around royalty."

"Oh, it's not you I'm worried about." He managed a wry, tired smile. "You get to leave Grand Bruan when this is all over; *I* have to live with her."

I mmediately after the murder Queen Jennifer Drake had withdrawn to her chambers, using her royal prerogative to override Kay's order that no one leave the great hall. The queen couldn't really be expected to mill about with the nobles under circumstances like these, and given the tension between her and the knights, she wouldn't want to subject herself to their constant scrutiny. So while I had waited in the closet for interrogation, Kay made sure she was safely locked in upstairs before he came to me.

I followed Kay through a door behind the thrones and up a stone, spiral staircase. The stairs were padded, the better to protect delicate royal feet.

Kay pulled me aside just before we emerged onto the next floor. He inserted the key in the disk, and the chain wound back up tight, pulling my wrists together. "Nothing personal, but you will be in the presence of the queen, and you still might be a murderer." He took a dagger from his belt and made sure that I saw him slip it, hilt-first, up his sleeve. A single flex and it would be in his hand; another flex and it would be in my back.

"Sure," I said. I couldn't argue with his logic.

"And I have one request. Please don't mention what I told you about Elliot Spears."

"Why would I?"

"I can't imagine. I just wanted to be clear on it."

"Being curious is my job, you know. Now I *have* to ask."

He considered his words before speaking. "Remember I told you that Elliot doesn't come around very often? It's because he and Jennifer had a very loud, practically public falling-out. No one knows for sure what started it, but barracks gossip says one of them broke off the affair."

"Which one?"

"Depends on who's telling the story. She never talks about it, though. And he's not around to ask."

"So if I mention it, she'll just say, 'No comment'?"

"No, if you mention it, she may hand you your teeth."

I was intrigued, but for the moment it didn't seem a priority. "Okay. I won't bring up Spears."

"Thank you." He seemed more afraid of this woman's disapproval than Agravaine's swords back in the service room.

When we emerged onto the landing, two armored sentries guarded her door. They saluted Kay and stepped aside as we approached. Kay knocked, and one of the young handmaidens opened the door wide enough to peer out. She had blond hair, an ample bosom thanks to the cut of her gown, and slender hips. "Her Majesty is not to be disturbed," she said.

"Tell her it's me," Kay said.

"She said no one."

"Rebecca—"

"Bob, I know it's important. But did you see her face down there? She's a mess. I can't let you upset her any more, not right now." The girl looked me up and down, taking in my cuffs. "Come back later, and I'm sure she'll be willing to talk to *you*."

I could tell Kay was about to accept this excuse, so I said softly, "Tell the queen that if she doesn't talk to us, we'll let everyone downstairs, including the knights, *know* she wouldn't talk to us."

Rebecca looked at me as if she'd scraped me from her boot. "I don't normally trouble the queen with messages from prisoners."

"I'm sure you're up to the challenge," I said.

Rebecca's eyes narrowed and she slammed the door in our faces. A few moments later she opened it all the way, curtsied and gestured that we should enter. "Her Majesty Queen Jennifer Drake will receive you now," she recited.

Naturally, Jennifer had the swankiest digs in the palace. Huge tapestries covered the cold stone walls, and a fire blazed in a hearth roughly the size of my office. Oil lamps provided an even glow, and the furniture was heavy, luxurious, and over-ornamented. Somewhere incense burned, and one of the other maidens strummed idly on a harp, never quite hitting a tune.

The queen awaited us before the fireplace. She wore a light

silk robe over her blue lounging gown, and her hair had been braided down her back. This close she was even more of a stunner, although something innately fragile about her brought up the desire to shelter and protect her from harsh things. I suspected she was well aware of this effect, perhaps even cultivated it, and probably watched to see if we fell for it. From the look on his face it was clear that Kay always did.

Rebecca, the harpist, and the two other maidens immediately withdrew to a couch in the corner as Jennifer strode to meet us. She put her left hand on her right shoulder, which caused her robe's billowy sleeve to sweep dramatically through the air. "I assume you've got news for me, Sir Robert?" She looked pointedly at me.

Kay bowed just enough for it to count. "Not the news you're hoping for, Your Majesty. We still don't know what happened yet."

"Yes, we do," I said.

She looked at me, and I got the full effect of her royal charisma. If I'd been a lesser man, I'd have curled up purring at her feet. "Are you confessing?"

I bowed. I'd been taught court etiquette since before I could speak, so it was point-perfect, even with my hands cuffed. "Edward LaCrosse, Your Majesty."

"He was the first one to reach Sam's body," Kay offered. "I don't believe he's the murderer."

She smiled wryly. "But you're not one hundred percent certain?"

"Not about many things, Your Majesty. But he says he's a private soldier who knows how to investigate crimes like this, and I've asked him to help."

This time she gave me a look I felt in my scabbard. "A *sword jockey*?" she said, with a little smile that spoke of royal treasures having nothing to do with jewelry. It was her way of asserting control in her male-dominated world. "Isn't that the common term? I always thought they were ragged little men hiding under beds or chasing charnel wagons."

"Not all of us," I said. "It may be a business of lepers, but I've still got most of my fingers."

"You said you knew what had happened," she said, ignoring my humor. Most women, royal or not, did that.

"It's not complicated. Someone wanted to kill Thomas Gillian in a very public way, which meant they had a point to make. Since you provided the murder weapon, that point may also have involved making you look bad. The victim got in the middle of it by sheer dumb luck."

"Surely you don't think I had anything to do with it." It was the obligatory denial, and she was a good enough performer that it sounded genuine. Which it might have been.

"I try not to think anything," I said. "I let the evidence think for me. Right now the evidence leads us to you. Hopefully it'll lead us further."

"And what 'evidence' might that be?"

I nodded toward the tray of apples, in plain sight on the sideboard. "The murder weapon. He wasn't killed with a sword or knife. Mind if I look them over?"

"Certainly."

I went to the tray. In the time she'd been alone with the apples, she could've done anything to them, including replace them all. But it didn't mean an examination would tell me nothing.

I picked up a knife from a nearby place setting. Immediately Kay stiffened and moved closer. I realized he was getting into position to protect the queen and gave him a wry smile.

Unable to grasp the knife in my puffy right hand, I used my left to awkwardly turn several of the apples. I looked for any discoloration that might show where the poison had been added. I found none. The killer apparently trusted that blind luck would have Gillian pick up the lone poisoned apple. "Are they all here?" I asked.

"As far as I know." She indicated herself and her maids. "We certainly haven't eaten any of them."

"Are these apples special?"

"In what way?"

"Can you find others like them anywhere besides the royal orchard?"

Surprised, she said, "I suppose one could. I'm no gardener, but I'm not aware that they're any rare variety."

I leaned down and sniffed. The same aroma I'd smelled from the late Sir Patrice was barely present. I looked more closely at the nearest apple and at last found what I sought: a tiny bump, easily missed, on the bottom near the calyx indention. I picked up the fruit with a napkin and said, "Look at this."

When Jennifer started to move, Kay stepped in front of her and said, "Hand me the knife first."

I did. Then Kay and Jennifer crowded close. "What is it?" Kay asked.

I transferred the fruit to the palm of my injured hand and tapped the bump with my fingernail. It fell off and revealed a hole no larger in diameter than a sewing needle. "A bit of wax to seal the hole. Do you still have the one that killed Patrice on you?"

Kay nodded and produced it, still wrapped in my handkerchief. I quickly found an identical wax seal in the same spot. "That's where the poison was injected into them, and then sealed."

Jennifer looked at me with either admiration or wariness; it was hard to tell. "So every apple was poisoned this way?"

"Let's see." Now that I knew what I sought, it only took moments to inspect them all. Roughly half of them were poisoned, and piled so that the lethal ones were on top.

Her breathtaking face creased with confusion. "But Mr. LaCrosse, they were with me the whole time. This could not have been done quickly; when would the killer have had an opportunity?"

I shrugged. "We'll know that when we catch him. Or her."

"I don't care for your manner, sir," the queen snapped.

"Neither do I. I grieve over it on warm summer evenings. But may I give you some advice? No one's accused you of anything yet, and when you jump at every innuendo, it just makes you look guilty. You might want to put on a thicker skin until we get this straightened out."

Her eyes opened wide, then narrowed, and the contempt that shot from them was enough to wither a cornfield. I understood Kay's reluctance to confront her. She straightened her back and raised her chin, which made her seem far taller than she was. With regal disdain she told Kay, "I would appreciate it if you'd show this *person* out of my chambers."

I pocketed Patrice's apple. "I apologize if candor offends

you, Your Majesty. If you think of anything that might help us, I hope your low opinion of me won't make you keep it to yourself." I made another perfect courtly bow. By the time I rose, Rebecca had scurried across the room and again held the door for us.

Halfway down the stairs to the main hall, Kay stopped, leaned against the stone wall, and sighed. He put away the dagger, then unlocked the disk to release the big loop of slack. "At least our heads are still attached. Thank you for not mentioning Elliot."

"No promises the next time." I raised my hands and extended the cuffs.

He shook his head. "No. Not yet."

The manacles had me both angry and a touch claustrophobic. "Come on, you saw the other apples. I couldn't have poisoned them, too."

"'Too'? Are you admitting you poisoned the first one?" he teased.

"Stop that. You know I didn't do it. Now get these things off me."

"It's for your own good, Eddie, seriously. If you're seen without those before we find the real killer, the folks who think you're guilty may decide to dispense their own justice."

"I'll take my chances," I said, adding in my head, *and I won't let the drawbridge hit me on my way out.*

"Not with that, you won't." He nodded at my injured hand. I could neither straighten nor curl my fingers now, and my knuckles were hidden under puffy, darkening skin. "Guess Iris was right. That'll sure hurt by tonight."

I couldn't argue; it sure hurt right *now*. "All right, so I'm still your prisoner. So tell me: how much can we trust what Queen Jennifer told us?"

"I've never known her to lie."

"You've never known her to murder anyone before, either."

He chuckled deep in his chest. "If you're going to suspect everyone even after you've questioned them, how are we going to make any progress? I'd like to solve this before we're both too old to enjoy it."

Yet again I wanted to smack him, but under the circumstances it still seemed like a bad move. So I took a deep breath, calmed down, and said, "Okay, you're right, I don't *really* think she had anything to do with it, but I *do* think she knows more than she's telling. But keeping secrets isn't a crime."

When we hit the banquet room again, it was worse than before. As soon as they saw me, the guests' murmuring escalated to shouts and catcalls. One of the courtiers, a white-haired fellow with eyebrows like caterpillars, bellowed, "Sir Robert, I *demand* you speak with us!"

"Great," Kay muttered. "You stay here," he told me, and strode over to the man. "Yes, Lord Shortridge, what can I do for you?"

"You can let us out of here for one thing. It's past sunset, and I for one did not come prepared for an overnight stay. Why, I don't even have the proper toiletries for my skin." Then he pointed a long finger at me. "And we all know he's the murderer, yet you keep him leashed at your side as if he were your favorite foxhound!"

The nobles chimed in with their agreement. Across the room, Gillian still watched me with his cold, implacable eyes. Agravaine was nowhere to be seen.

"I'm glad you're all so sure of things," Kay said. "But as long as Marcus Drake rules Grand Bruan, we'll approach this based on the law of the land. That law says a man must be assumed innocent until *proven* guilty." He looked disdainfully at the glass in Shortridge's hand. "And I don't think that proof will be found in the bottom of a wine bottle."

"You're using the king's law to protect a killer!" someone cried.

"Queen Jennifer can render justice in this case," Shortridge said. "She has the royal rank, *and* the full support of the nobles." The crowd chimed in its agreement. "We demand you convene a trial, followed by that man's execution."

"Demand all you want," Kay said. "But you're guests here, not rulers. Another treasonous outburst like this, where you openly advocate bypassing the king's law, and you can easily become prisoners." He turned and walked back toward me.

"Don't you dare accuse me of treason!" Shortridge yelled. "I am a lord of Grand Bruan!"

Kay dismissed him with a wave, but his face was grim as he approached me. "Listen, we've got to get you out of sight." He nodded toward yet another door. "Follow me and try to look nonchalant."

This wasn't another kitchen antechamber, but one of Nodlon Castle's private lounging areas. It was empty, and through the windows I saw the moon full and bright over the ocean.

Kay lit some lamps, and light from the tiny wicks reflected from myriad polished surfaces. Used as a refuge for the idle rich during tedious ceremonies, the decor was lush and sumptuous, redolent of fat bottoms and wheezing bosoms. The lingering smell of expensive cologne masked a subtler odor of sweaty desperation and decay, the common scents of any castle.

Kay opened the liquor cabinet, selected a really top-class vintage, and fished a corkscrew from a cluttered drawer. "This situation is way too close to getting out of hand," he said as he poured our drinks. He downed his in a single swallow. "I'm going to go get Marc."

"You're *leaving*?" I said.

"Don't worry, I'll assign someone to protect you. As long as you stay out of sight, you'll be fine. And once Marc gets here, you should be able to leave with no difficulties."

"So where is Marc?"

"At his main castle in Motlace. If I leave now and ride all night, I can be there well before dawn. Once he hears what's going on, he'll want to come sort it out himself."

"You sound pretty sure of that."

Kay grinned wearily. "I am." He nodded at one of the tapestries. "Do you know anything about him?"

The woven picture showed a man in hugely complicated regalia riding an equally decked-out horse across a flowered field. He carried a sword nearly as long as he was tall. At the far right of the image, apparently his goal, stood a woman with downcast eyes and a multipointed crown. Despite the artistic license, I recognized her as Jennifer Drake.

I looked more closely at the king's face, visible beneath his open visor. It was square-jawed and handsome, with long hair flowing from beneath his helmet. His beard was short and neat, and his eyes half-closed in either communion with the spirit world, or boredom. His lips were unnaturally red, a stylistic element I'd seen on a lot of Grand Bruan tapestries. "Just what I've heard back home."

Kay poured himself another drink. "He's the reason I have this job. He lived with me and my family in secret until he was fifteen and claimed the crown. We were raised as brothers. I used to make sure no one picked on him when he was little, and then after he put on six inches and fifty pounds the summer he turned fourteen, he made sure no one picked on me."

"Is he as honest as they say?"

"He's the best man I know. And I'm completely serious. Marc always tries to do the right thing, and he's smart enough to know what that is."

One tapestry showed Marcus on one knee, presenting a ring to Jennifer. Her dress had a train long enough to cross the channel separating Grand Bruan from the mainland. "How attached is he to his queen?"

"Watch the two of them together and you'll be lucky to get away without a toothache."

"So you want me to just sit around and wait for King Marcus to ride in and save the day?"

"It won't be all bad, I promise. I'll make sure you get a room stocked with liquor for three."

"Who are the other two?"

He grinned. "There are no other two. And once Marc is on the scene, everything will be all right. You'll see."

I sipped my drink and nodded, wishing I had his confidence. King Marcus Drake might be as spotless as Kay described, and I sure hoped he was. But as anyone who's ever polished armor knows, nothing attracts bird shit like a clean, shiny surface. And the buzzards were already gathered around us.

Left alone in the swanky lounge, I suddenly realized just how badly my hand hurt. My fingers would barely flex at all, and the swelling reached the second knuckles. I must've been really angry to throw such a clumsy punch. And the damn manacles hadn't helped.

To distract myself while I waited for my room, I looked over some of the other tapestries. One especially held my attention. It showed Marcus Drake as a teenage boy, pulling Belacrux from the tree where it had been embedded awaiting the island's true king. Behind him stood a younger but still recognizable Bob Kay, and watching over all this was a tall, husky man with a wide-brimmed hat. This would be Cameron Kern, who'd guided Drake's career from birth. His powers were so legendary as to be ludicrous: he could tell the future, turn the tide of battle, fly through the air, and transform into any animal he wished. He'd once magically caused an entire fleet of invading ships to burst into flame.

If he could've really done those things, of course, then he would've seen it coming when the king dismissed him and sent him packing. The rumors surrounding the reason were just as outlandish.

Another tapestry showed the Drakes' wedding ceremony, suitably exaggerated to include thousands of well-wishers outside the castle. Both king and queen looked young and idealistic, and again I spotted someone I recognized: Thomas Gillian, in armor and cape, waiting his turn to be knighted.

A pair of secondary figures caught my eye. They were depicted inside the castle, which gave them status, but far to the back of the witnesses. One was a small, dark-haired woman with enormous blue eyes, in an elaborate black gown that looked funereal. Beside her was a boy of about five, also black-clad and somehow more disturbing.

I held a lamp closer to these two. Their woven shapes were barely six inches tall, but the detail was extraordinary, so that the faces had the individuality of real life. Something about the boy seemed familiar to me, even though I'd never been to this island before. I couldn't place it, though, before a firm knock preceded the opening of the door.

Thomas Gillian entered. He carefully closed the door behind him, then locked it. He put his back against it, stood at ease, and said, "Sir Robert has put you in my charge."

"What precisely does that entail?"

"Where you go, I go. I protect you and, if you get out of line, restrain you. Up to, and including, execution." He said all this with absolutely no emotion.

"I guess I better behave, then."

"It would be in your best interest. Sir Robert has sent for the doctor to tend your hand, and she should arrive shortly."

The thought of seeing the dark-haired doctor again improved my mood. "Well, that's something. Kay opened a bottle; would you like a drink?"

He shook his head. "Given that someone has already tried to poison me once today, I think I'll stick to my own sources of refreshment for a bit."

Someone knocked softly at the door. Gillian unlocked it and stepped back.

Iris Gladstone entered. The dead room suddenly jumped to life. Or maybe it was just me. She said, "Hello, Tom. I'm here to check on Mr. LaCrosse's hand."

"Hi," I said.

She pulled off her coat, revealing a sleeveless tunic and skirt. To hide what those clothes revealed beneath a shapeless white coat seemed criminal.

Gillian relocked the door and assumed the exact same position. His eyes grew glassy, as if he were a million miles away. I knew better; he saw and heard everything. To Iris I said, "Working late?"

"Boy, nothing gets past you, does it?" She yawned and stretched, displaying far too many curves for a man in my weakened condition to endure. She ran her hands through her hair. "I had to examine several of the honored guests for various maladies brought on by the stress of their confinement. Alas, they'll all live."

"Survival is a courtier's main skill," I said. Watching her spread the contents of her bag on a side table was more enjoyable than it should've been.

She looked up and smiled. Having recently been dazzled by Queen Jennifer, I felt qualified to say that the royal grin paled next to this one, at least for me. She said, "I should probably offer to stitch your head back on since I bit it off before. Mary told me how you stuck up for her."

"Don't mention it." I gestured dismissively with my injured hand. The movement made it throb anew, and despite my best efforts it showed. It also rattled the chain between the manacles.

Iris turned to Gillian. "Tom, can you undo these?"

Gillian shook his head. "Sir Robert was explicit."

Iris's eyes narrowed. "Tom, I'm a doctor, and I'm here to treat this man's injury, which I can't do if it's halfway covered by these shackles. You can lock him up again as soon as I'm done, but for right now, I'm telling you, take them off."

Her voice grew firmer and louder as she spoke, so that by the end she was almost yelling. Gillian showed no reaction, but after a moment he picked up a padded barstool and crossed the room. He gestured for me to sit. When I did, he unlocked the manacle around my right wrist, then relocked it to his own. He stood right beside me, again as still and quiet as a statue.

Iris shook her head, laughed, and held out her hand. "Okay, let me see that broken battering ram of yours."

She turned my hand palm-up. "Wiggle your fingers for me." I did, though the movement was minimal. "Okay, I don't think you broke anything, but they're jammed up awfully good. Did no one ever show you how to throw a punch?"

"I'm self-taught. And impulsive."

"Be careful who you admit that to." She met my eyes, and the playfulness left her. "I need to straighten them out, and it's going to hurt. Do you want something for the pain?"

"No. I need to keep my wits about me."

She grinned with one side of her mouth; it was adorable. "Well, at least they shouldn't take up much room."

She turned her back to me and put my free arm under hers. I could smell whatever lavender concoction she used on her black, silky hair. She held my wrist with her left hand, and my index finger with her right. "All right, here's one."

If someone had driven a metal rod from my fingertip straight up my arm, it would've hurt less. The crack sounded like a sledgehammer hitting a rotted board. "That wasn't so bad," I squeaked. Sweat stung my eyes.

"Now two," she said without a pause. The pain was less intense, if only because I wasn't over the first one yet.

"Can I ask you something?" I croaked.

She wasn't one to be distracted. "Sure. Now three."

I was basically on fire from my right shoulder on down and gasped, "Do you know anything about poisons?"

"They're bad for you, as a rule. Last one. And this little piggy went . . . snap."

And, boy, did it. "Oh, we're done?" I said casually. I wasn't sure it was audible outside my own head.

"Wipe your eyes," she said as she released my arm.

After a couple of deep breaths, I realized my hand actually

hurt a little less and I could move my fingers a lot more freely. I slumped on the stool and said, "What about specific ones?"

"Specific eyes?" She poured me a drink from the decanter Kay had opened earlier.

"Specific poisons."

She test-moved my fingers and seemed satisfied with the results. "You're a sword jockey, aren't you?"

"Yeah. Do you disapprove?"

"Everyone has to do something. Right, Tom?"

Gillian raised one eyebrow. For him it was the equivalent of a burst of laughter.

Iris asked me, "So what poisons were you interested in?"

"Just one. Shatternight."

She didn't pause to think. "Acts very rapidly. Boils you alive inside. No known antidote. Distinctive odor. And it doesn't grow on this island."

"And it's what killed that knight at the banquet."

She frowned, and a stray lock of black hair fell over her forehead. "How do you know?"

I used my shackled good hand and brought out the apple. Gillian did not resist the movement. I held it for Iris to sniff. She said, "That's it, all right. You're a man of many talents."

"Especially when it comes to things that might kill me." I'd encountered shatternight where it grew wild, deep in the forests of Oconomo, and once narrowly avoided getting dosed with it. "So where on Grand Bruan *would* someone get shatternight?"

"Beats me. It has no medicinal value. And it would have to be brought from the south, across the channel, because it won't grow in this climate. Plus it loses its potency pretty rapidly once it's been picked, I believe."

"So whoever poisoned these apples would have been outside Grand Bruan in the recent past, correct?"

She cocked her head. "*You* came from outside Grand Bruan, I believe, didn't you?"

"True. But I'm not the murderer."

She glanced at my shackles and deadpanned, "That's a relief."

She took my injured hand and lightly massaged my fingers. Her touch was strong, sure, and yet delicate. Since I couldn't really seduce her with Gillian standing right there, I continued to talk about work. "I met Queen Jennifer earlier. Are you on good terms with her?"

Iris answered the question as casually as I asked it. "As good as anyone, I suppose. As long as you do your job and don't make any mistakes, she's easy to get along with. If you screw up, though, she'll eat you for lunch. Right, Tommy?"

As expected, Gillian did not comment, and I didn't look up to see if he raised an eyebrow. I said to Iris, "That sounds kind of harsh."

Her face, serious and so focused, was starry-night beautiful. "I've attended her during her miscarriages. That sort of thing brings out a woman's true nature. Hers isn't terribly pleasant." Iris looked down suddenly. "Forget I said that, will you? That was confidential doctor-patient information."

"It'll go no further unless it absolutely has to."

Iris smiled wryly. "You're good, though, you know that? I'm not easy to draw out."

"I'll take that as a compliment. Do you think she's capable of killing someone with poison?"

"Jennifer? If you mean does she have the resources, yes, of course. If you mean as a person . . . no. Not like this. Not watching them die. If she truly planned to murder someone, she'd arrange it to happen far away from her. But being bad-tempered isn't the same as being amoral."

"Lots of moral people have been murderers."

Iris laughed. "You *are* cynical, aren't you?"

"I've seen a lot of people's true natures, too."

"Well, if I were you—and I realize that's saying I'd suddenly be stupid enough to punch one Knight of the Double Tarn in the face while I was under suspicion of murdering another one—I wouldn't waste my time looking at the queen. I'd look *around* her, for someone who wants to make her look bad. And who doesn't care if someone dies to do it."

Her theory matched my own, a sure sign that she was brilliant as well as beautiful. "You think that was the main reason? Not to kill my bodyguard here?"

She snorted. "Tom could be killed anywhere. No offense," she asided to him. "He's a soldier. But to kill him here, under the queen's nose, using the queen's gift, clearly means they want to implicate . . ." Iris paused, then smiled. "Now come on, you can do it . . ."

I grinned at her teasing. "The queen?" I closed my fingers gently around hers.

She glanced up sharply, and for a moment I was afraid I'd crossed a line. Then she smiled. "Ah, Mr. LaCrosse," she said almost wistfully. "I'm flattered."

"And interested?"

She looked down almost guiltily. "Yes, and interested."

"But?"

"No *but*. Except that you are, after all, a prisoner. And my patient."

"I'm *very* patient."

She chuckled. "And if you're here tomorrow night, we might be able to pursue it."

"Why tomorrow night?"

She looked up at Gillian. "Turn the other way for a second, Tom." I felt him do as she asked. She released my hand and put her forearms on my shoulders, her wrists crossed behind my head. She stepped so her body was against mine and her face close. Since she was standing, I had to look up at her, which I certainly didn't mind.

She said quietly, "Because right now it's late, I'm exhausted, and my feet hurt. And even though I've worked on you, you're going to be in some *real* pain soon."

I started to protest, but she continued, "And since I *do* want to see you tomorrow to check on your hand, perhaps— and that's not a promise—we can arrange something less professional. If you've managed to clear your name by then."

"Are you this hard to get for all your patients?"

She laughed and tossed that bothersome lock of hair from her face. "Mr. LaCrosse, I work around eligible young men every day, and you've gotten farther than any of them ever has."

"She's right," Gillian said calmly, and we both looked up in surprise. He still had his back to us.

"Besides," Iris continued, "no one in Grand Bruan would

have dared punch Dave Agravaine in the face, even though
he's needed it for a long time. I admire that, and I like you.
You're funny."

She paused, and her voice took on a low, sultry quality I
recognized, although it never failed to surprise me a little when
it was directed at me. She leaned even closer and said too quietly for Gillian to hear, "Tomorrow, we'll see what happens.
For tonight—"

She touched her lips to mine. I followed her lead and kept
it soft, gentle, respectful. No tongues. But she did nip my
bottom lip a little as she drew back.

"—I prescribe bed rest and sweet dreams."

My own voice was a little ragged, and not from pain. "I always do what the doctor orders."

"Then do one more thing for me. Even with Tom here
on your side, watch your back. There are a lot of secrets in
Grand Bruan, and you may trip over others without meaning
to. Some people might go to extremes to keep things hidden
that have nothing to do with Patrice's murder, on the off
chance you might expose them by accident."

I would've agreed to anything after that kiss, so I had no
problem saying, "Thanks. I'll be careful."

But I wasn't. When she left, I sighed with almost teen-age happiness, which lasted precisely as long as it took Gillian to uncuff himself and remanacle me. "You," I said, "are a mood-killer."

"Duty before pleasure."

"That's why I'm my own boss," I muttered. I poured my-self another drink. My arm had begun to ache almost up to the elbow.

To my surprise, Gillian poured himself a drink as well. He raised it in salute, then tossed it back in one gulp. "Have you got any questions for me?"

"I will. I assume if you thought you knew anything, you'd have volunteered it by now."

"True. Like you, I'm still collecting information and con-

sidering how it fits together. It's a bit disconcerting to be plot-
ted against."

"Even for a Knight of the Double Tarn?"

He smiled for real. "Don't believe everything you hear in
those ballads. Remember how the queen said I was knighted
on her wedding day?"

I nodded.

"What she didn't mention was that I was barely fifteen. I'd
lived a sheltered life on a windy piece of rock out in the northern sea. I knew the skills of arms because we had nothing else
to do. But I'd never faced a real opponent determined to kill
me until Marcus came recruiting."

"How did he convince you? Appeal to your patriotism?"

For the first time, Gillian presented a genuine, full-face
smile. "Remember, he wasn't much older than me. He convinced me that girls would like my scars."

I laughed and gestured at the tapestries decorating the
room. "You seem to have risen to the challenge. Was he right
about the girls?"

Gillian's smile turned wistful. "Let's just say he was, and
leave it at that."

Since he was being so open all of a sudden, I pressed forward. "So tell me, straight up: *Do* you think the queen tried
to kill you? Or have you killed?"

"I don't know." He pondered for a long moment. "Do
you know why we're called the Knights of the Double
Tarn?"

I shook my head.

"The next-to-last battle of the wars of unification took place on a narrow isthmus between two tarns. Do you know what a tarn is?"

Again I shook my head.

"It's a lake that's deceptively deeper than it should be. Some are claimed to be bottomless. And they have currents at different depths that often go in opposite directions. At any rate, when we'd won, Cameron Kern declared that our brotherhood of arms needed a name and chose that."

I waited. Gillian wasn't a man to be rushed, and if I prodded him, he might drop the whole thing.

"The tarn is a good representation of Grand Bruan society as well. It looks placid from the outside, but it's made up of levels and currents that often run in opposing directions and at cross-purposes. I have tried to stay above these considerations and simply do my duty, but even that can generate unseen conflicts."

I risked a comment. "It's hard to imagine you and Dave Agravaine in the same organization."

"I agree with you," he said with another little smile.

"So you believe you might've inadvertently antagonized the queen?"

"That's what I'm trying to decide. She and I have never been close, but since her marriage we *are* family, and I've respected that."

He looked off into one of the tapestries, and I chanced another question. "Are the rumors about the queen and Elliot Spears true?"

He did not look at me. "Only the two of them know the answer to that."

"What do you think?"

His gaze returned to me, and the little glimmer of candor vanished. "I think it's time for you to be sequestered somewhere else."

Visions of dungeons and torture implements filled my head. "I can sit quietly in the corner, if you're tired of talking to me."

"I don't mean a cell. This castle has plenty of secure rooms that are quite comfortable, and Sir Robert ordered one readied for you. I'll go see if it's done." He went to the door and paused before opening it. "If I reach any conclusions about today's events, or if any useful information comes my way, I'll pass it along."

"Thanks."

"In return, I'd like your word that you won't try to escape."

"Sure," I said.

"That was fast. Do you always give your word so casually?"

"Nothing casual about it. Even if I got out of the castle, I'd still have to get off the island. I believe in luck, but not in miracles."

"I see. Well . . . enjoy your drinks, and I'll return shortly."

He closed the door, and the bolt slid into place. I took another sip of my drink and shook my head. The man had to be the straightest arrow in the quiver, all right.

I paced around the room some more, pondering what Gillian had told me. Well, trying to ponder it. The promise in Iris Gladstone's kiss kept intruding, so I finally gave up. I leaned back against the one tapestry-covered wall and let myself fantasize.

And promptly fell into the open doorway hidden behind it.

When I got free of the heavy cloth, I saw that the short passage ended at a stairwell that led both up and down, and women's voices came from beneath me. They spoke in whispers, but the tone was unmistakably urgent. I gathered the manacle chains in my hands to silence them, tiptoed down the dark stone stairs, and stopped when the words became clear.

"I cannot allow this, Your Majesty!" one woman hissed.

The answering voice was unmistakably Queen Jennifer Drake's. "Are you pulling rank on me, Rebecca?"

The girl Rebecca, the same one who'd been so snotty to Kay and me earlier, snapped, "Rank isn't important. What if someone sees you? How will you explain it?"

"The queen's spending some time alone in the moonlight after a particularly trying day. Who would care?"

"The queen of Grand Bruan does *not* worship the moon goddess."

"No, but apparently I wear jewelry in my most intimate feminine parts," she said bitterly. "Who would start a rumor like that? Who would *believe* it?"

"I'd rather them believe that," Rebecca said, "than know you're a moon priestess."

My eyes had adjusted enough that I saw moonlight streaming in from an open door at the bottom of the stairs. Two figures cast long shadows onto the landing.

"I know you're scared," Rebecca continued firmly. "So am I. But I forbid this."

"Then you *are* pulling rank."

"Marc will be here tomorrow. He'll take care of everything. Like he always does."

Jennifer said something so softly I couldn't catch it, but the defeated tone conveyed its gist.

Rebecca was having none of it. "Then let them pin it on that man with Kay, LaCrosse or whatever his name was. Let them convict some stableboy, or some old enemy of Gillian's from the wars. It doesn't matter who takes the blame, as long as it's not you. Marc needs you, Jennifer. Grand Bruan needs you. And so do we. You're *so close*."

Jennifer said nothing. I saw her move into the light and head up the stairs toward me. As fast as I dared, I rushed up and closed the door to the lounge. She passed me on the stairs without seeing me in the darkness.

But I saw her. Beneath the cloak that billowed behind her in her haste, she was totally naked.

Rebecca followed. A few moments later a door opened and closed above me, and I heard the unmistakable noise of a big dead bolt slamming home.

I stood in the dark going over what I'd heard. *I'd rather them believe that than know you're a moon priestess,* Rebecca had said. Which meant the queen was breaking her own laws. But why was that against the law in the first place?

And what exactly was she "so close" to?

I pulled the handle on the door behind me. It did not budge. I felt for a latch, but found none. I pulled as hard as I could with my good hand and leaned my weight into it. Nothing. I didn't know if I'd accidentally locked it or it was just stuck, but either way it wasn't going to open from my side. The only way out was the staircase.

If I went up, I'd find the equally locked door of the queen's private chambers. So I went down and emerged into a small courtyard, with tasteful shrubbery and a lone tree providing shade during the day. Faceless stone walls fifteen fight high surrounded it. I saw no other exit, which made sense if this place was intended for royal recreation. Or surreptitious moon worshipping.

For a moment the night sky mesmerized me. I'd been inside, under ceilings, since I got to Nodlon Castle. This sudden reminder that there was, in fact, a world beyond these walls made me smile.

Then, from out of the tree's shadow, emerged Cador, Hoel, and Agravaine.

They fell into formation, Agravaine in front, the other two behind and to either side. They had shed their armor and wore loose civilian clothes. They weren't visibly armed, but they were professional soldiers, so against what they saw as an over-the-hill amateur, they didn't need to be.

Running wasn't an option. Neither was calling for help. I couldn't believe I'd walked into such a blatant trap.

"Where's the queen?" Hoel said, puzzled. "We have a message for her—"

"Shut up," Agravaine warned. Then he glared at me and said, "Well, if it isn't the asshole." His nose was huge by now, swollen and crusted with blood at the nostrils, so that his words came out as *Ip it ibn't the asshobe.*

I looked around. The moonlight provided plenty of illumination and confirmed that not a single weapon-size object lay within reach. I had the emergency knife in my right boot, but with my useless hand and the manacles, I'd never get it out quickly. I was screwed.

"We have business to finish, and this is as good a place as

any," Agravaine said as he approached. His distorted voice would've been comical in any other situation. "You killed Sam and want to pin it on the queen. Now we'll show you what happens to people who mess with the Knights of the Double Tarn." He stepped right up to me, fearless because of his backup. He pushed me in the chest like a schoolyard bully.

My rage flared. *Well, hell,* I thought. *If I'm going down, I'll go down swinging.* And then once more I punched him in the face with every bit of my strength. And like a moron, I instinctively used my right hand again.

This time the sound was like two bags of muddy gravel crashing together, and if the fresh pain that shot up my arm was any indication, it must've been agony for Agravaine. He let out a shriek and stumbled backward, his hands clutching his face. I won't comment on the sound I made as my fingers gave way like a bundle of dry twigs.

My punching hand was now officially out of commission, although I used my forearm to block the handle of the spiked club Cador swung at my head. Where the hell had *that* come from? I kicked Cador in the balls, just before Hoel sucker punched me in the kidney. I fell to my knees but had time to sweep Hoel's legs out from under him with the manacle chain. He landed on his back and his head struck the ground, hard. He was out.

Before I could capitalize on this, Agravaine roared out of the dark, blood streaming down his face, and hit me with his whole body. The impact knocked me flat, and he jumped on my chest. Moonlight twinkled on his dagger as he raised it high over me. "I'll cut your fucking heart out!" he yelled.

Then he felt *my* knife under his chin. Drawing it left-handed and with my hands cuffed had not been easy, but I was highly motivated. He froze; his arm was raised to strike, but there was no way he could sweep it down into my chest before I buried my own knife in his neck. If I died, *we* died.

Blood from his nose dripped on my face. The only sound was our mutually labored breathing and, for me, the cacophony of my heart.

"Who goes first?" I asked. I hoped it sounded more like a cool whispered threat than a panicky gasp, but I wouldn't bet on it.

One of the other knights moaned. Neither of us dared glance away to see who. I couldn't make out Agravaine's eyes clearly, but I knew the dark rage and arrogance in them warred with the realities of his situation.

"Hello?" a male voice called from upstairs inside the secret passage.

"Someone's coming," Cador said in a pained squeak.

Agravaine slowly rose. I sat up with him and kept my knife under his chin. As soon as I could get my feet under me, I scrambled backward out of range, trying to look as if I always held my knife left-handed. Cador lifted the unconscious Hoel onto his shoulders, and Agravaine slipped his blade back out of sight. Without a word they vanished back into the shadows beneath the tree. The hinges of a hidden door creaked.

I backed into the nearest wall and slid to the ground. My hand hurt like my first broken heart. I waited to see what fresh threat would emerge from the secret passage.

It was Thomas Gillian. "Mr. LaCrosse? Are you down here?"

"Yeah." I slid the knife back into my boot before he appeared from the stairwell. He looked at me with a schoolmaster's disapproval. I said, "Would you believe I wasn't really trying to escape?"

"Of course. You gave me your word that you wouldn't." If he was being ironic, it was too dry for me to catch. "You seem to be bleeding."

"I tripped over my new jewelry."

"I see," he said, as calmly as if he saw this sort of thing every day. "Are you in any condition to make it back up? Your room is ready."

"I'll make it," I assured him.

chapter

EIGHT

We went up the stairs, through the lounge, and crossed the main hall so quickly that the nobles didn't have time to demand my head. We went through another door, up a second flight of stairs, and down a wide corridor. We were now above the royal chambers; it meant that, unless you were a lizard capable of scaling sheer rock walls, you couldn't leave your accommodations without passing the queen's guards below.

Gillian opened the huge wooden door at the end of the hall. "Here you go. I think you'll find everything in order."

My hand throbbed with every heartbeat, but I still wondered why Gillian accepted my lame excuse so easily. He couldn't be *that* oblivious. He gestured for me to raise my hands and removed the manacles from my wrists. The sense of relief was akin to a burning man's hitting the water. "Thanks. I'd tip you, but I'm tapped out."

"Since I'm a Knight of the Double Tarn, that would be considered an attempted bribe. Best you don't pursue it."

"Fair enough."

He nodded and, without another word, left.

They'd given me a small but lavish guest room. The main door was reinforced, and bars protected the windows; I was as safe as if I'd been in prison, and that may have been the plan. But double mattresses and Bob Kay's promised supply of ale went a long way toward making jail bearable.

I rubbed my wrists, careful with my right one. Numbness had set in, but I knew that wouldn't last. I wanted to sit down, drink myself stupid, and awaken anywhere but in Grand Bruan. Instead, after washing Agravaine's blood off my face and eating some of the fresh bread set out for me, I paced the room and methodically studied it. All castle rooms had secrets, whether openings into passageways or peepholes for observation. Royalty liked to keep their enemies, as the saying goes, even closer than their friends, and anything embarrassing about the personal habits of a rival was as good as a freshly edged battle ax. Many treaties had been signed, to the consternation of the general populace, to preserve the dignity of a king with a soft spot for little boys or livestock.

I spotted two peepholes right away and plugged them with pieces of the bread. Then I searched even more closely because those were *so* obvious, I suspected them as decoys. Sure enough, I found a third hidden ingeniously in the mortar between two wall stones, positioned to give a good view of the entire room, especially the bed. I stuffed the sharp end of a quill into that one, on the off chance a peeper might put out his own eye before he noticed it. I found no hidden seams indicating a secret passage and finally declared the room secure.

The closets and dressers contained clothes that were close enough to my size. I sat on the edge of the huge canopied bed and wrestled my boots off with my good hand. I took off my shirt, soaked Agravaine's blood out of it in the basin, then hung it up to dry near the fire. I put my trousers neatly between the mattresses, an old bachelor trick to restore the creases. I changed into some comfortably baggy black pants and a nice pullover tunic. All this domestic effort took the last of my energy, so I fell back on the mattress and stared up at the canopy's design. Like everything else here, it depicted another scene of battle triumph for King Marcus Drake.

I fell asleep staring at it. My own memories of battle easily conjured the appropriate sounds.

I awoke to a fanfare of horns and cheering. My first thought was, *That's more like it*. It was the least I deserved after what I'd been through.

Then I winced. Way too much sun blasted into the room, and judging from its angle, I'd slept until noon. I rolled out of bed and nearly howled as my injured hand came back to aching life. I stumbled to the window, blinking against the glare, to see what caused the commotion.

People filled the central courtyard below. Many were the irate guests from the previous night, but now they cheered as if this parade had been the whole reason for their trip. The rest were castle staff and, of course, the entire complement of the Knights of the Double Tarn.

Another blast of music announced the arrival of, I assumed, King Marcus Drake. Certainly the number of men in armor standing in neat, shiny rows along the parade route implied the visitor was important. Then Bob Kay rode slowly through the gate, followed by a tall man with long brown hair, a beard, and a flowing purple cloak.

I dressed as quickly as I could. As I wrangled my boots with my good hand, Kay unlocked the door. He looked exhausted beneath a coating of road dust. "You made good time," I said.

"I knew Marc would insist on coming immediately." Then Kay exclaimed, "Shit! Didn't you see the doctor?"

I shrugged. The knuckles on my right hand were black, with yellow circles outlining them, and the rest of my hand was bright red and swollen. "Yeah, I saw her."

"Dr. Gladstone usually does a better job."

"She did a great job. Agravaine and his pals ambushed me again after you left."

Kay scowled darkly. "I'll take care of it," he said, but with less than his normal certainty. He indicated my hand. "And I'll make sure that gets taken care of as well."

"That's not the only strange thing. Can I talk to you privately somewhere?"

"Not now. I'm glad you're already dressed, because the king wants to see you immediately." Before I could react, Kay locked the manacles around my wrists again. I started to protest, but by then I'd resigned myself to it. In his place, I'd have done the same thing.

I followed him downstairs into the hall where the fatal banquet had been held the evening before. The food was gone, but it was again filled with people. The clatter of armor echoed from the high ceiling as pages helped their knights out of their parade battle dress. Sun streamed in through windows and the open main doors; in daylight the room was far less glamorous, and the tapestries looked faded and threadbare.

It appeared Marcus Drake had brought the rest of the Knights of the Double Tarn with him. They were a varied crew, similar only in their cool, unimpressed demeanor. I saw no sign of Agravaine and his cronies, although Gillian nodded a greeting. It was moderately friendlier than before.

"Marc!" Kay called. Then suddenly, with no real time to prepare for the moment, I stood face-to-face with the most famous king in the known world.

Actually, face-to-chest is more like it. If I thought the Knights of the Double Tarn made me feel small, then next to King Marcus Drake I was a dwarf. He stood six and a half feet tall, and his shoulders were as broad as one of the serving tables. His tunic, undoubtedly custom-tailored to him, nonetheless drew tight across his muscular arms. In contrast, his brown hair fell boyishly into his face, and he tossed it aside to reveal his clear, surprisingly kind eyes. I'd met my share of important people, and usually something about them immediately disappointed me. But everything about Marcus Drake measured up to his larger-than-life reputation.

He'd already removed his armor and was restrapping his sword belt as we approached. I wondered if the scabbard held the legendary Belacrux. Like everyone, I imagined this weapon as always gleaming, freshly polished, and razor-edged. Up close, though, the sword at his waist looked just like any other well-used battle weapon, the worn leather hilt grip stained with sweat and blood. If this was Belacrux, then it was the only letdown.

Drake saw me looking. "Yes, this is Belacrux." I expected a huge, booming voice to make the rafters quiver, but instead h : spoke with casual, conversational ease. "And, no, I'm afraid you can't hold it."

I said nothing. He grinned when he saw Kay. Despite his size, his smile was easy and genuine.

"Your Majesty," Kay said formally, and knelt to Drake. I belatedly did the same.

"Rise, Sir Robert," Drake responded in kind.

Kay gestured to me. "Marc, this is the man I told you about. Edward LaCrosse."

I bowed. "Your Majesty."

"Bob thinks quite highly of you," Drake said. "Bob, loosen those cuffs. So give me the quick version of what's happened here."

"Didn't he tell you?" I said as Kay unlocked the disk and let out the chain's slack.

"Of course," Drake said. "But I want to hear *you* tell it."

Comparing stories was the oldest trick in the scroll; besides, I had nothing to hide. "Your man Patrice took a bite from a poisoned apple that was pretty clearly meant for someone else. No one else here had the sense or gumption enough to try and help him, so I did. I guess that made me look guilty to some people. Kay understood I had nothing to do with it and asked me to help find the real culprit."

Drake looked at Kay, who nodded. The king said, "And you believe Thomas Gillian was the true intended victim?"

"Right now I do. I'll change my mind if the evidence changes."

Drake looked around. "And where is Jennifer?"

"In your quarters," Kay said.

Drake regarded me seriously. "Do you believe the rumors that the queen is involved?" He did not lower his voice or whisper, and I couldn't politely look away to see if the other knights within earshot reacted to the question.

"I don't believe anything, I just follow the evidence. And right now there's no evidence of that, except that she brought the apples."

"That's enough for some people."

"I think some people wanted her to be guilty before there was even a crime."

Drake's eyes widened. I could've been more tactful, but my hand hurt and I was tired of being treated like a criminal.

"Well," he said after a moment, with a tiny smile, "nice to see I don't intimidate you."

"I'm quivering on the inside."

His grin grew. It was one of those grins that made you want to be his pal just so he'd grin at you again. Some men cultivated that; with Drake it seemed both inadvertent and sincere. "Then I suspect we'll get along." He noticed my hand. "That looks recent."

I nodded. "Yesterday. I punched something thick a couple of times."

"Dave Agravaine's head," Kay added.

Drake scowled. "Ah."

"Your Majesty!" a new voice cried, and there was a commotion at the main doors. A mob of the nobles pushed against the guards trying to restrain them. "King Marcus, we demand an audience with you at once!"

"Hell," Kay muttered, then yelled, "Get that door shut! Get those people out of here!"

"No, wait," Drake called to the guards. "Let them in." They obeyed, and the mass of pampered flesh surged toward us. I resisted the urge to step behind Kay.

At the head of the mob was Chauncey DeGrandis, his gaudy yellow color scheme replaced with sky blue. He wiped sweat from his face with a handkerchief. "Your Majesty, I apologize for my rudeness, but this confinement is intolerable. Here is the man responsible for the murder." He pointed at me. The others murmured their assent. In back, I saw Lord Astamore vigorously nodding.

Drake put a large, gentle hand on the puffy man's shoulder. "Calm down, Lord Chauncey, or you'll blow up and bust. Now take a deep breath—that's it, all the way down, let it out slowly—and tell me in simple words what you're so upset about."

DeGrandis did as the king commanded, wiped his face again, and continued in a much calmer voice, "That man murdered one of the Knights of the Double Tarn. We all saw it. And now *we're* the prisoners, and *he's* being protected by Sir Robert."

Drake smiled. His tone was even and infinitely patient. "I understand why, if you believe that's the case, you're so upset. I would be as well. Now I want you to answer my questions in the same calm way. Can you do that?"

DeGrandis nodded.

"Excellent. Now—why do you think this man is a murderer?"

"We all saw him standing over the body."

Drake nodded. "Ah. I see. But to beg your pardon, I've been told that the unfortunate Samuel Patrice had already fallen before this man reached him. Is that true?"

DeGrandis licked his lips before speaking. Drake's rank, size, and paternal demeanor took the wind from the soft man's outrage. "Well . . . I wasn't watching at the time. Personally, I mean."

"Then I'm sure you have a reliable source, someone who saw this man with Patrice before he fell?"

DeGrandis laughed nervously. "I . . . it's just general knowledge, Your Majesty."

Drake's eyebrows went up. "'General knowledge'?"

DeGrandis sighed, knowing he'd been defeated by the king's logic. "Yes, Your Majesty."

The others murmured among themselves, reconsidering their positions. It had nothing to do with my true guilt or innocence, and everything to do with staying on the king's good side. DeGrandis was a casualty in the eternal battle for royal favor, and the mob felt no loyalty to the man who'd led them a few moments earlier.

Drake, his hand still on DeGrandis's shoulder, shook the other man in a friendly gesture that probably rattled his teeth. "Lord Chauncey," he said with a little laugh, "do you remember all those years ago when we put down the new law codes? You were there, I believe. You sat to my left, about two rows back, didn't you?"

DeGrandis did not look up. He sounded like a small child. "Yes, Your Majesty."

"Does 'general knowledge' fall under any of the categories of proof we agreed on? Especially for capital crimes?"

"No, Your Majesty."

"I've just arrived, Lord Chauncey. I know what Kay's told me, and now what you've told me. I've heard what the man you accuse had to say as well. And I may ask some others to tell me what they saw. Now, this 'general knowledge' you mentioned must have started with someone. Whom would you recommend I talk to, to find out more about it?"

DeGrandis looked up sharply, realizing here was a chance to pass the blame to someone else. "Er . . . well . . . Lord Astamore has been the most vocal in his condemnation of that man."

The look on Astamore's face was enough to balance all the crap of the previous day. He looked around, but all the exits were guarded and his former friends moved diplomatically away. I made eye contact with him and smiled, just as he'd done to me the day before. I didn't normally traffic in revenge, but, hey, when it's handed to you by a king . . .

Drake nodded. "I see. Well, then, I'll be sure and talk to him." Then he looked over the other nobles. "Does anyone else have anything to add to what Lord Chauncey has just told me? Anyone? . . . Very well. I'm going to go upstairs, visit my wife, and wash off some of this trail dust. I'm sure you'll all understand that I need you to remain here as my guests until we resolve this tragedy. Thank you in advance for your patience, and remember, this is the law, *our* law, at work. And the law, gentleman, is what puts the *grand* in Grand Bruan."

The room bowed to him and he turned to Kay and me. In a low voice he said, "Gentlemen, let's get out of this circus, shall we?" Without waiting for an answer he headed for the door, and we followed. No one else did.

In the stairwell, Drake paused between floors and ran a hand through his hair. Thanks to the sweat and wind from his ride, it stayed in a rather unflattering position. "What a nightmare," he muttered.

"Sorry, Marc," Kay said. "I tried to handle it, but nobody listens to me. They'll only pay attention to you."

"I know you did your best, Bob."

Kay turned to me. "Other than running into Agravaine again, did anything else happen while I was gone?"

"I learned some more things. The poison the killer used was shatternight. That's important for two reasons: one, it doesn't grow anywhere in Grand Bruan, and two, it loses its potency soon after it's picked. That means that whoever used it came straight here from some place where it *does* grow."

Kay and Drake exchanged a glance. Kay said quickly, "That was the first thing I checked. She's not here. I promise."

"Who isn't?" I asked.

"My sister Megan," Drake said. "She's . . . well, she has issues with me. And with my kingship. That's why she left the island."

"She's a lunatic," Kay said.

"That's too harsh, Bob," Drake corrected. "She has the strength of her delusions, and that makes her dangerous. But she hasn't been seen on the island in five years. And she was never a good one for being discreet, so if she ever *did* come back, everyone would know it." He looked at Kay. "Although you *did* check, right?"

"I checked."

"What's she got against you?" I asked Drake.

"That's personal," Kay said gruffly, and crossed his arms.

"No, that's all right, I think Mr. LaCrosse deserves to know so he won't think we're keeping relevant secrets." Drake paused a moment to organize his thoughts. "Megan is only my half sister. She believes, and sadly she may be correct, that my father raped our mother to conceive me. Only my former adviser Cameron Kern knows for sure, and he refused to discuss it with me."

"That's one of the reasons," Kay interjected, "he's now a *former* adviser."

"Bob," Drake said warningly. "At any rate, Megan is two years older than me, so she remembers how being thought of as the king's whore affected our late mother. And on top of that, she left the island as a young woman and became a moon priestess, and we all know their opinion of men in general. Because of all that, she feels I deserve the punishment my father never received in his lifetime."

"Awkward to have treasonous family," I agreed.

Drake smiled with a sad little sigh. "Yes."

"And entirely beside the point," Kay said. "I'll look over the guest list and see if any of them have traveled outside Grand Bruan recently, to somewhere they might acquire shatternight."

"What about the other knights?" I asked. "Have any of them been off the island?"

"Three of them went to Sartoba to help train their army," Kay said. "They got back two days before this incident."

"Check it out," Drake said. Kay nodded. To me the king asked, "Anything else?"

Your sister isn't the only moon priestess in your family, I could've said. But I decided this wasn't the best time. "I'll let you know as soon as anything occurs to me."

"Good. Let's talk again in a bit after I've cleaned up and visited Jennifer. I owe her some private time, especially since we'll have to hold court very soon and make some public statement."

Kay and I both bowed, and Drake continued up the staircase. Just before he reached the next landing, he stopped. "And, Mr. LaCrosse? There's a very good doctor here. Gladstone, I believe is her name. Go see her about that hand, and tell her I sent you. She'll fix you right up." Then Drake disappeared upstairs.

I turned to Kay and grinned. "Have to obey the king, you know."

"I'll send Gillian with you again," Kay said. "To watch your back and such. Make sure you don't get ambushed again."

"Please, no. His charm is too overpowering."

Kay laughed. "You got that right."

"Besides, Agravaine's not the kind to try something in broad daylight. He's like a cockroach, he needs shadows to function. I noticed he wasn't in the hall when Drake arrived."

"You can be sure Marc noticed, too. All right, I'll take you down to the infirmary. Come on."

T he infirmary consisted of one big room filled with cots, and a smaller room for examinations. In the glow from the windows Iris was even more breathtaking. Her black hair, deliciously tousled the previous evening, was now neatly parted and combed, and a touch of artificial color shone on her eyelids and lips. Her white coat was immaculate, and beneath it she wore a powder-blue gown. The calves revealed below the hem were certainly good medicine for me. She sat writing something on a jar's label before she put it on a shelf. Then she turned, saw me, and smiled.

"Good morning, gentlemen," she said as she stood. Then she spotted my hand and scowled. "Well, *that* tells me you didn't follow doctor's orders. What happened?"

"I used it to make a point. Emphatically."

"I bet it hurt."

"It sure got *my* attention."

She smiled knowingly. It was only adorable. "You know what's ironic? First thing this morning I saw a broken nose that had also gotten twice as bad overnight. Damnedest thing. Two self-increasing injuries in one day."

"Something must be going around," I agreed.

"Bob, take those manacles off. And step outside, will you?"

"I think I should stay—"

She gave him a significant look. *"Bob."*

Kay sighed, unshackled me, and went back out into the hall. He closed the door, but left a small gap. "Close it all the way, Bob!" Iris called. He did.

She nodded toward the examination table. "Now hop up there, little boy. I should warn you, though, that if you're going to keep playing so rough, I'll have to speak to your father."

I jumped onto the edge of the table. She lifted my hand and gingerly pushed my sleeve up my arm. When she ran her fingertips lightly over the bruise, I winced. She said, "That tough-guy veneer really *is* just skin-deep, isn't it?"

"If that."

"You can cry if you want to, I'll never tell. Now wiggle your fingers." I did so, and she pushed on a couple of them. "I think you did some real damage this time, soldier. You need a cast."

As she poured fresh water into a basin and placed it on the table beside me, I said, "I noticed that the beds in the other room were all empty. How's the girl Mary?"

"She left. Said she wanted nothing more to do with castles and knights."

My professionalism managed to get my attention. "And you let her? She was a witness to a murder."

She shrugged as she withdrew a roll of cloth and began cutting it into strips. "She wasn't my prisoner."

"Do you know where she went?"

"Back to whatever small town she was plucked from, I suppose. She'll probably marry her childhood sweetheart and start squeezing out babies."

I said nothing. Mary probably couldn't tell us anything else, but then again, maybe I hadn't asked the right questions. I wondered if Agravaine had gotten to her.

Iris said, "I heard King Marcus is here."

"Yeah, he got in this morning. Gave me a royal command to come see you, in fact, when he saw my hand."

She poured some white powder into the water, and it immediately turned cloudy. "That's a relief. He's a good man, and he'll straighten out these metal-plated idiots before someone else gets seriously hurt."

Since my career as a knight was aborted pretty early, I never had the luxury of fighting directly for king and country. Certainly I had never served under anyone who inspired the loyalty of Marcus Drake. My warrior years were spent as a mercenary, a sword-for-hire battling for anyone who paid me. I didn't care who the enemy was, or why we were at war with them. During those years I killed lots of people with no more thought than I'd have swatting a fly.

And our medical facilities were nonexistent. If we got cut, we stitched each other, and if we got stabbed anywhere vital, we died. If we were too wounded to fight, we were dumped: no parades, no medal ceremonies, no bards singing of our deeds. Certainly no neat rows of beds in an airy, clean castle, or beautiful young doctors to bolster both our flesh and our spirits.

As Iris checked on the progress of the thickening liquid in the bowl, I said, "So Agravaine came to see you?"

She nodded. "He said he ran into a door going to pee in the middle of the night. I don't think his nose will ever set right now."

"That's too bad."

She smiled again. I could watch her do that all day. "Treating his injuries is always a pleasure. I look forward to his final one."

"That's a bit callous."

"Doctors have to be callous. If we got emotionally involved with our patients, we'd go nuts."

That wasn't terribly different from the way a soldier had to think; it was one reason I was no longer a soldier. "So you *never* get involved with patients?"

"Never," she said at once. She dipped one of the cloth strips in the bowl, then draped it over my knuckles. It was wet and heavy, and she immediately overlapped it with another. She pressed the dangling ends against my skin, and they stuck there. She began threading strips between my puffy fingers.

I tried not to react when it hurt, but I didn't fool her. "Will my hand be better than his nose?"

She smiled. "Don't worry, I've treated this kind of thing on the battlefield many times. You'll be fine. And I know a neat trick."

By now the cloth around my hand and wrist had begun to stiffen. She produced a sword hilt, the blade neatly removed, and pressed the grip into my injured palm. "Now hold this as tightly as you can while the bandages harden. That way the cast will set in the right shape. You won't have as much wrist movement, but you also won't drop it every time you parry a blow."

I did as she instructed while she cleaned up the remaining cloth strips and leftover plaster. In a few minutes, she removed the hilt from my hand, and sure enough, the cast retained the shape of my grip.

"See?" She put the sword hilt back on its shelf. "You won't win any swordsmanship awards, of course."

"I wouldn't on my best day."

She handed me a black sling. "If the pain gets too much, use this to keep your hand above your heart. It might also remove the temptation to use it as a battering ram. But the more you can stand having it down, the faster it'll heal."

I put the sling in my pocket and hopped off the table. "Not bad. Where'd you learn to do that thing with the sword, anyway?"

"I apprenticed during the last years of King Marcus's military campaigns, doing battlefield triage. If a soldier wasn't dead, he needed to be able to return to the fight. I worked this out myself."

"Was your teacher a moon priestess?"

Her eyes flashed with a surprising degree of anger. "No. Medicine is a science on Grand Bruan, not some superstitious hocus-pocus."

In every other kingdom I'd visited, moon priestesses were respected as healers. "I've seen them do some pretty amazing things," I said cautiously.

"Yeah, well, knowing you have to stop the bleeding is easy. Understanding where the blood comes from is a hell of a lot harder."

"I'm not trying to pick a fight, you know."

She took a deep breath, then sheepishly smiled. "Sorry. If your fingers get numb, come see me immediately. It means either your hand's grown more swollen or the cast is too tight. Either way you could end up with gangrene."

"Oh, I can practically guarantee I'll need to come see you."

She flashed those magnificent eyes at me. "You don't give up, do you?"

"I will if you really want me to," I said seriously. And I meant it. I gave her a moment to respond, but she let it pass. "So can I ask you something off topic?"

"Off which topic?" Her smile returned full strength.

I smiled back; heck, I grinned like the last man alive after a three-day battle. "It's about Queen Jennifer. What kind of woman is she?"

"Out of your league, I'm afraid."

"No, seriously. You said you'd seen her true nature, and I need some insight. This place has more secrets than flies on a manure wagon, and I don't know who to trust."

"You seem to trust Bob Kay."

"Sure. He has the keys to my shackles. And I trust you."

Her eyebrows went up. "That a fact?"

"You know it is. But after you two, I'm flapping in the breeze. Drake seems decent, but he's thrown his lot in with Jennifer, who"—I glanced at the door to make sure no one stood waiting for the doctor and overheard me—"I definitely don't trust."

"Why?"

The words to tell her about the previous night left my brain, passed through my throat, and made it all the way to my teeth before I choked them back down. "Instinct," I said instead.

"You really think she's a poisoner?"

"It's a woman's way. No offense."

"None taken. It'd be my way, too. We all use the talents we're given."

"And, no, I don't think she did it. But that doesn't automatically mean I trust her. How well do you know her?"

Iris wiped her hands with a towel. "Hm. I first met her right after I'd finished my apprenticeship. They were both really young, you know. We all were. Marcus was crowned when he was fifteen and married Jennifer when he was seventeen. And that was . . . wow, nearly twenty years ago." She shook her head at the passage of so much time. "When did I get to be thirty?"

"Do you like her?"

She laughed. "Who I like is completely beside the point in this job. But between you, me, and the mice in the walls, no. Not at all. Okay, wait, that's not entirely true. I didn't like the snotty little girl Marcus courted. The woman she is now . . . she's different. Stronger. More dedicated."

"What changed?"

Iris shrugged. "Who knows? Back then she was a teenager. Now forty's peeking over the horizon. People change a lot in those years."

Again I wanted to tell her what I'd overheard the night before, but decided to hold back until I better understood the

Grand Bruan dynamics. I trusted Iris, but my instincts were not infallible. "So do you think she could do what she's accused of? Poison a knight as a warning to the others?"

Her face crinkled delightfully as she thought about it. "The spoiled girl Marc married?" she said at last. "Yes, I can believe it. But the woman she is now? No."

"I see. Well . . . thanks. I have to meet with the king again, so I should probably be going."

A touch of mischief again shone in her eyes. "I *would* like to check the cast before you leave to go back to wherever you came from. So we'll see each other at least once more."

"At least. And after that?"

"After that is after that." She tossed the rag into a bin. "I'm a military doctor. I go where the battles are."

I held up my bandaged hand. "I doubt I could manage a whole battle, but I could put on a hell of a skirmish."

She laughed and shook her head. "I'd love to discuss tactics with you, but I have work to do. I *will* see you later, though." And the kiss she gave me was the best promise I'd ever had.

As I wound back through the castle corridors behind Bob Kay, my wrists again secured, I scanned every hallway junction for Agravaine's crew. They never appeared. If they weren't hunting me, what were they doing?

By the time I met again with the king and queen, my cast itched something fierce.

I joined Bob Kay and the royal couple in the same room where Jennifer had received us the night before. Once again Bob wound up the slack in my manacles, just in case. Drake greeted us dressed in casual trousers and an old favorite shirt with the sleeves ripped out to accommodate his considerable arms. Jennifer wore a simple dress and a lone strand of pearls, and her hair hung loose and unadorned. The queen's maids, including Rebecca, had withdrawn to give us privacy. I wondered if they were listening behind a door, or peering through a hidden peephole. I'd gain nothing by embracing my paranoia, though.

Drake bolted the door behind us. "So, we seem to have both a murder and a public relations crisis. I believe if we resolve the first, the second will take care of itself." He nodded at my hand. "Iris fixed you up, I see."

"She did." I hoped he would also tell Bob to release me, but that didn't happen.

Instead he continued, "So we're agreed there's a murderer in the building somewhere, who wants to make the queen look guilty."

"No," I corrected him. I'd finally pondered my way through something that had bothered me all along. "Even as a frame, this is a poor job. There are lots of kingdoms where the queen might kill someone with impunity, but not this one. We know murdering Patrice wasn't the goal, and neither was killing Gillian or framing the queen."

Jennifer spoke for the first time. "Then what *was* the point, Mr. LaCrosse?"

I shook my head. "Haven't gotten that far yet. I suppose it could just be a way to disrupt things. Sow dissent. Start people talking. And whoever planned it didn't care if someone had to die."

"Or they simply wanted Gillian dead," Jennifer said. "Why must there be a plot behind it?"

"Gillian has his enemies, sure," Kay said. "Every soldier does, especially one as prominent as he is. But he fights in every tournament; they get their shot at him."

"*If* they're the sword-and-sandal type," I said. "If he pissed off a bard or someone's lady-in-waiting instead, though, it's unlikely they'd meet him on the field. But I still don't think killing him was the main thing."

Drake told Kay, "I like what your man LaCrosse says. I

think the target of this is, ultimately, sedition. Someone wants to topple the crown, but indirectly."

"Thanks," I said, "but it's only one theory. There's also the idea that the queen did it and deliberately made it look amateurish and sloppy so she'd have plausible deniability. That's a pretty good plan, too."

"I am *not* a killer," Jennifer said. Her glare at me was so cold I needed a sweater. "How often do those words have to be said?"

"*Please*, Jennifer," Drake almost snapped. I wondered what they'd been discussing before Kay and I arrived. "No one here thinks you're a killer."

Jennifer did not back down. "Are you certain?"

I caught Kay's eye and wondered if we should slip out. He minutely shook his head.

Drake put his palm against her cheek. Their size difference made the gesture even more tender. "This is exactly what he wants, Jennifer. You and I at each other's throats. The Knights of the Double Tarn looking at each other suspiciously. The nobles convinced there's a cover-up of something."

Jennifer would not be calmed. "Who's 'he,' Marc?" It was half-taunt, half-accusation. She pointed at me. "This man? Some disgruntled knight? Your old friend Kindermord? Someone else none of us know?" She stared up at him, daring him to answer.

Drake started a little at the name *Kindermord*, but only a trained observer such as me would notice. The name also made Kay purse his lips a little. Drake recovered instantly and said at last, with more patience than I expected, "Jennifer, this isn't helping."

"You're still going to hold court?" Kay interjected.

Drake nodded and turned away from his wife. Her gaze followed him with something very like contempt. "First thing tomorrow morning. We'll let everyone speak, get their grievances into the open. No secrets."

A sharp knock sounded from the door. Everyone except Drake jumped. Kay strode across the room and opened it. "Who the hell is knocking on the king's private—"

He stopped suddenly. Thomas Gillian waited just outside. He wore shining dress armor and stood at ease with his hands clasped behind his back, polished boots apart. "Your Majesties, I offer my sincere apologies for this interruption."

"Tom," Drake said patiently, "we're kind of in the middle of something. Is this urgent?"

"I believe it is."

"I'll take care of it," Kay said, and stepped outside with Gillian. He didn't shut the door all the way, but they spoke in low tones none of us could hear. I risked a glance at the queen, but her expression was unreadable.

Kay came back into the room and closed the door. He grimly faced Drake and Jennifer. "Gillian wants to speak to both of you," he said darkly. "He's got some of the others with him."

"Show them in," Drake said, sounding perplexed at Kay's tone. "If it's so important he—"

"Maybe you should speak to him alone," Kay suggested. "I'll tell the others to wait in the hall."

Drake's eyebrows went up at the interruption. "No," he said firmly. "That would just spread more rumors."

Kay started to protest again, but thought better of it. "You're the king," he said wearily, and returned to the door.

He stepped aside as Gillian and three other knights entered the room. Like Gillian, the soldiers wore their best go-to-court clothes and were clean and neatly shaved. In unison they knelt before Drake. The metal shin guards on their boots clanked against the stone floor.

"Permission to rise?" Gillian said.

Drake frowned a little at the formality, but he went with it. "Yes. Welcome, Sir Thomas, Sir Harold, Sir Peter, Sir Jordan."

Gillian and his companions stood. He held his chin rigidly parallel with the floor. Ironically, he conveyed far more of royalty's innate nobility than Drake. "Sire, I have come to a deeply troubling conclusion about yesterday's attempt on my life."

Drake crossed his arms. "And what's that?"

"Sire, I have reflected on my past misdeeds, my deepest sins, and those whom I have wronged. In each case, I considered those affected by my actions and their possible desire for revenge. I have come to the conclusion that none of them could possibly have been involved."

There was a moment of silence. "And?" Drake prompted.

Gillian nodded at me. "This man is clearly not the culprit, despite what the nobles may say. I have expressed this certainty to the other knights, all of who agree with me. With the usual three exceptions."

"Dave Agravaine," Kay asided to Drake. "And Hoel and Cador, of course."

Drake said to Gillian, "I have to say my conclusions are pretty much the same as yours."

Gillian nodded. "I would expect that, Your Majesty. You are a wise and intelligent man. But I and the other knights have come to an additional conclusion that you will no doubt dispute. Yet we are convinced it is the case. We believe," Gillian concluded, his words utterly devoid of passion, "that the queen, already morally suspect for her past conduct, was behind the entire event."

Drake showed no reaction, Kay sputtered in outrage, and Jennifer hissed, "That is *absurd*!"

Drake shushed everyone with a small wave of his hand. Except for the red flush of anger, he showed no outward sign. His voice remained steady. "So *why* would Jennifer try to kill you, Tommy?"

Gillian's composure broke slightly, and for an instant, no longer than a bee's wingbeat, real emotional pain showed. Then it was gone. "After much thought and prayer, I believe the queen intended to murder me as a warning to those who have publicly discussed her past conduct."

"Tommy!" Jennifer gasped.

"How dare you!" Kay thundered simultaneously.

"Quiet!" Drake snapped. The effort to control his temper caused sweat to pop out along his hairline. Through clenched teeth he said, "That's a very serious accusation, Gillian."

"Yes, sir," he responded. The knights behind him had neither moved nor spoken and, now that the king's wrath was about to boil over, seemed anxious to be mistaken for furniture.

Kay had no regal image to maintain. "Why in the hell would the queen want to kill *you*?" he demanded. "*You* never gossiped about her to anyone."

Gillian turned just enough to meet Kay's eyes. "That is true, Sir Robert. But the first rumors of the queen's misconduct came from the Knights of the Double Tarn. I have achieved some prominence in that organization, second only to Elliot Spears. Therefore, by killing me, the others would be frightened into silence."

"Tommy, you're my *friend*." Jennifer's disbelief and hurt certainly sounded genuine. "We're *family*."

"Indeed, Your Majesty, I once thought so."

"Tommy, be reasonable," Drake said, still calm. "You can't seriously think Jennifer would go to such lengths just to quiet some rumors."

"And those rumors are *ancient*." Jennifer's voice shook with emotion. "I've had no opportunity to be indiscreet with Elliot in *years*. And I never *have* been."

"I regret my lack of conviction in your response." Gillian's gaze did not waver.

"So what do you want me to do, Tommy?" Drake's voice rose as he spoke. "Lock Jennifer up? Burn her at the stake? Chop off her head and stick it on a post? Would that satisfy all of you? Or do you just want to pass her around, so that what one knight got, you all get?"

By the end Drake was roaring, and Gillian's three pals wilted under this royal onslaught. But Gillian was unbowed. "When you hold court tomorrow, sire," he said in the same infuriatingly even tone, "I will ask to settle the matter in trial by combat."

Drake laughed humorlessly. "No one's settled a dispute that way in years. We have courts and laws now."

"That is true, and were this any other crime, I would

expect nothing else. But this is a crime of both treason and blood betrayal. As she said, the queen is also family. As such, this can only be expunged through spilled blood. Mine, or the queen's through her champion."

"Tommy, please," Jennifer said, and approached him. Tears shone on her cheeks. "Look at me. I've known you since before you could shave. You've been my friend and confidant. How could you believe this of me?"

He turned those blank, serious eyes on her. "I assure you it was not an easy decision. And it broke my heart to admit it to myself." Then he faced Drake again. "Because of the seriousness of the accusations, I ask that the combat be scheduled as soon as possible. Since Elliot is not here, I must insist that we not wait for you to summon him. You must choose a champion from among the knights present."

"I'm not choosing anything," Drake snapped. To the three silent witnesses he added, "Nor am I denying Gillian his request." He stood to his full imposing height, and his voice grew official. "But since it involves the crown directly, I *am* claiming royal prerogative and will take the day to think it over. I suggest all of you do the same. If you go through with your intention to raise the issue at court . . . I'll make my decision then."

"As you say, Your Majesty," Gillian said. He knelt again, and the three men with him followed suit. They stood and strode from the room without waiting to be dismissed. The door closed behind him with a solid, funereal thud.

"I don't *believe* that," Kay seethed. "Who the hell does he think he is?"

"A man with the moral high ground," Drake said wryly. He turned to Jennifer. "So *now* what should we do?"

"You're asking me?" she replied, and added a derisive "Hmph."

"This is all *about* you," he almost, but not quite, snarled. "By tonight, every Knight of the Double Tarn will know Gillian asked for trial by combat, and that one of them will be asked to stand in for Elliot."

"How will you get out of it?" Kay asked.

Drake shrugged. "If Gillian really demands it, I'll have to let him have it."

"Are you serious?" Jennifer gasped. "You'll let my honor, your *wife's honor,* be decided by two thugs with swords?"

"I have a country to run, Jennifer. The loyalty of the military is essential to that, and they already think you're guilty. I have to overcome that somehow."

Jennifer stepped toward him slowly, trembling with fury. "So you, my husband, the man who shares my bed, would give in to these demands just to *save face.*"

"To save Grand Bruan," he corrected.

"This is absurd," she said again, and turned with a swirl of her silk gown. "I'll be in my sewing room. When you have some rational thoughts, please let me know." Her door slam was far more emphatic than Gillian's.

Drake sighed and dropped into the nearest chair. He looked up at Kay and me. "Okay, fellows. I'm open to suggestions."

"Is there any way to get word to Elliot?" Kay asked.

Drake shook his head. "I'd have to send one of the knights, and then everyone will know it's because I don't think anyone else will stand up for the queen's innocence."

"*Will* anyone?" I asked.

No one answered.

Drake pondered a moment, then said, "I suppose, as Jennifer's husband, *I* could fight Gillian."

"No," Kay said quickly. "You are the king, you have to stay above it all and pass judgment."

Drake chuckled. "Not in a trial by combat. The winner's sword is all the judge they need. You just don't think I can beat Tommy, do you?"

Kay said nothing.

Drake turned to me. "You've got a unique perspective on this, Mr. LaCrosse. What do *you* think I should do?"

"Put off this fight as long as you can," I said. "Let Kay investigate this further. The killer is here, and he'll find him. Maybe he's this 'Kindermord' the queen mentioned."

Drake shook his head. "There's no time. Somebody will have to fight Gillian, unless I get a lot smarter between now and tomorrow morning." He paused. "And there's no one named Kindermord. It's just old gossip, older even than the stuff about Jennifer."

Kay sighed. "Marc, I'm really sorry about all this. It happened on my watch."

Drake smiled. "Bob, if it *hadn't* happened on your watch, Jennifer's head might already be decorating the main gate." Drake heaved his large frame from the chair. "And now, if I don't get in there and make peace with her, *my* head might be up there in the morning."

"I'll do what I can, Marc," Kay said.

"Bob," Drake asked quietly, "do *you* believe she's guilty?"

"No," Kay said at once.

Drake turned to me. "And you?"

I held up my hands. "I'm a prisoner, I have no opinion either way."

Drake indicated my manacles. "Do we really need those, Bob?"

"I'm ninety-nine percent sure he's not involved," Kay said. "But it only takes one percent to kill you."

Drake nodded. "That's true. I suppose I should go attempt to mollify my own one percent, then. Bob, keep me posted. Good evening, gentlemen."

Drake went into the other room where Jennifer awaited. I almost expected crockery to fly past his head when the door opened, but it closed behind him uneventfully.

"You have no ideas about anything?" Kay demanded. "That makes me look real good for building you up to the king. Thanks."

I clenched my fists; well, at least my left one. He was lucky I didn't shatter my cast on his skull. I snapped, "You really want to know what I think? Even if you had a *dozen* guys like me, you'd never get to the bottom of this. A royal court is always full of secrets, and this one is no different, although it *is* impressively complicated. I mean, hell, maybe this was all to force Gillian into a tournament; I'd look real hard at anyone who volunteers to fight for the queen."

"I'll keep that in mind," Kay said, still fuming.

For some reason this disapproval made me even more determined to defend myself. "And even if I stayed and cleared up this mess, another one would just spring up in its place. That's how it works."

I must've sounded condescending, because Kay's angry

redness deepened almost to purple. "I don't expect you to understand, you being a sophisticated outsider like you are. But this court, this king, this *country*, is *different*. We've earned the chance to make a safe, secure future for our children, instead of adding their blood to what's already soaked into this island. That chance means each of us has to do everything, *everything* to make it work, to hold this dream of Grand Bruan together."

He gestured at a nearby painting that showed a triumphant Marcus Drake on horseback, sunlight glinting off his upheld sword. "You see this? There has never been a single, unified government on this island in recorded history before this one. Now no one dares to attack us with swords and armor anymore, so they come after us with ideas, with gossip, with death by damn poison. And that poison spreads with every lie and accusation that gets made. It can't be stopped with armor and swords, only with *this*." He touched his temple. "And those of us who have learned to fight only with our hands *need* the help of people like you, who know how to fight that way."

This passionate tirade, coming as it did from a big, square-headed soldier who at first glance might not appear to know any two-syllable words, moved me far more than I wanted to admit. Still, I held up my wrists and rattled them for emphasis. "It's not my fight, Kay. And it's only my problem until I get these off for good."

Kay looked at me for a long, silent moment, searching my face for the idealism he was sure lay hidden there. He didn't find it. Finally he sighed, "Damn it, Eddie," then turned away and struck the stone wall with the flat of his hand. The noise echoed. Without looking he said, "I'll take you back to your room, then, until I can make arrangements to get you safely out of the castle."

The relief I felt at those words was tempered by the guilt at disappointing Kay. "I'm sorry, Bob."

"Me, too."

he door to my luxurious prison once again closed behind me, and the lock clicked in the silence. I felt as if I'd just kicked the crutches out from under a one-legged man.

For good measure I wedged a heavy chair against the door handle. If that mob of angry lacehounds somehow got past the guard and wanted in, they'd at least have to get mussed up a little. And more important, it would alert me should Agravaine decide to make a strike; he'd have to work harder than this to catch me off guard.

I closed my eyes and sighed. I couldn't believe I was actually trapped in a castle like some fairy-tale princess, but here I was. Half the people around me thought I was a murderer, the other half wanted an innocent woman to burn at the stake, and the world's greatest king was hamstrung by his own code of honor and law. I'd be immensely glad to be away from here and back in the real world.

I worked my shoulders to get out the stiffness from being in chains all day, but only dislodged a big, heavy yawn. Everything I told Kay was true: it wasn't my fight, it wasn't my problem, and Grand Bruan's internal politics were none of my business. But two things continued to nag at me despite my efforts to ignore them.

One was the look on Kay's face when he spoke of his dream for Grand Bruan. I was so used to dealing with cynical, counterfeit feelings that I was unprepared for his genuine emotion. If something could affect a grim, gritty soldier to such a degree, perhaps it *was* worthwhile, and worth my time. Maybe I should do something because it was right, not just to save my own hide.

The other was the certainty that, once she knew my reasons for leaving, Iris Gladstone would never speak to me again, no matter how many times I broke Agravaine's nose.

Outside the window the evening sun cast its golden glow all the way to the opposite horizon. Past the city walls, dust rose from wagon wheels as merchants headed home after a day hawking wares at the market. Smoke trickled from chimneys as wives dutifully prepared evening meals.

Once no such community could have survived beyond the castle's barricade. The historical Grand Bruan wasn't a place for nice families and hardworking tradesmen. Raiders and rivals would have slaughtered anyone they found, burned all the crops, and destroyed the buildings. Now, though, children played in the dusk with a reasonable chance they might never in their lifetime have to fight anyone with a sword. They could go to school, learn to read, and build a secure future for their own children. In this bloody, violent world, that was a hell of a gift.

But not *my* gift, I reminded myself. Not *my* problem.

I looked down at the rock-hard bandage on my hand. I remembered the way her hair smelled as she wrenched my fingers back into place. The thought of never kissing her again was not pleasant, but so what? Women were everywhere, and eventually I'd intrigue another one. It's not as if I wanted a wife, or a mother for my children. Those things were not options for me, and I was quite happy that way. At best I could get some brief companionship, and it would be no real effort to find a working girl in a tavern with short black hair, and dancing eyes, and a biting wit, and a touch that brought every bit of me to life, and . . .

Ah, *hell*. I had it bad, all right. And from just one real kiss and a bunch of cracked knuckles. I turned to get a drink from the bar.

King Marcus Drake, all six and a half feet of him, stood less than three steps away.

I know I jumped. I probably let out an undignified, girlish yelp. I threw myself back against the barred window and my hand shot reflexively for my sword, except that I didn't have one and my hand was useless. "Shit!" I said, although I barely heard it over the thundering in my chest. How had he crept up behind me without my hearing him?

"Sorry." Drake filled the room like a stallion in an outhouse. "Didn't mean to scare you."

The chair still blocked the door. "How the hell did you get in here?" I demanded as I caught my breath.

He waved a hand at the far wall, where a section of brick had opened to reveal a dark hallway beyond. "Secret passage. The place is loaded with them."

I'd thoroughly searched the walls for any seams that indicated hidden doorways and completely missed that one. That made me neither look nor feel very smart. "I thought you were making peace with your wife. Did she chase you in here, or is there some other reason for sneaking up behind me like that?"

He blinked at my disrespectful tone, but his voice was calm when he said, "Actually, Mr. LaCrosse, I'm here on business. I want to hire you."

I did not kneel as etiquette demanded. Instead I went to the bar and poured myself a drink. I didn't ask Drake if he wanted one. I tossed it down, shivered at its bite, and said, "Is that a fact?"

"I know you haven't been treated terribly well—"

I held up my bandaged hand. "You think?"

"—but . . . well, Mr. LaCrosse, I need your help."

I closed my eyes in supreme annoyance. He didn't say *we* or *Grand Bruan* or *the country* needed my help. If he had, I could've easily stayed angry. It was a personal request, spoken without self-pity or whining or any sort of royal posturing. And just like Kay's damn speech, it got through to me.

He stood there expectantly, huge and mythical in the normal-size room, and awaited my response. I must've been light-headed from the stench of genuine idealism, because even though Drake and I were about the same age, his mystique was so intense I had the fleeting thought that I wanted to be him when I grew up.

I said, "Let me guess. You want me to fight Thomas Gillian."

He laughed. "Good lord, no. No offense, but he'd have you carved into pork chops before your sword cleared its scabbard." Then, realizing he'd been a bit too disparaging, he added, "Because, of course, it wouldn't be a fair fight with your injury."

"Right."

"I'm sorry, I don't have time to banter. The king can't disappear for very long without someone noticing. I need you to go to Blithe Ward and bring back Elliot Spears. He's the only man who can either talk some sense into Gillian or beat him in a fair fight."

"Who or what is Blithe Ward?"

"Elliot's castle. It used to be called Bitter Ward, but when he took it over, he renamed it."

"Where is it?"

"On the other side of the island. A day's ride, if you switch horses regularly and don't stop to relieve yourself too often."

"Will he come?"

"Yes. He's my best friend, and as the queen's champion it's his job."

Drake was one of those men who effortlessly made people crave his approval, so most jumped to do what he asked. I didn't. "Don't you have errand boys for this sort of thing?"

"If I send one of them, everyone would know it. I have to appear impartial."

"But you're not."

His big shoulders sagged a little. "No. I *will* be impartial in my judgment, should that become necessary, but never in my heart. How can I be? I love Jennifer, and I believe she's innocent. Nothing can change that."

"Not even the facts?"

"You said yourself that the facts are on her side. There's no real proof, only conjecture, but it plays on people's feelings. It's those emotions that I have to worry about. Jennifer isn't terribly popular, and a lot of people wouldn't mind seeing her suffer."

"Look, I appreciate the spot you're in, but this is none of my business. Really. I just want to get out of here, and if it's all the same to you, cut Grand Bruan out of all my future travel plans. You people are just too high-strung for simple folk like me."

He said quietly, "You think the way things are now, you'll get out of the country in one piece?"

I was silent for a moment. Finally I said, "It's unseemly for a king to threaten a commoner. Makes him sound petty."

"No, it's a warning. You *will* get safely out of Nodlon, but it's a long way from here to the south coast. If anything happened to you, you'd very easily become the scapegoat for yesterday's events."

I felt a slow chill that had nothing to do with temperature. History showed that Drake was a hands-on king not afraid to get a little bloody. I'd hate to fight him with two good hands, let alone just one. "That *would* get Jennifer off the hook."

"But it doesn't expose the real killer. If we don't do that, he'll strike again. And I won't be able to sleep thinking his next target might be Jennifer."

"Or you."

"Or me. And that would be the worst thing, not for me, but for this country. The peace and unity we've created depends on my being invincible. I'm not, of course, but I can't let that get out." He said this last with a wry little smile.

I sipped my drink more carefully this time. So the great King Marcus Drake wanted my help and expected it simply because it served this sparkly dream of Grand Bruan. Just as Bob Kay had done a few minutes ago, and as I knew Iris Gladstone would if I saw her again. Before I even realized I'd formed the words, I said, "I get twenty-five gold pieces a day, plus expenses."

"That's all?" he asked, genuinely surprised.

Yeah, that's all, I thought sardonically. *That's the price of my clear conscience.* "There's not much money in this business if you're honest."

Marcus smiled a little. "Then you must be the most honest man around."

I didn't laugh. "I'll need something with your seal on it so this Spears will know I'm legit. And a good horse." I recalled the recalcitrant, mule-stubborn one that had brought me here from Lady Astamore's and would be glad to never see it again.

"All taken care of." He produced a folded parchment, sealed with embossed wax. "Give this to Elliot. Show the seal to anyone who questions you. Bob's already arranging the horse. There are messenger stations all along the route where you can change mounts."

"Awfully sure of yourself, aren't you? Good thing I said

yes, or you'd have looked pretty silly." I pocketed the items. "Normally I get half my fee in advance."

He put one hand on my shoulder. The weight, both physical and moral, was considerable. "I don't pretend to believe you're doing this just for the money, Mr. LaCrosse. I've been lucky enough to encounter more decent men than not in my life. I'm glad you've continued that trend." He paused. "And you'll find your *entire* fee with Bob."

I didn't laugh in his face, but the urge was pretty damn strong. Instead I said, "Can I ask you something?"

"Of course."

"What if you go to all this trouble and Spears loses?"

"Only someone from off this island would ever ask that. Thank you again, Mr. LaCrosse."

"Wait," I said suddenly. "Since you're getting my services so cheaply, I want you to throw in a favor."

"What?"

"Ten minutes alone with the queen."

He blinked, and his expression subtly grew harder. I'd seen that same look on the faces of many irate husbands; it was nice to know that he was, deep down, so typical. "Why?" he asked with frightening calm.

"Use your imagination."

"That's not funny."

"And I'm not joking. I've spent the last two days investigating a murder an awful lot of people believe the queen committed. I'd like some resolution just for my own sake."

"She won't come."

"She will if you tell her to."

"And I'd pay for it for the next three weeks."

I wasn't sympathetic. "Crowns are heavy, aren't they?"

He thought for a moment. "All right, I'll send her. But she won't be pleasant."

Neither, I thought, *will I.* But I kept that to myself.

I poured two drinks and had just stoppered the decanter when the secret passage opened again and Queen Jennifer Drake emerged. She started to close it behind her, but I said, "Leave it open. That way I'll know no one's on the other side listening."

She stared at me with a mix of surprise and contempt. She looked soft and feminine in her casual finery, but the fire in her eyes was as sharp as ever. "I am yours for ten minutes, Mr. LaCrosse. Don't waste it being clever."

"Occupational hazard," I said, and offered her a drink. She looked at it and back at me, making no move to take it. I shrugged, put hers back on the bar, and sipped mine. "I overheard you and your serving girl Rebecca in the courtyard last night."

The reaction was so minuscule I almost missed it. "I was in a courtyard?" she asked coolly.

I nodded. "And you were . . . underdressed."

She looked back at the open passage, then took a casual step toward me. Most men would've thought nothing about the movement. I said, "That's close enough. Anyone can be dangerous if they get within arm's reach."

"I merely wanted the drink you offered."

I mock-bowed and handed it to her. She turned it up and drank half of it. It got no more reaction than my revelation.

"So were you skulking about in the shadows last night?" she said. "That's what your kind does best, isn't it?"

"It was entirely an accident, believe it or not. But it did leave me with the nagging question of why a queen would let her lowly attendant rip her a new one that way."

Jennifer smiled slightly. "You turn a colorful phrase, Mr. LaCrosse. You didn't ask *why* I chose to be naked."

"Didn't have to. I've met moon worshippers before."

This time a red flush crept up her face. It could've been a delayed effect of her drink, of course.

"And," I continued, "I've met queens. But never one so demure to a lesser mortal."

"Will you accept," she said after a moment, "that both my presence in the courtyard and the conversation with Rebecca have nothing to do with the murder of Sam Patrice? And therefore are no concern of yours?"

I shook my head. "You've forfeited your right to be taken at your word, Your Majesty."

I'd basically called her a liar to her face, but she showed no reaction at all. At last she said, "What did Marc say?"

"You know I haven't told him."

"And why is that? I'd think the opportunity to bring down a queen would be too strong to resist."

"Oh, I'm good at resisting. Besides, you're not *my* queen, so I really don't have a knight in this joust. I just want to know why you let Rebecca talk to you that way."

"And how will that help solve this crime?"

"I won't know until I get an answer."

She chuckled without humor. "Very well. In all ways I am her superior, except in matters seen under the moon. Last night she came to me in that role, and in that role she had the right to speak to me as she did."

That made sense based on what I knew about moon priestesses. Their rank had nothing to do with age or their station in life, so a lady-in-waiting *could* have seniority over a queen. "Are you in league with your husband's sister? She's a moon priestess, too, I hear."

"Hardly. Megan Drake is a single-minded creature bent on revenge for a wrong committed against her mother by Marc's father. For that reason, she's been banned from the island. And for that reason, so has worship of the moon."

She took another drink, and anger fueled her words. "Oh, it still occurs; it always will. But it's furtive now, hidden, disreputable. If the great King Marcus hates it, it must be a bad thing. That's how the common thought goes." She looked at me. "Can you imagine his reaction if he found out his own queen, his own *wife*, took part in it behind his back? That one day *she* would become a priestess able to lead rituals?"

"Is that what Rebecca meant when she said you were 'so close'?"

"Yes."

"I don't know, Marc seems a pretty levelheaded guy. He might support it. And even if he didn't, you *are* the queen."

"Make no mistake, Mr. LaCrosse. In Grand Bruan, Marc is the jewel; I am merely the setting. I can be replaced."

I raised my glass. "You turn a colorful phrase yourself."

She bowed slightly to acknowledge the compliment. Then she continued, "He allows me great freedom, but he expects his few absolutes to be followed. And one of them is that moon worshipping is forbidden."

"So if I tell him what I saw, you're screwed."

"Pithy. And accurate."

"You also mentioned someone named Kindermord. Who is that?"

"I don't know. It's a name that came up a lot back when Marc was first crowned king, but I never met the man. And Marc never talks about him anymore."

"He said it was old gossip. What about?"

"I really don't know. It's been twenty years, at least." She finished her drink. "Is there anything else?"

"Did you really have those apples with you the entire time?"

Her hard expression softened enough to show real fear. "Mr. LaCrosse, with the moon as my judge, I picked them myself, brought them in my personal baggage, and never let them out of my sight except for the five minutes prior to the actual banquet, when I left them in the extremely crowded kitchen in the care of some pretty young serving girl I'd never seen before in my life."

"Who got beaten up by your man Agravaine."

Her face darkened. "He is not *my* man."

"He's one of the few knights who seems blindly loyal to you."

Through clenched teeth she said, "That may be. I have no control over his unhealthy obsessions. But whatever he's done is at the whistle of his master, not me."

"Who's his 'master'?"

The distaste in her voice was enough to sour milk. "Marc's nephew. Medraft."

That name, spoken so casually, brought me up short. "Not *Ted* Medraft?" I asked softly.

My reaction didn't surprise her. "Yes. The infamous 'Dread Ted.' You know him, then?"

This was unexpected, and unpleasant. And I should've thought of it myself. During my final campaign as a mercenary, just before I woke up as the only survivor of a whorehouse massacre and vowed to change my ways, we got a visit from a contingent of young Knights of the Double Tarn cadets. They were there to get a taste of actual combat, something no longer possible on Grand Bruan.

I couldn't tell you who the others were. But Ted Medraft stuck with me. Part of it was his youth: he was barely a teen, dark-haired and bare-cheeked. He was soft and rather overrefined for a knight, and the rumor was he'd got his commission through connections rather than merit. At the time, I could not have cared less.

The exchange program ended before it really started, though. Our unit commander, a grizzled old soldier who'd seen more corpses than a village full of gravediggers, sent the cadets packing without even time to rest their horses. When they were gone, and the commander had got suitably drunk, he told us why.

It seems young Medraft sat in on an interrogation and offered to help motivate the subject. What this involved was kind of vague, but it made one officer in charge pass out and then desert the unit. The other later beat someone senseless for merely asking about it.

By now Medraft would be grown, and the talents he demonstrated as a youth would be refined and perfected. That's not something I wanted to contemplate.

And I had no idea he was Marcus Drake's nephew. "By reputation," I said to answer her question. "Then his mother is . . ."

"Marc's sister Megan."

I poured another drink. "If I'd known he was involved, I'd have raised my rates."

"Yes. Ted takes an 'interest' in me. The way a man takes an interest in a friend's wife. I've never encouraged it, but he's let me know that, should I ever be threatened, he will make sure the threat . . . goes away. And Agravaine, who's always underfoot, is like the younger brother who fancies his elder sibling's girlfriend. He makes sure Ted knows everything, secretly hoping Ted will lose interest and he'll be able to step in."

"A charmer."

"Which one?"

"Both."

"Indeed. Although Ted actually *can* be charming. And he has quite a flair for love poetry." She paused. "Is that all?"

"It's all I know to ask. Is there anything you want to tell?"

"I did *not* poison those apples. Nor do I know who did. That is all I can tell because that is all I know."

"Then I guess we're done." I bowed. "Thank you, Your Majesty."

Her eyes narrowed. "You have a surprising sophistication, Mr. LaCrosse. You haven't always been a 'sword jockey,' have you?"

"No, I used to be a shoemaker. But my sole wasn't in it."

She smiled, lopsided and wry. Despite everything, I liked her; if she was stringing me along with lies, then maybe I *should* be a shoemaker. She left through the hidden door, which closed silently behind her. I finished my drink, considered another, then thought better of it. My observational skills had got bad enough without more help.

There was a knock at my door. Before I moved the chair, I said, "Yeah?"

"It's Bob Kay."

The bolt slid aside and Kay entered. I held out my wrists for the manacles. He sighed, "Oh, stop it." He closed the door behind him and said in a low voice, "Marc sent me to explain the plan for getting you out."

"Can't I just walk out the door?"

"Agravaine and his pals know you're leaving. They'll be waiting for you tonight at the main gate."

"How do they know?"

"Because I told them. I *want* them waiting at that gate. They also know that Gillian's asked for trial by combat. Unless they can pin the crime on you, specifically a *dead* you, they know the queen will be found guilty."

I scowled. These vaunted knights, purveyors of chivalry and all that was good in men, sure didn't live up to their publicity. "How did you guys manage to get this shining-armor reputation again?"

"There was a time," he said sadly.

"Do all the frilly important people still think I'm guilty?"

He nodded. "The longer we keep them locked up here, the more certain they are, even after Marc's little show. That's why Agravaine wants to make quick work of you, so they can post your head at the gate and get Jennifer off the hook."

"So Agravaine's after me, and that means, indirectly, that Ted Medraft is after me."

Kay's eyes narrowed. "How do you know about Medraft?"

"How does anybody?"

"Well, lucky for you Medraft's not here. Marc keeps him assigned to the northern posts, where his particular skills are best used. He may barely be a man age-wise, but just knowing he's in the area gives a lot of raiding parties second thoughts."

I had to laugh. "And Marc thinks I can just waltz out and go fetch his pal Elliot."

"Marc asked me to make sure you get out of the castle without running into any problems, and I'll do that." Kay walked past me to the window and looked out. "Come here. See that hill right there, the one that lines up with that archery notch on the wall? When the moon touches the top of it, it'll be well past midnight. Come downstairs into the banquet hall. It'll be empty. There's a serving-room entrance hidden behind the Battle of Tarpolita tapestry; can you find that?"

"Yeah."

"Go into the hallway behind it and find the grate in the floor. Lift that and climb down. It's a drainage tunnel that runs under the castle so the cliff doesn't erode out from under us. It's mostly dry this time of year. I'll meet you at the end of it with a horse."

"And then what?"

He unrolled a small parchment on the bed. "This is a map of the route, although I doubt you'll need it. The road from here to Blithe Ward is a major thoroughfare, and it's practically a straight line right across the island. There are a few crossroads towns, but they shouldn't confuse you. And here are the courier stations where you can switch horses. You can't miss them, either."

"There's one thing nobody's faced up to," I said. "What if Spears says no?"

"He won't," Kay said with certainty.

"But if he does?"

Kay sighed, the weariness of a man carrying more than a single lifetime's disappointment. "Then I hope you like heat, because this island will burn."

fter Kay left, I locked the door again and walked to the window. It was dark now, and the shadows in the courtyard below told me the moon was just rising. It would probably not reach the hilltop for a few hours. Not only would that be past midnight, it would be awfully close to morning and wouldn't leave me a lot of darkness to use. I figured I might as well try to get some sleep, and the drinks I'd guzzled during my interviews made that actually feasible.

I stretched out on the bed, fully dressed down to my boots; I wasn't quite ready to relax all the way yet. But with some forced deep breathing, I got calm enough that my mind drifted, and I assume I did sleep a little.

Until another knock, softer than Kay's, snapped me wide-awake.

I slid from the bed, drew my knife with my left hand (I was

getting better at that), and pressed myself flat against the wall beside the door. Mock-sleepily I said, "Yeah?"

"It's me," a female voice said, too quietly to be recognized.

"*Me* is half of what a cat says."

"It's Iris."

I put the knife away and opened the door. She wore a dark cloak with a hood. I could see only her lips, chin, and the hollow of her throat. But I recognized her just the same. The sweep of her shoulders and the little smile lines at either end of her mouth were unmistakable; I'd know her at a hundred yards in the fog.

"'*Me* is half of what a cat says'?" she repeated drily.

"*Ow* is the other half."

"Oh, I got it," she assured me.

"Late for a house call, isn't it?"

"I go where the injuries are." She pushed back the hood to reveal a serious, though no less lovely, face. "Bob Kay asked me to check your hand before you left. He said you might run into trouble and wanted to be sure you were as sturdy as we could make you."

"Really?" I did my best not to grin. I was only partially successful.

"Aren't you a little old to keep acting like a horny teenager?" she said, but with a smile. "This could just be a trick to get close enough to do you in."

I closed the door behind her. "A man's got to die from something."

She slipped the cloak from her shoulders and tossed it over the back of a chair. "Truer words were never spoken."

My grin faded. She held a long, shining straight razor.

She scowled when she saw my expression. "Oh, for God's sake. I'm not going to slit your throat. I just thought that if you lost your beard, you'd be harder to recognize."

"Oh."

"You're paranoid."

"It's served me well."

"Yeah, well, not tonight it hasn't." She quickly arranged a pitcher and bowl on the table, turned a chair toward the lamp, and motioned for me to sit.

"*You're* going to shave me?" I said dubiously.

She put one hand on her hip. It accented her curves, as did the long, low-cut dress, complete with black lace at the wrists. I suddenly realized that she'd *dressed up* for me. "The first surgeons were also barbers," she said wryly. "Trust me."

The skeptical old soldier in me listed all the ways this could be a trap. "Uhm . . . maybe you should just keep me company while I do it."

"That should be fun to watch, unless you're left-handed."

She had me there. Still, it would be a brilliant way to get me off guard and finish me with little fuss.

"You either trust me or you don't, Eddie. But I have to tell you, if you won't let me close enough to shave you, you'll *never* get me into bed."

At last I said, "Well, since you put it *that* way . . ."

I took off my shirt, a little self-conscious of my less than youthful belly, but I figured a doctor wouldn't mind. When I turned to face her, though, her eyes were wide with something very much like awe. "My *God*," she whispered.

For just the tiniest fraction of a second I thought my physique had rendered her speechless, then I realized what she meant. "Yeah," I said. "It was a long time ago."

She bent close to examine the three-inch puckered scar near the center of my chest. Then she scurried around to look at my back. "It went all the way *through*?" she gasped.

I nodded.

"And you didn't drown in your own blood? Or die from gangrene?"

I shook my head. "I was off my feet for a while, though."

"I'll bet." Now she regarded me with a mix of pity, admiration, and tenderness. "What *happened*?"

"It was a long time ago," I repeated, and stared at the wall. I couldn't meet Iris's eyes because I might see Janet's instead. And then I'd hear her screams.

After a moment Iris said, "Okay. It just surprised me on a professional level. Most injuries like that don't get the chance to develop into scars."

I shrugged. "We all get surprised sometimes."

I took the offered seat. She wrapped a towel around my neck, then lathered me up with something she produced from her bag. It smelled pungently fresh, and I was alert for any change in awareness the fumes might bring about. When nothing happened, I finally relaxed. It was a tremendously luxurious feeling.

She ran the blade up the side of my neck and just over my jawline. It went *shckt* as it sliced through my whiskers. I said, "So how come you haven't bagged one of these handsome, wealthy knights?"

"Who says I haven't?" She rinsed the blade in the water basin.

"No ring."

"Most doctors don't wear jewelry. Tends to snag on the edges of wounds."

"That's nice to know. But you didn't answer my question."

The razor skitched up my cheek. A big blob of soapy beard dropped onto the towel over my chest. She said, "I don't care for soldiers much. I know lots of women swoon over a man in uniform, but I've seen them at their worst. Once a man is taught to be violent, it becomes his first instinct. And when there's no war to fight, way too many of them turn it toward their women."

"I was a soldier once. And my current job requires violence on occasion."

"I know."

"But you're here."

She rinsed the blade in the bowl. "You're different. You stuck up for that girl when you didn't have to."

"I just happened to be there. Any decent guy would have."

"My point exactly. There aren't many decent guys in armor. Some are better than others, of course. Bob Kay comes close. But even he wouldn't take a swing at Dave Agravaine. And believe me, that guy's needed his face smashed in for a long time."

She began working around my mouth, so I stayed quiet. I felt the swell of her breasts against my arm as she leaned over me, and I smelled her light perfume. I resisted the urge to glance down when the neck of her dress gaped slightly. Well, I mostly resisted. I felt like a kid entranced by the thought of seeing his first naked female body.

Finally she finished, wiped my face with a towel, then nodded toward the mirror above the mantel. "Check yourself out."

One glance at my unadorned features reminded me why I'd grown the beard in the first place. I had to admit, though, that I looked completely different. "You've successfully removed that ugly growth," I said, "and revealed the uglier one beneath it."

"So the patient will survive?"

I turned to her. "The patient will grow it back as soon as he can. But he appreciates the effort."

She stepped forward, so close that I reflexively put my hands on her waist. She pressed her hips against me and let my arms take the weight of her upper body. Her hands lightly touched my bare cheeks. "Now that you won't scratch me up if you kiss me," she said in a husky, unmistakable voice, "let's discuss my fee."

"I thought you worked for the government."

"I do. But you don't. You've run up quite a tab, what with an office visit and two house calls."

I felt her breath on my upper lip. Her hands moved down to my chest, and one fingertip ran along my scar. I said, "I certainly wouldn't want to stiff you."

She giggled. "Are you sure about that?"

She was so close I could hear her slightly ragged breathing. "*Now* who's a horny teenager?" I said.

The smile left her face, replaced by the kind of look men dream about inspiring in women like her. She said, "I'm no teenager, sword jockey."

Then she proved it.

★   ★   ★

LATER I looked up at Iris as she sat astride me in bed. The moon was now centered in the window, and its light cast her in pale blue, edged with orange from the dimmed but persistent lamp. Her skin glistened with sweat, and her lips had that delicious puffy quality some women get when they're aroused. She rolled her hips slowly and bent over me; her breasts slid against my chest. With her eyes closed, I wondered for a moment if she pictured someone else beneath her. Then she smiled down at me and traced her fingers along my hairless cheek. "You clean up nicely."

"And you dirty up well."

She laughed and kissed me. I looked past her shoulder at the moon, did some quick calculations, and decided it would reach the pinnacle of the hill within the next half hour. "I have to go soon," I said into the kiss, which showed no signs of stopping.

"I know," she agreed, and pulled back enough to look into my eyes. She ran a hand through her sweaty hair. "I should probably mention that this is not characteristic of my normal behavior."

"Or my normal luck."

She laughed again and wiped the perspiration from her eyes. She had a slender, trim shape under her clothes that spoke of her active life, and a couple of scars of her own that I intended to ask about someday. "I've just never met anyone like you," she continued. "And I knew I'd regret not doing this if I never saw you again."

"Really." It wasn't a question so much as a statement of disbelief; I did not generally inspire unrestrained lust in intelligent, beautiful women.

She nodded. "I know myself, Eddie. I know what I respond to. It's not the shallow surface, no matter how handsome or wealthy it is. You can believe me or not."

I rose and put my arms around her waist, feeling the muscles of her back move beneath her skin. "I believe you." I rolled her onto her back. She went willingly, opened herself to me, and together we pounded out the last of our lust with much noise and effort. We finished with barely enough time for me to dress, pack, and head downstairs. Getting out of that bed was one of the most heroic things I've ever done.

We made no awkward promises, except the unspoken one that was in our kiss as I slipped out the door. My last sight of her like that, naked in the moonlight, would stay with me for a long time.

chapter FOURTEEN

Even indoors my newly bare cheeks felt the night's chill, and my footsteps, despite my attempt at stealth, sounded loud against the stone.

The rush from the time spent with Iris, which left me feeling as if I could kick the whole world's ass, had burned itself out by the time I reached the top of the staircase. I paused for a moment and listened for any movement or voices. Only silence reached me. I took the steps two at a time, knowing that I'd come out near the door to the great hall.

My typical luck held. At the bottom I ran smack into a trio of men starting upstairs.

They stared at me. I stared at them. Two of them were pudgy, dressed in expensive clothes a bit too small for their corpulence. The burgundy veins stood out on their noses and ears, marks of their long-term dissipation. I didn't know them, but they seemed typical wealthy landowners and had no doubt been among the courtiers howling for my entrails for the past two days.

The third I recognized at once as my old pal Ken Spinkley, the Lord Astamore. But his face was as blank as the others.

A long moment passed when no one moved or spoke. "Well?" said the nearest man, who wore amber eye shadow. He humphed with impatience. All three were drunk, and one had to lean against the stairwell door for support.

"I think I'm going to be unwell," the leaning man said, his voice thick from drink.

"Ladies are unwell," Eye Shadow said. "Gentlemen vomit."

"Would you kindly step aside?" Astamore snapped at me, making no effort to hide his annoyance. "We've been run out of the great hall."

Suddenly I realized what was going on: they *didn't recognize me*. I was clean-shaven and dressed differently, and they were pig-porking drunk.

The leaning man warned, "Watch your shoes, here it comes."

"Oh, no, get out of the way!" Eye Shadow demanded, and pushed me aside. He grabbed leaning man under the arm and hauled him to his feet. They stumbled up the stairs toward the guest floor, but the retch-and-splash sounds that followed told vividly that they didn't make it.

"Morons," Astamore muttered. He looked at me again, and a glimmer of familiarity gleamed behind the drunkenness. "Say . . . I know you, don't I?"

It was late, I was on the spot, and I pulled out the only name I could think of at that moment. With immense dignity

I tucked my injured hand behind my back and looked imperiously down my nose at him. I let a bird twitter in my voice when I said, "I, sir, am Lord Huckleberry."

Astamore blinked. "Oh. I'm sorry. Kenneth, Lord Astamore, at your service."

I pursed my lips in annoyance. "If 'my service' includes roughing me up with your boorish gallivanting, then that is true indeed. Perhaps I should have a word with the king, whose company I have just left."

"No, I assure you, we meant no harm," Astamore quickly said. Nervous sweat popped out around his hairline. "We were simply looking for the way back to our rooms, there's certainly no need to bother King Marcus about this. Is there?" He added the last so pitifully I almost laughed in his face.

"Perhaps not." I swept past him. "But should you inconvenience me again, I shall certainly take measures." I didn't see the look on his face as I went through the door into the great hall, but I'm sure it was suitably aghast.

As promised, the room was empty. The only illumination came from moonlight through the narrow windows. I crossed the room to the Tarpolita Hill tapestry and slipped behind it into the designated serving room. I snagged one of the small table lamps, lit it, and went into the darkened corridor that connected the rooms. The drain cover creaked as I lifted it. I climbed down the ladder, paused to pull the grate back into place with my good hand, and dropped with a splash into an inch of running water. I turned the lamp up all the way.

As with everything else in this damned storybook kingdom, the tunnel was ridiculously clean. They must've sent people down here once a year to make sure no vegetation or wildlife was able to take hold. The lamplight reflected off the eyes of a lone pair of rats, but it was nothing compared to the horde I'd have found in any castle off this island.

How the hell did Marcus Drake *do* that? This went beyond any sense of duty, into a realm of pride in one's kingdom that I'd never before seen. Sure, you could order men to clean these tunnels, even force them to do it. But they wouldn't do it *this* well unless they felt they had a personal stake in it.

I realized, of course, that I knew exactly how Drake did it. He did it the same way he'd got me to take this stupid job.

Annoyed with myself, I looked behind me and saw the vertical bars that covered the cliffside opening. Beyond it stars burned in the clear sky. I turned landward and began to walk. The tunnel's ceiling was about half an inch shorter than I was, which kept me in a crouch, and the passage sloped gradually upward. Steplike notches lined the floor just below the water, so that if you fell, you wouldn't slide all the way to the spout. My lower back did not take long to express its disapproval, followed quickly by my knees and, in sympathy, my busted hand.

This distracted me enough that I didn't spot the body on the tunnel's floor until I was almost on top of it.

I stopped immediately and took in the scene before moving closer. The body lay on its side, the water trickling around it to continue downhill. Its feet were bare, and ropes tightly bound its ankles. I couldn't see its face or tell its gender from its wet clothing. A handful of rats waited nearby, disturbed by my light but not frightened off.

I waved the lamp, and the vermin scattered. I knelt beside the body. Its hands were tied behind its back. The small fingers curled limp, and the ropes hadn't bitten into the skin. That told me the corpse was bound after death.

I also saw it was a woman.

I slowly turned her over. The long, wet hair hid her face, so I had to brush it aside. I recognized her.

It was Mary, the serving girl.

Yet it *couldn't* be. There wasn't a mark on her face.

I stared at her for a long time. I was absolutely sure it was her. I'd watched her closely in the great hall, just before Patrice fell dead. Yet Agravaine had given her a black eye and a split lip just two days earlier. Those injuries simply *couldn't* heal that quickly.

I ran my finger along her cold cheek. Her eyes were closed, and her features slack. She hadn't drowned. Using just my good hand, I sought the fatal injury beneath her clothes and found it quickly enough: a single knife thrust between her ribs, no doubt angled toward her heart. The edges were white and puffy, washed clean of blood by the steady water.

Her joints were stiff; she'd been dead at least several hours. She could've been killed anytime after Iris said she left the infirmary.

But why was she *here*? I looked back down the tunnel toward the cliff grate, which blocked anything bigger than a rat. She couldn't just wash out to sea, even if there was enough water flow to carry her. There weren't enough rats to dispose of the body, or even render it unrecognizable. So the only explanation was that it wasn't dumped here, but *stored* here. To be disposed of later.

I looked at her face, verifying the impossible truth that

there was no trace of her injuries. The flesh was unmarked, unswollen, unsplit. There was still a touch of baby fat in her cheeks, and an innocence that had survived her death.

I'd mocked her possible future back in the great hall before the murder. At the time it had been the worst fate I could imagine for her.

I considered carrying her with me to meet Kay. She deserved better than this, lying facedown in a glorified sewer for the crime of being in the wrong place at the wrong time. But there were more undercurrents than just the water in this tunnel. Had I been set up to find this girl? Was a contingent of armed men waiting for me to emerge with the proof of my guilt tossed over my shoulder?

Against all my better instincts, I carefully put her back the way I'd found her. Wherever her spirit now resided, I hoped it understood.

THE tunnel opened at the bottom of a small, empty pond. The even, bowl-like sides were lined with round rocks to prevent erosion when rainwater filled it. At the top of the slope, Kay sat smoking a pipe, eyes heavy with exhaustion.

He smiled as I emerged into the moonlight. "Well, hack off my legs and call me Shorty. You look ten years younger without the beard."

"I'm in disguise." I did not tell him about Mary's body, or my run-in with the courtiers, or that I'd claimed to be the mythical Lord Huckleberry. Nodlon Castle was a surprising distance away, down the slight slope toward the cliffs. I hadn't realized the tunnel was quite so long.

He fingered my jacket's lapel. "You might be a little over-dressed to be inconspicuous."

"Once the road dust settles on me, I'll be fine."

"There's your horse." Kay indicated a nearby tree where the animal was saddled and tied. "She'll do fine for a long, fast trip. And here." He handed me a sword and scabbard.

"I guess you trust me now."

"I'm not sending you out unarmed. But I should warn you: If you intend to leave Grand Bruan without completing your job, Marc will send Tom Gillian after you. And Gillian won't stop until he's found you, and one of you is dead."

I sighed and shook my head. "I knew it was too easy."

"Yeah. And here's this."

He tossed me a small money bag. From its weight I could tell it included more gold than I'd asked for. While the threat of Gillian's retribution was definitely a factor, this was the real reason he could trust me. Not the money itself, but what it represented: my word. I said, "For what it's worth, if I take payment for a job, I see it through."

"I hope so. Because so does Tom Gillian."

I put the money in my jacket pocket, then with great diffi-culty, thanks to the cast, I buckled the sword around my waist. Kay offered no help. When I finished, I said, "One more thing. Seriously, how will Spears take it when I show up and tell him to drop everything and come here?"

Kay snorted. "It's Jennifer. If she says spit, he'll ask how far."

"So there *is* something to the gossip?"

He shook his head wearily. "Hell, I don't know. Maybe,

once. When we were all a lot younger, we all did things we're not proud of now. But it's old news, and the people involved have made their peace with it. Bringing it up now does no one any good."

That comment set my mind working. "Bob . . . who *would* benefit if Marc lost the crown?"

"No one. He doesn't have an heir."

"Isn't that unusual?"

Kay shrugged. "It's not from lack of trying, believe me. Those two are all over each other. It just hasn't happened yet."

"Then he has no next of kin?"

"Just his sister. She'd never be accepted as a ruler, though. And neither would her son. *I* hope she's dead in a ditch somewhere on the mainland." He looked up. Although the moon was still overhead, the sky to the east was growing visibly lighter. "You should really get going. If anyone from the castle sees you, this'll all be pointless."

"All right. I'll be back as fast as I can."

"You're coming back? I thought you'd drop off your message and then haul ass back home."

"Well, with the threat of Tom Gillian hanging over me, I have to follow through to the end."

"Right," Kay said with a knowing little smile. "It has nothing to do with a certain feisty castle doctor, does it?"

"Nothing at all. But if you happen to see her, tell her to be sure to remember the *ow* until I get back."

"Inside joke, I assume."

"Yeah."

"I'll tell her."

We reached the horse. She was a beauty, dark with a few white patches. In the dim illumination I couldn't see if her base color was brown or black. She tossed her head in either greeting or intimidation.

I was, in the estimation of my old riding instructor, a piss-poor horseman, probably because I hated horses. They were too big, too smart, and too enigmatic for me to ever trust. This began in childhood, and at the time nothing had yet changed my opinion. In fact, most of my experience reinforced it.

Once I'd seen a cavalry officer, Colonel Bierce, approach an obstinate stallion that kicked him in the head so hard it actually tore away his jawbone and sent it flying out of the corral. From the upper teeth to the throat it left a great red gap fringed with hanging shreds of flesh and splinters of bone. The worst part was that the injury wasn't immediately fatal; the poor bastard never even lost consciousness.

The road was deserted as I started the long trip to Blithe Ward. Many things bothered me, not the least of which was that I still didn't know who really killed Sam Patrice. I was sure Jennifer Drake didn't, and that gave me the moral clearance to take this job; but the list of suspects had otherwise gotten no shorter. And how had Mary the apple girl ended up miraculously healed and dead in the sewer?

The greatest crimes are always the small ones; a man who kills his unfaithful wife in a moment of passion will arouse the outrage of all, while a man who orders the death of thousands will barely rate a comment for it. Before this was over, a relatively simple murder would become a legendary bloodbath. And I would always live with the thought that, had I been just a little bit smarter, I might have prevented it. Because I'd just seen the crucial clue, right in plain sight, and hadn't understood what it meant.

S omeone tossed a fresh log on the tavern's dying hearth fire. The popping sparks and surge of fresh warmth reminded me that these things I was describing happened years ago, and that I could no longer change the outcome. Nevertheless, in telling the story I found myself wishing I'd been smarter, more courageous, *better* somehow. I wished I'd been worthy of the dream of Grand Bruan, even though I understood now that its failure was inevitable.

The group gathered around me was larger, too. I'd been so engrossed in my tale that I hadn't noticed the newcomers arrive. For someone in my profession, that kind of obliviousness was not reassuring.

They all watched me expectantly, their faces scrunched in concentration. I had no idea I was such a riveting storyteller. Then again, the subjects of my story were Marcus Drake,

Elliot Spears, and Ted Medraft, who carried many less worthy tales told on cold winter nights. Even seven years after that fateful day, peddlers still brought new broadsheets recounting more and more outlandish adventures of King Marc and the Knights of the Double Tarn. At least *my* outlandish adventure had the virtue of being true.

Finally Callie broke the silence. "So was he really as tall as they say?" she asked softly.

"Who?" I asked.

"King Marcus," she said with the same reverence I'd heard priests use to invoke their gods. "One of Tony's songs says, 'His crown tapped the ceiling beams.'"

Tony was Callie's no-account minstrel boyfriend, addicted to giggleweed and other girls. He left before the first snowfall, promising to return and marry her. She was the only one who believed him.

"He was a big guy," I agreed. "He had to be, to swing Belacrux. That sword weighed a ton."

"So you handled his sword?" Angelina asked, deliberately sarcastic. It was her default mood when she wasn't sure how to respond, and I knew it for the defense mechanism it was. That didn't stop it from annoying me.

"Angie, please," Liz quietly scolded. She was the only one in the room who'd dare stand up to Angelina in her own tavern. I squeezed her hand where it rested on my leg. She winked.

"So did you really get to hold Belacrux?" Ralph the leatherworker asked, childish eagerness making his voice go high. "Did it really have a pommel made of emerald?"

"Yeah," I said. "I did. And, no, it wasn't really covered in jewels. They wouldn't stand up to as much pounding as that sword got. It was just a big sword for a big man."

"But it *was* sharp enough to cut a butterfly's wing, right?" seamstress Esme asked.

I felt like a nanny explaining a bedtime story. "I didn't get a chance to try that. But it seems unlikely."

"Oh," she said, disappointed.

I tapped my ale mug, which I didn't remember finishing, either. "My throat could use some lubrication."

"This story isn't *that* good," Angelina muttered, but gave me a refill anyway.

I took a long drink from my fresh mug just as the door opened to admit yet another new listener. Sharky Shavers quickly closed the door and blinked in surprise at the group gathered around me. "Did I miss something?"

"Eddie's telling us about King Marcus Drake and the Knights of the Double Tarn," Callie said. "He *knew* them."

"Really," Sharky said skeptically. "So this doesn't have anything to do with the coffin outside I nearly tripped over?"

"I'll get to that," I said.

"Yeah, he'll get to that," Angelina said, "about the time this keg runs out, I'm sure."

"Good, I'm curious about that, too. The boy who delivered it asked me where to find you," Sharky said.

I sat up straight. "Boy?"

"Yeah, he came up the river trail about three hours ago. Rode a big horse pulling that coffin. Looked about sixteen or so; his voice hadn't changed all the way, even. Had a little scar on his cheek. Knew the name of the town, and your name, and that was all. I told him your office was here."

Liz turned to Gary Bunson. "You said it was an old man."

"It *was* an old man," Gary said defensively. He was used to being on the defensive, usually because some white lie had collapsed beneath him. But I sensed his outrage was sincere. "Why the hell would I make up something like that? Wasn't it, Eddie?"

The click in my head as everything fell into place was so loud I'm surprised no one else heard it. I wanted to laugh, but not because it was funny; it was the sheer unbridled *audacity* of it. I'd looked the old man right in the eye and hadn't seen it. Back when I'd been on Grand Bruan, I dismissed all the claims of magic that tried to intrude into my theories. Now, after some of the things I'd seen the past few years, I knew better. But still . . .

Liz noticed the change in my expression. "What?" she asked softly.

I grinned and shook my head. "I'll tell you later." I took another drink and said, "All right, let's get back to the story. Up until now everything had happened pretty much in one place, Nodlon Castle. Now I was about to cross almost the whole island. Being outside, on a fast horse and with a goal to accomplish, felt great after all that court intrigue. But . . ."

I saw a painting once, hanging in the castle of a king who'd hired me to verify his chamberlain's honesty, called *Sunrise on Grand Bruan*. It depicted the aftermath of the Battle of Tarpolita far differently from the tapestries in Nodlon Castle. In the painting bodies covered the slope, while at the top young Marcus Drake stood leaning on the pole that bore his standard. He was realistically depicted as weary and wounded, and the sun cast a red glow over everything that simultaneously hid the real blood and made the whole image look blood-soaked.

That same sun rose before me as I headed due east toward Blithe Ward, showing me fields and forests of blood. I was too preoccupied to recognize it for the omen it was.

The landscape outside Nodlon was ripe and full with late-summer produce. Prior to Drake's rule no one would have dared plant such huge fields with a single crop, fearing they'd be set alight as part of some military action. Now I saw at least one barley field stretch to the horizon.

The horse Kay had provided was pure muscle and single-mindedness, bred and trained to carry messengers. I was heavier than she was used to, and my horsemanship was dire, but she had a strong sense of professionalism and didn't let me slow her down. We made astoundingly good time.

Part of this was the ease of the road itself. It was paved with flat, even stones, with ditches on either side for drainage. At first light it filled with horses, men, and wagons loaded with produce and trade goods, all heading toward Nodlon Castle. Eventually I passed the tipping point, and traffic began to flow *with* me toward whatever awaited ahead.

As the sun peeked over the top of the forest, I noticed a distant, obviously man-made cloud hanging in the morning air. I couldn't tell if it was smoke or dust. It was to the northeast and grew larger as I watched, which meant it was coming this way. If it was smoke, it was a hell of a fire; if it was dust, then it was a hell of a lot of people. Either way, it was a long way off and I'd be well gone before it reached the road.

I stopped at the first messenger transfer station, a small building attached to a corral where a half dozen horses milled about. Smoke curled from the chimney, and a man stood outside smoking pensively on a pipe. As I rode in and dismounted, the horses all came to the fence, eagerly jostling to be the next one selected.

The man on duty looked at the seal on my message, then at me. After a moment he gave a shrug and, with little wasted movement, took the saddle and bridle from my horse and put them on a new one. I was on my way within minutes. "Ride like the wind, messenger," he said flatly, by rote.

I passed through a small town where the day's market was just being set up, the destination for all that local produce. At least if it was market day everywhere, I wouldn't stand out on the road so much. People waved at me in that guardedly cheery way rural folks greet strangers. On the other side of town a few late farmers headed in with their produce. They also waved.

I galloped over a hill and down into a low stretch. To my left I glimpsed a small burst of flowers along the otherwise grassy shoulder. From the midst of them protruded what looked like the hilt of a sword. I figured I was making good enough time, so I wheeled the horse around and returned to look it over.

It *was* a sword, old, weathered, and driven deep into the ground among the planted flowers. Several pieces of vellum, some so old the rain had beaten them into the dirt, were tied to the hilt. I dismounted and knelt so I could read them.

The first read, *We miss you, Daddy.* Another, in a child's hand, said, *Sleep well, Grandpa.* I wondered how the honored dead had met his end.

This isolated and empty stretch of road seemed perfect for bandits, but I saw none. My horse whinnied impatiently, anxious to return to work. I also had a sudden flash of Thomas Gillian sharpening his sword while he watched an hourglass drain away my time, so I returned to the saddle.

I topped a hill and saw a line of wagons impeded by something. With the barest tug on her reins, the horse hopped the ditch and proceeded along the shoulder as if this were nothing unusual. The ground was too soft for the heavily laden carts to take the same detour, so they had to wait for the way to clear. The farmers and peddlers glared jealously at me as I passed them.

Finally I reached the reason for the backup: a cart bearing new flagstones, and three men watching a fourth as he replaced broken ones in the road. Slowly.

"Come on, guys, my taxes pay for this!" one farmer yelled from the seat of his two-wheeled cart. It had no visible effect on the workers.

"You can't travel five miles on this goddamned road without getting caught behind construction," the farmer said. I heard murmurs of assent from his fellow travelers. I doubt it sped things up.

We returned to the road, which was clear all the way to the next low hill. I felt the morning wind on my newly bare cheeks.

AT midmorning I arrived at a crossroads village where two of the stone thoroughfares met. A sign announced it as Astolat, and the road that crossed at its center traveled north/south just as mine did east/west. Farmers and merchants busily sold their wares at the edge of town, but the few buildings were quiet. The tavern was open for business, though.

At the transfer station I climbed down and stretched my legs, wincing at the pain in my lower back. That had become more frequent the older I got and had nothing to do with how seldom I rode horses. It was the lingering reminder of a spine-crushing blow delivered by a club the size of a calf, wielded by a black-haired maniac against a cocky young mercenary who had ignored the advice of older, smarter soldiers. That mercenary, now a much wiser sword jockey, subsequently paid a lot more attention when other people spoke. And when he started to forget this lesson, his back reminded him.

I narrowly avoided being drawn into conversation with the young man on duty at the station. He wanted to know all about the situation at Nodlon, and I was amazed all over again at how fast and thoroughly bad news could spread. I made polite excuses and decided to take a quick break for a drink. Surely Thomas Gillian wouldn't begrudge me that.

The tavern, called the Crack'd Mirror, was smaller and dirtier than anyplace else I'd been in Grand Bruan. When I walked in, I had to wait for my eyes to adjust to the dimness; there seemed to be no light other than the hearth fire, and what sunlight managed to pierce the cracks in the walls and ceiling. Luckily there were a lot of those, and in the hazy air the light shafts resembled chaotic prison bars.

I hung my jacket on a wall hook beside a hooded cloak, then sat at one of the tables. My butt and backbone were both grateful for something that wasn't bouncing. I rested my injured hand on the tabletop, glad to no longer feel the weight of the cast tugging at my shoulder. Still, I was alert. Even coated with road dust I was overdressed for the place, and that could lead to trouble.

A large human shape moved back and forth behind the counter, but made no move to ask me if I wanted anything. No one else was in the room, so at last I whistled for his attention. When he turned my way, I said, "What's a fellow got to do to get some ale in this place?"

He did not reply, but picked up a mug and opened the tap to a keg. I turned and nearly jumped out of the chair.

A woman had appeared next to my table. I hadn't heard her approach or sensed her nearness, both of which were uncharacteristic of me. Were people in Grand Bruan just stealthier than anywhere else? I said, "If you scare me to death, I can't pay my tab, you know."

She put one foot brazenly on the chair beside me, which hiked her tattered skirt enough to show a smooth, surprisingly clean calf. She leaned down to give me a clear view of her admirable cleavage. "All by yourself today, stranger?" she said, her accent heavy, raw, and untutored.

"Yeah. Just stopping for a drink."

Her hair fell down in her eyes and hung close to her cheeks. I couldn't tell how old she was, only that she wasn't elderly. The parts of her I *could* see were certainly worth the look. She asked, "What'd you do to your hand? Rub it raw pulling your ladle?"

I smiled and said nothing.

"My name's Elaine. I've got all my teeth. Want some company, then?"

"No, thanks. I've only got a few minutes."

She grinned and licked her lips. "I only need a few minutes, love. I can take you from trickle to fountain before you know what hit you."

"No thanks," I repeated.

She glanced at the silhouette behind the bar, who stood immobile. I couldn't be certain he watched us, but what the hell else would he be looking at? "Please," she said softly, her smile fixed and fearful, "look around. Nobody ever comes in here, and he takes it out on me. One day he'll knock out my teeth, and then where will I be? I promise, you won't regret it,

I'll let you do anything you want to me, just please don't let him see you turn me away."

The hairs on my neck stood up the way they always did to alert me to danger. I slouched in the chair as if trying to appear cool and sophisticated, when really I just wanted to get my good hand close to my boot knife. "You don't look like he beats you."

"He doesn't do it where customers can see it," she said, eyes down.

She could be telling me the truth; she could also be playing on my sympathies to get me alone and slip a knife between my ribs. "Why do you stay?"

She shrugged again. "He's my father; where would I go?" She sidled behind my chair and began to rub my shoulders through my clothes. "Oh, you're a strong one, aren't you? You don't look like you would be, all dressed up like that. Usually people in these sorts of clothes are soft as butter. *Everywhere*," she added with a lascivious chuckle.

I didn't like the idea of not being able to see her. "I'm full of surprises," I said, took one hand, and pulled her back in front of me. I pressed a gold coin in her hand. "Show this to your father, it should make him happy. And then bring me my ale."

She looked at the coin, and her eyes widened. "Is this real?" she whispered.

Ordinarily I wouldn't have flashed so much cash in a place like this, but it was the smallest coin I had. "It's real. Now go get my drink."

I winked and slapped her on the behind, for her watching father's sake. She jumped and for a moment glared at me with a superior, overwhelming outrage that was totally out of character for a tavern whore. It vanished at once, replaced by a cool smile, and she flounced over to the counter for my drink.

Then a man appeared in the tavern door, blocking the light from outside.

Like me, he waited for his eyes to adjust. He was broad-shouldered and slender and wore a blood-red cape that fell to his knees. As he stood, he pulled off his riding gauntlets one finger at a time, then tucked them in his belt in a style I recognized at once. He might not be in uniform, but he was definitely military, and not some yeoman, either.

There was a stillness about him I'd noticed in other military men, the truly dangerous ones. It was a kind of confidence that ran so deep, it precluded any need to show off his prowess. If people were foolish enough not to see it for themselves, then they deserved whatever trauma he dealt them. When it was needed I could project it, too, so I knew it was for real.

The girl returned with my ale, plopped it down so hard it splashed the table, then sauntered over to the newcomer. "Well, hello there. Two new gentlemen in one morning. Must be a girl's lucky day."

The man did not respond as she put her hand on his chest and pressed herself against him. "Now that gentleman over there, he was generous, mighty generous. Think you can match him?"

"I don't know," he said cautiously. His voice was young and rather high-pitched. "I'm not sure what you mean by 'generous.'"

She rose on tiptoe and whispered something in his ear. He

smiled and chuckled. "Well, I don't know if I can be *that* generous. But I can certainly compensate you for your time."

"I don't know what those fancy words mean, dear heart, but I trust you. My name's Elaine." She slipped her arm through his. "And, look, I've still got all my teeth."

As she led him past, he stopped and looked at me. I couldn't make out his features, but I felt a bit like a rabbit must feel when the wolf looms over it. I smiled.

"You made quite an impression on Elaine here," he said.

I shrugged. "Treat a whore like a lady and a lady like a whore. They both like it that way."

He smiled. It lowered the room's temperature. "I must've missed that bit of wisdom growing up. Where did you hear it?"

Elaine tugged on his arm. "Come on, love, there's time to chat later. Besides, you can tell me anything, I love to listen."

The man's gaze didn't leave me. "I'm sure. Well . . . good day to you, sir."

"Likewise," I said with a nod.

As Elaine led him toward a door at the back of the room, a shaft of light fell on him and I finally got a good look at his face. If I'd had a mouthful of ale, I might've spit it out at that moment.

It was "Dread Ted" Medraft.

He was older, of course, now in his late teens without the baby fat he'd had before. But I'd recognize him anywhere. I watched as cautiously as I could, not wanting to draw his attention again.

He and the girl went into a back room, and in the silence I heard the latch slam into place. As soon as it did, I slapped another coin on the table and ran for the door, grabbing my jacket as I passed. The last sound that reached me was her loud, muffled giggle.

Medraft's horse was tied at the tavern's hitching post. It was an evil-looking white mare, its tack decorated with small, decorative spikes. Had he spotted mine at the transfer station? Would he connect it with me?

For that matter, why was he *here*? Kay had said he was in the far north of the island, which put him many days, if not weeks, away. So this wasn't just a casual visit.

I climbed onto the new horse as quickly as I could and nudged the mare's ribs. She did not seem to find this sudden departure unusual and took off at a quick trot. If Elaine was as good as she said, I wouldn't get much of a head start.

In moments we were out of town and had vanished over a hill. If Medraft chose to pursue me, he'd have a three-out-of-four chance of picking the wrong road. Which meant I only had to worry about Gillian if I failed at my task. Comforting.

The big cloud was still to the north, but behind me now. That meant it was traveling south down the road that led to Astolat. In the full sunlight it was plainly dust, not smoke, and only one thing sent that much dust into the air: an army.

But if the king and the majority of the Knights of the Double Tarn were at Nodlon, then whose army was on the march?

chapter SEVENTEEN

I assumed Elliot Spears, the greatest knight in the world, would have a palace to rival that of his best friend, Marcus Drake. When I saw it, though, I realized I was off the mark about the house, and possibly the man.

Blithe Ward was a palace, but it was nothing like a castle. There were no outer defensive walls, no moat, no drawbridge or watchtowers. There was just a big stone manor house on a hill, surrounded by gardens and orchards, apparently unguarded. I guess when you have Spears's reputation, you don't need a lot of peacetime security.

I arrived as the sun hung low in the sky behind me, illuminating Blithe Ward with a palette of vivid colors. A pair of servants lowered the flag bearing Spears's crest, and one of the chimneys smoked as cooks prepared the evening's dinner. A feminine figure stood at the rail on the widow's walk, but I could make out no details. She had gone by the time I passed through the stone archway at the gate.

I rode up the sweeping drive and dismounted the fifth and last of my messenger horses. I hadn't spent an entire day in the saddle in a long time. My back had passed through pain to numb acceptance, but I knew as soon as I stopped moving, it would express its displeasure. I was starving; except for some apples bought off a passing wagon (and, yes, I checked them for poison), I'd eaten nothing all day. Encountering Ted Medraft had made me want to keep moving.

A breathless stableboy ran up to me and said something in a language I didn't know. He tied a small tile marked *3* to one of the stirrups, then pressed a matching one into my palm. He took my horse's reins and led her toward the stables.

I faced the big double door. Both halves bore Spears's standard, a shield with three red stripes, above huge metal rings. I lifted one and let it slam down under its own considerable weight. It made a sound like a distant clap of thunder.

After a moment a rough-looking man in formal attire opened one side of the door. Although I knew he wasn't, I asked, "Spears?"

He scowled harder. "You said what?"

"Spears, Elliot Spears, the fellow with the shining armor."

"I don't know anybody by that name."

"You're standing in his house, and you don't know him. That's pretty funny."

"So you've got a funny sense of humor. Take it away and play on it somewhere else."

He tried to close the door but I blocked him. I produced the message from Drake and waved the official seal under his nose. "You know where to find Spears, and I've got a message from the king for him. Don't you think we should at least talk about it?"

He looked at the seal, at me, then shrugged as if it were a mere inconvenience. "Sure, if you think you've got something."

He stepped aside and I entered. When he closed the door, he produced a small, light sword of the kind designed for use indoors. He gestured that I should raise my hands. "Do you mind?" he asked, masking his sarcasm behind a bland smile.

I was too tired to take offense. "No, I'm used to it."

I let him take my sword and pat me down, turning and spreading my feet to accommodate him. He missed the knife in my boot; was I the only one who used that trick? Then as he was about to speak, a woman's voice called, "Clove? Who was at the door?"

"A messenger from the king for Lord Elliot. It's all under control, milady, just . . . go back to your quarters."

The voice sounded familiar. I tried to peer around him to see who had spoken, but he deliberately moved to block me. A door closed somewhere in the voice's direction.

"Clove? Your name is Clove?"

He returned my sword and sighed. "It's pronounced *Clah*-vay, but I'm under strict orders not to make an issue of it. Follow me, please."

The long, narrow foyer led to two big doors that, I assumed, opened onto the main hall. Smaller doors were along the walls. Clove gestured to a large upholstered bench. "Wait here while I inform the master."

Alone now, I looked at the artwork decorating the walls to

distract me from my protesting stomach. The odor of cooking taunted me. Surely a man such as Spears would have a spare place for an unexpected guest.

A lot of the paintings depicted the same scenes as in Nodlon: great battles won by Marcus Drake, with Elliot Spears always by his side. But the largest painting held my attention. It showed Jennifer Drake, not in her capacity as queen, but simply as a woman seated at her dresser, brushing her hair. She brazenly displayed one bare shoulder, and her expression was suitably faraway and longing.

Now *this* was a surprise. Not that Spears would own such a painting so much as that he would display it here, so all his guests would have to pass it. For a man rumored to be linked romantically with the queen, it was both confirmation and provocation. It could've been a gift, I supposed, or a simple sign of Spears's status as queen's champion. The informal nature of it seemed to work against that.

I stepped close and studied Jennifer Drake's expression. The artist had captured it, all right. There was the same strength, the same intelligence, even the wary quality that lurked under everything else. I raised my hand and risked a touch of the fine brushstrokes that composed her face.

I heard a soft, feminine gasp and turned in time to see a door close behind me. I rushed to it and found it locked. Someone had been there watching me, though.

Clove emerged from the main hall. His boots rang out on the stone floor as he approached, and he did not speak until he reached me. "Lord Elliot will see you now, sir."

"Is Lady Elliot with him?"

"There is no Lady Elliot, sir."

"I saw a woman watching as I rode up."

"Perhaps one of the maids, sir."

"Then who did you call 'milady' before?"

He ignored the question. "If you will follow me?"

He pushed open the double doors to reveal a standard great hall, much like the one at Nodlon but smaller. The main table had place settings for two. The lord of the manor rose from his seat and strode toward us.

In person Elliot Spears looked exactly as he should: taller than me, slender but not skinny, with a clean-shaven, square-jawed face. He wore loose, simple clothes that belied his status. His hair was short and unruly, adding to his boyishness, but the touch of gray at his temples implied maturity. He had the same stillness as Ted Medraft, but without the accompanying aura of incipient violence. You sensed he could kill you a dozen different ways if he chose to, but unlike Medraft he wouldn't enjoy it. If you had to dream up the image of the perfect knight, it would look just like him.

"Welcome to Blithe Ward." His accent was slight, betraying his origins from outside Grand Bruan.

I bowed but did not kneel. "Lord Elliot."

"And you are?"

"Edward LaCrosse. No particular rank."

"I've found rank only useful for placing blame, anyway. Clove, you may return to your duties."

"Yes, my lord," the servant said, although a look passed between them I couldn't interpret; maybe it was just Clove's gratitude that Spears pronounced his name correctly. I almost asked Spears if we could talk over dinner, but it would've been gauche. Then again, who was the second place setting for, if not me?

"You seem to have an injury," Spears noted.

I shrugged. "I'm accident-prone."

He looked me over with a slow, sweeping gaze that told him everything he needed to know about me. Then he gave me a friendly, lopsided smile. "I've had the same sort of accidents in the past. Who tended you?"

"Iris Gladstone at Nodlon Castle."

"Ah. I have scars that would be far worse had she not been there. Of course, that was many years ago when she was a mere girl. I have not seen her in some time."

"She's grown up." Then I produced the message. "King Marcus wanted me to give this to you personally."

Elliot took it casually and broke the seal. As he read, though, his entire countenance changed; his muscles drew taut and he seemed to stand taller, taking up more space and becoming more solid. When he looked up from the note, his expression actually scared me a little.

"Is this true?" he said with no inflection.

"I haven't read it."

"It says Queen Jennifer is suspected of murder, and that the situation is so serious that her champion is needed to defend her."

"That much is true."

"What's not?"

"I don't think she killed anyone."

He took a step toward me. In this mood he had the presence of a shifting glacier, and it took every ounce of my self-control not to back away. He said, "You seem to enjoy the back-and-forth of questions and answers, but I must say I don't. I'd much prefer that you tell me everything you know."

"Sure." I did, leaving out the personal bits with Iris, of course. But I made sure to include that Gillian would track me down and kill me if Spears didn't show.

When I finished, he said, "There's a hand behind all this. Pulling strings, nudging pieces across the board."

"Ted Medraft."

He frowned. "Medraft?"

"He's pulling Agravaine's strings, apparently. And he's not where he's supposed to be. I saw him in Astolat on my way here."

Spears tapped a corner of the note against his chin as he thought about this. "No. Medraft is clever, and his interest in Jennifer is no secret, but he's not devious to this degree. There's a deeper power at work."

"Who?"

He smiled, with the kind of humor a man has when he's about to pull the spear from his own belly. "I don't wish to say. Not because I believe I'm wrong, but because I don't wish to give it reality should I be mistaken."

I felt the sense of being watched again. The hall was big enough it could be from any of a dozen places, and I took a quick scan around the room with just my eyes, without turning my head. I saw nothing, which meant the watcher was behind me. "So you're going to Nodlon?" I said to keep the conversation going.

"Of course. I'm the queen's champion. This is my job. My *only* job, in peacetime. I . . ."

As he spoke, I turned slowly, feigning nonchalance as I searched for a sign of movement. I spotted it behind a tapestry, where the fabric bulged out just enough to give away the person hiding between it and the wall.

With no warning I rushed over and reached behind the cloth. My fingers closed around a slender feminine arm, and I yanked the watcher into the open, saying, "All right, what's the big idea—"

My words cut off like a cask spigot. I held the wrist of no serving girl or minor noblewoman, but of the queen of Grand Bruan herself, Jennifer Drake.

chapter

EIGHTEEN

I stared at her. She stared at me. Spears, I assume, stared at us both. But he was the first to speak.

"Jenny, what are you doing spying on us? I've told you about that. Get back to the kitchen where you belong." He pulled her away from me and and shoved her toward the door. Over his shoulder he said to me, "Sometimes the help forgets their place."

"Hold it, hold it," I said. "What the *hell,* Spears? You think I don't *recognize* her?"

She was dressed in a simple but expensive gown, with her brunette hair braided and twisted close to her head. Yet the lips and eyes were unmistakable. Although even when she feared for her life and marriage back in Nodlon, she never looked this frightened. She blurted, "It's not what you think."

"It never is," I said wearily. "Surprise me."

"No, really, it isn't what you think," Spears said. He'd lost that superior attitude and put his hands protectively on her shoulders.

"Let me explain," Jennifer said.

"Let *us* explain," Spears corrected.

I held up my hands. I was sore, hungry, and monumentally weary of complications and intrigues. "Please, no, don't bother. I really don't care." Then I added to Jennifer, "Except about one thing: how did you get here before I did?" It was a straight shot from Nodlon Castle; even if she'd somehow passed me while I was swapping horses or dawdling in Astolat, I'd easily have overtaken a queen's slow-moving retinue on the open road.

Spears and Jennifer looked at each other. "Tell him," Jennifer said.

Spears finally said, "I suppose if I don't, I'd have to kill you to keep you from inquiring further."

I said nothing, but shifted my weight so I'd be ready to move. Being killed by a legendary warrior was actually a lot classier than most of the ways I assumed I'd die, but I wouldn't go down without a fight.

Jennifer smoothed wrinkles from her gown and recovered some of her dignity. "I don't think that will be necessary. Are you in the king's service?"

"He's paying me," I said.

"Then this can be handled, I'm sure, with an appropriate amount of . . . compensation?" She looked at me with haughty, defensive disdain.

I frowned. Surely she knew me better than that by now. "I kept your other secrets, didn't I? Give me a good reason and I'll keep this one. But I don't bribe."

Again they looked at each other, as if they knew something important I didn't. It got on my nerves.

Finally Spears said, "There's something you don't understand, Mr. LaCrosse." He looked at Jennifer. "She is not who you believe she is."

"She's not Queen Jennifer Drake of Grand Bruan?"

"No," she said. "I'm not."

I'd heard my share of lame excuses, but this might beat them all for sheer nerve. "You called her Jenny," I pointed out.

"My name *is* Jennifer. But . . ."

Like a guilty teenager, Spears blurted out all in one breath, "She is the half sister of the woman who is now queen of Grand Bruan."

Now it was my turn to stare at them, especially at her. I said, "No way." But there were differences, subtle and hard to spot but definitely present if you took the time to look. Mostly it was in her bearing; Queen Jennifer never looked as deer-in-torchlight frightened as this woman.

"It gets better," Spears said, then nodded at Jennifer, or whoever the hell she was, to continue.

She took a deep breath. "Jennifer Drake and I have the same father. Around the time his wife became pregnant, he also had a liaison with one of his servant girls. Both the servant and his wife gave birth on the same day, both bore girls, and both girls were named . . ." She looked down and sighed at the absurdity. "Jennifer."

I made no effort to hide my skepticism. "That's a little hard to believe."

She shrugged. "I know that. It doesn't make it untrue."

"I realize how ridiculous this sounds," Spears said. "I know a bit about breeding both horses and hounds, and the chance of two identical offspring from a single father and two different mothers is . . . well, unlikely. But"—he spread his hands helplessly—"there you are."

"So your mother was a serving girl," I said.

"No," she said, chin high. "*My* mother was the lady of the manor."

This took several moments for me to process. My stomach growled in the silence. At last I said, "Maybe I'm just tired, but I'm not following this at all."

"Some days it confuses me, too," Spears said.

"I am the daughter of Lord Leo Camiliard," she said. "I met Marc Drake shortly after he'd been crowned king. He was young, handsome, and forceful; he overwhelmed me with his attention. I fell in love, agreed to marry him, and become the queen of the newly united Grand Bruan. But . . ."

She began to cry, the kind of silent tears that strike before you're aware of them. Spears gently took her hand.

"The thought of being queen terrified me," she continued. "I hated being stared at, being expected to speak and be gracious and follow court intrigues. I loved Marc the way you'd love a god, as something not human; it wasn't . . . wasn't *real*. And then I met Elliot."

I saw where this was going. "So you switched places with the other girl who looked just like you."

She nodded, delicately wiping her eyes. "Marc spent very

little time with me before we were to be married. He was creating a whole new government, after all. So whatever differences there were, my sister overcame them. She's much better suited to being a queen than I am."

"Even though she's a commoner."

"Nobles, commoners, what difference does it make?" Spears said. "Marc has his queen, and I have my love."

I closed my eyes in annoyance, weariness, and just plain disbelief. "So *this* is why people think you and the queen are fooling around."

"Yes. We have visitors, and Jenny usually manages to stay out of sight. But not always. A glimpse here, an overheard comment there . . ." Spears shrugged.

"You had a very public fight with the queen, they tell me."

"Yes. It was about whether we should go public with the truth, now that the days of war and conflict were over. We chose not to."

It explained a lot: why the Knights of the Double Tarn distrusted the queen, and why Spears was scarce now that the wars were over. It didn't explain why someone tried to kill Thomas Gillian and make it look as if the queen did it. "Well, be that as it may, the woman currently wearing the crown needs to see you by tomorrow or things could get ugly."

He nodded. "Of course. I'll be ready to go within the hour."

"Elliot," Jenny said. She stepped close and added softly, "You can't just leave me here."

"You'll be fine. Just stay upstairs, and—"

"No!" she almost shrieked. "I can't do it! Here all alone, wondering if you're all right—"

Spears smiled. "It's a joust of honor against Thomas Gillian, Jenny. It's not that serious. And I never lose."

"I won't stay here alone." Her voice was firm even though she looked down at the floor. "I'm tired of hiding."

"She's got a point," I said. "Drake seems like the kind of guy who—"

"Don't tell me about Marc Drake," Spears snapped, fury in his eyes. Again I fought the urge to step back. "Our blood mingled on too many battlefields for me not to know him better than even his queen does. If I thought even remotely that he'd understand, I'd have told him long ago. But he wouldn't."

"There's another reason she shouldn't stay," I said. "Whoever's behind this may know about the two of you. With you gone, she'd be pretty vulnerable."

"See?" Jenny said.

Jenny and Spears looked intently at each other, a contest of wills I wasn't sure who would win. After a moment I risked interrupting them to say, "Now that my message is delivered, if it's all the same to you folks, I'll be leaving. Best of luck with the joust."

Spears held up Drake's message. "That's not what it says here." He read, "'Mr. LaCrosse has my utmost confidence. Anything you ask of him will be the same as me asking it. I'm convinced of his honesty and integrity.'" Spears folded it with a wry scowl. "Looks like you're still on the royal payroll, if you're an honorable man."

Of course I'm honorable, I thought. *The second-best knight in the kingdom will come after me if I'm not.* God, I wanted off this island. But the whole situation had become so incredibly *goofy* that now I had to see it through for myself. "All right, whatever.

We'll bring her along back to Nodlon. I suppose if she's in disguise—"

"No," Spears interrupted. "I want you to take her to Cameron Kern."

Jenny gasped. "Kern!"

"Yes. Most people think he's dead, and those who know better won't think to look for Jenny there."

"Apparently I'm supposed to escort you back to Nodlon," I pointed out. "If I don't, your friend Gillian will come after my head."

Spears looked at me as if I'd said the silliest thing in the world. "Mr. LaCrosse, I give you my word, I will go to Nodlon. And if I do have to fight Tom, as much as I may hate it, I'll win." He sounded as certain of his victory as he was about the next full moon.

Suddenly Jenny noticed my cast. "But you're injured! Your hand, how can you protect me?"

"He won't need to fight," Spears said evenly.

"But if he does—" She turned to me. "You can fight, can't you?" she asked desperately.

"Yes." *Especially if you'd give me some damn dinner,* I thought, but didn't say.

"I have something that will help," Spears said. He went to a large standing cabinet that, when opened, displayed an array of swords, maces, and other weapons for hand-to-hand combat. He returned with a sword in a strange-looking scabbard.

He slipped the straps of the new scabbard around my arms, so that it was held in place along my spine. A belt attached to the bottom of the scabbard then went around my waist. He guided my right hand up over my head; sure enough, the hilt of this new sword snapped into my rigid grasp, and I drew it with little extra effort.

"Wow," I said, impressed. The sword's polished blade gleamed golden in the lamplight. Its cross guard was a simple bar, and the pommel was an unornamented solid ball. It felt perfectly balanced. "Not bad, as long as I've got a high ceiling above me."

"Putting it back is a little tricky at first," Spears said with a smile. "But you'll get the hang of it. And you'll find it's actually a faster draw than a sword at your waist."

He showed me how to grab the bottom of the scabbard with my left hand to steady it while I carefully slid the sword back into it. It would take practice, but the quick draw made it worthwhile. I left the sword Kay had given me on the table; carrying too many weapons just makes you feel silly.

Jennifer—I mean, *Jenny*—watched all this silently, arms folded. When I'd practiced the draw a few more times, she finally said, "So when do we leave, Mr. LaCrosse?"

"How far away is Kern?" I asked Spears.

"Maybe a day, depending on traffic. You need to travel so as not to attract attention."

I looked blatantly at Jenny. "That's going to be difficult."

She nodded. "Yes. If you gentlemen will excuse me, I'll go fix that. Then I'll be ready to go. Under the protection of a one-handed swordsman who apparently hasn't eaten in a week." She flounced indignantly from the room.

We stared after her in silence. Finally I said, "They're a lot alike, too."

"Oh, yes."

I turned to Spears. "So why isn't this Kern guy advising the king anymore?"

"I wish I knew. Whatever it is, it was so serious Cameron left without any sort of farewell. He just walked out of the king's chambers, out of the castle, and into the night."

"And no one knows why?"

"Cameron does. And Marcus. To my knowledge neither has ever spoken about it."

"And you never asked?"

Spears smiled. He *was* a handsome thing, all right. "Have you *met* Marcus Drake? No, I never asked. But I've always wondered. Now—come with me."

chapter NINETEEN

I followed Spears through the corridors of Blithe Ward. Everyone we met immediately dropped to one knee. Spears motioned for one man to walk with us and spoke to him rapidly in their shared native language. The man rushed off to whatever task Spears gave him.

None of this slowed Spears down. He strode with such purpose that I had to work to keep up, and as a result I missed lots of no doubt interesting details. Many paintings and weapons were on the walls, and I wondered if they were souvenirs or mere decorations.

I did pause when we passed through the armory. The way the polished bits of protective gear and bladed weapons reflected lamplight made the room look like a golden treasure chamber. Each glossy piece, its straps and linings long repaired from the days of battle, hung neatly with its fellows, ready should the master of the house need them again. Some of the weapons I'd never seen before, and was unsure exactly what they did.

One item brought me up short, though: a magnificent two-handed broadsword hung point-down on the wall, an altar beneath it with two candles burning. The blade gleamed like quicksilver, the hilt was wrapped in supple-looking black leather, and the pommel sported an enormous ruby. Nothing marred its reflective surfaces. It looked, in fact, the way I'd expected Belacrux to look.

I didn't even realize I'd stopped until Spears cleared his throat from the doorway.

I nodded at the sword. "What's the story behind this one?"

He thought about it a moment, then shrugged. "It's not a secret. This is Arondite. My father's sword, and his father's, going back as far as anyone knows."

"It's something," I said sincerely. I'd seen a lot of beautiful swords forged only for display, and a lot of ugly ones created simply to kill. This one combined the best of both.

"You have a good eye," Spears said with a hint of pride. "They say one of my forefathers first used it to rid my homelands of a rampaging giant that was decimating the population. It was made from a metal that fell from the sky, cooled in the blood of a dozen virgins, and struck by lightning when it was first held aloft."

"Do you actually use it?"

"Oh, yes. When I need the certainty of a weapon that will never fail."

"Will you use it against Gillian?"

"I have no intention of fighting Tom. My foe is not my

brother knight. Whatever is behind this, its goal is clearly to sow dissent, and we must close ranks against it."

I noted his use of the word *it* instead of *him* or *her*, but didn't comment. He was clearly as circumspect as he was lethal. I gazed at the other combat-related objects. "You've got quite an arsenal here. Do you know how to use all these things?"

"Of course."

"You still practice?"

"Every day. I can't slow the process of aging, but I can make sure that I compensate for my weaknesses as they appear. When I lose a bit of speed in a thrust, I start using a longer blade. That sort of thing."

I shook my head. "I have to say, I'm impressed. You live up to your reputation."

He smiled, a slight and sad expression that carried more weight than it should have. "No one could live up to my reputation, Mr. LaCrosse. In many ways it saves me a lot of trouble, because it does half my job for me. But one day I know I'll encounter a sword or a mace or an arrow with my name on it. Dying of old age is not really an option."

I could think of nothing to say to that. I looked over a large shield painted with a row of red griffins against a wavy red background. The image was chipped and dented in places, and one strap end had torn free. Whatever had happened to it, the damage was apparently more important than using it again. "No restoration for this?"

He chuckled. "No. I fought ten men that day, all at once. Good men at arms. I slew them all. I keep this as a reminder that my greatest day is behind me, and that every victory since then has been by the grace of fate. Or luck."

He ran a finger along the edge of the shield. "But enough of the past. Grand Bruan's new enemy is very much of the present, and I must address it. Come along."

I trailed him through more hallways and doors until at last we emerged into the well-lit stables. By lamplight, pages and grooms attended the various animals; my borrowed horse gleamed from a fresh brushing in one of the stalls. Elaborate saddle blankets and snake-smooth tack hung neatly on the walls, an equine version of the armory. The boys chatted among themselves until they noticed us and fell silent. They bowed as we passed them, then resumed their diligent work. *Doesn't anybody slack off on this island?* I wondered.

Spears spoke to the stableboy who'd first greeted me, again in their common language. The boy listened and gave a flying nod as he ran off.

A four-wheeled wagon, worn with use and age, waited with two horses already hitched to it. Spears turned to me. "Good, it's ready. This wagon will help you blend in with the locals a bit more. Although your clothes could be problematic. Not too many local farmers wear a suit from court, even one as battered as yours."

"Do you have peasant clothes just hanging around for emergencies?"

"No, and it would take too long to find some. Ah, well, it should be fine. I sent Jack to fetch the map with directions and to tell Jenny we're waiting."

"What do I do when I get her to Kern's?"

"Tell him the situation. Hold nothing back. Make sure Jenny is safe and comfortable. I think at that point you may consider your duties discharged. By then I will have established the queen's innocence and hopefully ferreted out the hand behind all this."

And explained to Gillian why he doesn't have to track me down and kill me? I thought but didn't ask. "You still say it can't be Medraft?"

"No," Spears said with certainty. "But if he is involved, a logical culprit suggests itself."

"His mother, the king's sister?"

"I can neither confirm nor deny. If I am right, I will deal with it. If I am wrong, I don't want to add to the web of gossip."

Spears walked to the stable doors and looked out into the night. He cut a dashing figure even lost in thought. It couldn't be easy to be the top sword in town; I wondered how many challengers he faced in a given year, all hoping to be the man who slew Elliot Spears. Eventually one would be, and he knew that. That had to weigh on him.

"When I first came to this island, Mr. LaCrosse, in the middle of Marc's wars of unification, this house looked nothing like it does now. The insides were raided bare, the grounds overgrown, and a clan of near-cannibal brigands used it as a base to waylay travelers. In the countryside I saw farms burned, dead men's legs protruding from ponds, and livestock rotting by the side of the road. Nobody dared go out in public after dark. The land was ugly and scarred."

"It's better now."

"Yes, it's better." But he said it sadly, as if he didn't believe it was real.

"May I ask you something?"

He nodded.

"Why did you come?"

"I came to fight. I *stayed* to help build . . . this." He gestured at the world beyond the stable. "A land where the next generation might never know the sound of sword striking in anger against armor. Tell me, where are you from?"

"Arentia," I said guardedly. It was true, but I didn't like talking about myself.

"A fine country. The young king seems to know how to rule well. But then, he inherited a stable land from his father. Marc did not. He forged it with his will and his blood." Spears smiled again, wistfully. "And mine also. That is why I stay."

"Not for Jennifer?"

"Jenny," he corrected with a smile. "Not at first. But now, she is linked inextricably with the dream."

He turned and bellowed a loud order. Instantly the boys stopped what they were doing and ran out into the night, whooping and hollering. Spears smiled after them. "They do their jobs so well, sometimes I forget they are still children. I must remember to dismiss them early more often."

I nodded in their direction and asked, "Do they know about Jennifer? I mean, Jenny?"

"They know she is the lady of the house, and that she is . . ." He paused as he sought the right word. "Reticent?"

"Shy," I suggested.

"Yes, that's it, shy. Since none of them are likely to ever meet Queen Jennifer, the resemblance is not an issue."

"Drake never visits?"

"He intends to, on occasion. The queen always finds a way to dissuade him. She has as much to lose as we do."

"It's funny. You trust me because Drake says so, and yet you're trusting me with things he doesn't know."

Spears looked at me with that cold warrior look. "I'm trusting you, Mr. LaCrosse, because I have no choice."

Before I could say more, Jenny emerged from the same passage. Her hair was down and hung in waves close to her face. She wore a floppy, sweat-stained hat with a wide brim. Her dress was simple and threadbare. Her eyes were red from crying, but there were no tears now. She carried a canvas bag and, more gloriously, a basket laden with food. "I couldn't help noticing you seemed a bit peckish," she told me wryly.

I tore off a piece of fresh, oven-warm bread. "I apologize in advance for my lack of table manners," I said as I chewed.

"There's no table," she said, her smile widening.

When I finished, I tossed her bag into the back of the wagon. A puff of dust and a few sprigs of hay bounced in response. The horses shuffled in place.

"Nice disguise," I said to her, then gestured at my own dusty but expensive clothes. "I'm not exactly dressed as a farmer, though."

"It won't matter," Spears said. "It's night, and the roads are safe. Between here and Kern's place, no one will bother you."

Jenny climbed onto the wagon seat. She neither asked nor waited for help from either of us. She arranged her battered dress as if it were court finery. The boy Jack returned, and Spears gave me the map. "This will get you to Kern. He will probably act like he expected you; he's that way."

"Is he a wizard, like they say?" I asked through my second bite of bread.

"He likes to provoke. His wisdom is considerable, and he is able to see into the hearts of men to a degree that might well be magic. But he primarily enjoys keeping people off-balance."

"Should I trust him?"

"Yes."

I looked over the map, which seemed pretty simple. The route took us about halfway back to Astolat, where we'd turn onto a secondary road that wound through forests and hills. I tucked it inside my coat, then yawned; I'd had about four hours' sleep in the last day and a half, and it began to wear on me.

"And now, would you excuse us a moment?" Spears said quietly. He cut his eyes toward Jenny, and I nodded.

I wandered to the stable doors. The path beyond them led to a service gate down the hill from the house. This end of Blithe Ward had no visible lights. The trees, shrubs, and shadows provided plenty of opportunities for ambush, but who would dare it under Elliot Spears's nose?

I wiggled my fingers in their cast, noticing there was more room; the swelling had considerably diminished. I shifted my shoulders, trying to find a position where the new scabbard didn't seem uncomfortable. It improved my posture, although the sword's bare-metal pommel kept tapping the back of my head. A nice leather wrapping would make it a lot more bearable.

I glanced behind me. Spears and Jenny were still deep in soft, serious conversation, their faces close.

I yawned again. I didn't entirely buy the loony tale of identical half sisters; it sounded more like a bedtime story than real life. Whatever its source, though, the resemblance between Queen Jennifer and Jenny was extraordinary. Still, my job was just to make sure *this* Jennifer got to her destination, after which I'd have a healthy purse and a clear conscience and could decide then what to do about Iris Gladstone.

Eventually they kissed. Spears took the nearest horse by the bridle and led the wagon to the stable door. I climbed onto the seat beside Jenny. "Have a safe trip," he said to me, but his eyes never left her. "I'll send word as soon as I can."

"Yes," she said firmly.

I took the reins and urged the horses forward. Spears walked beside us to the gate and opened it. Beyond it, the moonlit road stretched into the darkness. Jenny turned and watched the gate close behind us.

For a long time neither of us spoke. I continued to raid the picnic basket until my stomach stopped berating me. We rode west on the same road that brought me here, and the wagon made a lot of noise on the flagstones. A whistling farmer taking home an empty cart passed us headed east, and we exchanged neighborly waves. Finally I said to Jenny, "So who else knows about your . . . situation?"

I couldn't see her face in the darkness. "The other Jennifer. Cameron Kern. Elliot, of course." I could hear the slight smile in her voice. "And now there's you."

Abruptly I yanked the reins, halting the wagon. Ahead the road rose up a slight hill, and three riders were silhouetted against the night sky, stopped and apparently conferring. They could've just been ordinary locals on their way home—it wasn't that late, after all—but I was taking no chances. We were at the bottom of the slope, in a pool of shadow beneath a tree; if they hadn't heard our clattering approach and we didn't give ourselves away, we should be invisible. To Jenny I whispered, "Be very still."

The three riders had not moved. Their voices reached us, but not clearly enough to make out. Were they coming our way, or headed toward Astolat?

They finished their conversation and started down the hill at a fast trot. There was no time to jump from the wagon and hide, certainly no chance of turning around and outrunning them. So I did the only thing I could.

I pulled Jenny into my arms and kissed her.

Even at the time, part of me appreciated how rare this moment was. She was a beautiful woman, and when I held her close, I felt the shape of her slender, strong body against me. I was experiencing the same embrace as both Marcus Drake and Elliot Spears; that was some pretty rarefied company.

She strained against me at first, then amazingly began to relax. I felt her lips part slightly, and her arms went around my neck. It became less of a ruse than I intended.

Then one of the riders said from beside us, "What've we got here?"

I looked back at them. Shadowed by the tree, I couldn't make out their faces, which meant they couldn't see mine or notice how overdressed I was. I said, in what I hoped was a fair approximation of the local country accent, "Do you mind? We'd like a little privacy here."

I felt a sword tap my cheek. "Don't get smart, farm boy."

I spread my hands. It was dark enough they couldn't tell I was armed. "Hey, whoa, I'm not trying to start any trouble. We're just out for a ride, you know?"

The next voice both raised my hackles and made my temper wind to the breaking point. It was the sneering, unmistakably broken-nosed whine of Dave Agravaine. "Forget it. We don't have time. Come on."

The sword did not move. Then it tapped my cheek playfully. "Too bad, or we'd share her with you. Maybe she'd like a couple of real men."

"Come on!" Agravaine snarled. It came out *Cub ah!*

I watched until they disappeared in the distance, back toward Blithe Ward. I heard Jenny draw a breath to speak and quickly touched her lips with my finger. Still watching over my shoulder, I snapped the reins. The horses pulled us up over the hill and into the open, where at least we couldn't easily be ambushed. I said, "Okay, but speak softly."

"Elliot would have you gelded for that."

"I'm sorry, it was all I could think of."

"Your first impulse in a moment of danger is to kiss the nearest woman?"

"Yes."

She was silent for a moment. Then she giggled. She choked it off at once, but there was no denying it. After a moment she added, "My experience with kisses has been limited to one man, but yours was not . . . unpleasant. I wouldn't make it a habit, though." She leaned close and gave me a small but deliberate peck on the cheek.

I might've blushed. "I wanted them to think we were just local folks out for a good time and completely uninterested in them. And since they were Knights of the Double Tarn, it was definitely the right call."

"Knights of the Double Tarn?" she gasped.

"Yeah. One was Dave Agravaine, so I assume the others were Cador and Hoel."

"Why would Knights of the Double Tarn be here?"

"If they don't know about you, then those particular knights were probably out to ambush Elliot. If somehow they *do* know about you . . ."

"Then we have to get to Cameron's place quickly. Hurry!" She reached across and tried to grab the reins from me.

"Stop that!" I said roughly, and pushed her back. "There's no reason to panic." I held her shoulders until she stopped struggling. "Nice to see you worry about your husband," I snapped.

"Elliot doesn't need my help," she said, still shaking. "But if they catch me, if they hurt me, I can't bear it—"

"Nobody is going to catch you. You may not believe it, but I know what I'm doing. They're going the other way, and we've got a good head start. Now calm down."

The wagon seat trembled, conveying her shudders. She was totally unlike the other Jennifer, and I realized that the long-ago decision to switch was right. But I also understood why Drake might see it as treasonous betrayal.

I stopped the wagon and took her in my arms again, not as a man takes a woman but as you'd hold a frightened child discovered far from home. I recalled Mary the servant girl trembling on her stool, face battered from Agravaine's tender care. That made me even more aware of my responsibility. I kept one arm around Jenny's shoulders and snapped the reins with the other. The sooner I got her to safety, the better. For everyone.

chapter TWENTY

L uckily the turnoff was marked well enough that I spotted it in the dark. We left the stone-paved road for a more traditional worn path across the countryside. Here and there hearth fires shone through the windows of small farms, and we startled a group of young people skinny-dipping in a lake. The sound of their joyous panic was both sweet and, in its fragility, somehow ominous. If they knew what was going on at Nodlon Castle with their king, they might not be in such a hurry to run around so vulnerably.

We went around a bend, and out of the corner of my eye I saw a man on horseback just beyond a stand of trees. "Don't move!" I hissed. I yanked the reins with one hand and reached for my sword with the other.

Jenny laughed. "That's a statue, Mr. LaCrosse."

By the time she said it, I'd figured it out myself. It was

life-size, made of stone, and mounted on a low pedestal. The horse reared on its hind legs, and the knight riding it had his sword above his head.

I sighed in relief and embarrassment. "Who the hell puts a statue out in the middle of nowhere, anyway?" I snapped.

"You can find these all over Grand Bruan. There was a decisive battle in the wars of unification on this very spot. Old Pernil—that's the knight's name—came out of retirement to fight alongside Marcus and Elliot. He took a javelin meant for Marc and died." She paused for a moment. "Pernil used to visit our castle when I was a little girl, long before Marcus came to power. He did little sleight-of-hand tricks to amuse me. I wanted to marry him when I grew up."

Looking around at the countryside, I was again amazed at how quickly and thoroughly the citizens of Grand Bruan had put aside centuries of differences and united under one ruler. The battle she described left remarkably few scars on the landscape. I'd seen fields so salty from spilled blood that nothing ever grew there again.

Near midnight we left the open country and went back beneath the forest boughs. Owls and nighthawks called, and deer darted from cover ahead of us. The insect chorus expressed its contentment, countered by the *barrumphing* of frogs. Like those isolated stretches of the main road, this would be prime bandit cover anywhere but Grand Bruan.

"I saw you admiring my painting," Jenny said. "Back at Blithe Ward. I apologize for spying, but you understand why now."

I was glad she'd decided to talk, because I was losing the battle with my eyelids. "Was the model you or the queen?"

"That one was me. Elliot painted it himself."

"I'm impressed. He's a man of many talents."

"No, only a few. But he excels at them." She paused. "You thought it was Jennifer?"

"Well . . . yes. At the time I didn't know you existed."

"Then may I ask you something as a man?"

"I'm not sure I'm qualified to represent all men."

"I think you'll do, if that kiss was any indication. Who is more beautiful, the queen or me?"

I laughed. "Any answer to that question might lead to bloodshed."

"Please, I'm serious. I know we look similar. Even identical to a casual glance. But there must be differences."

"There are. But they don't make one of you more beautiful than the other."

"What are they?"

"Why do you want to know?"

Her voice grew small in the darkness. "She makes Marc happy. I once wanted to do that with all my heart, and failed. I've often wondered if that meant she was somehow a better person than me."

"You make Elliot happy. I doubt very seriously if the queen could do that."

"Making Elliot happy is no effort."

"Maybe making Marc happy is no effort for the queen. I'd say you both ended up where you needed to be. I'm sorry it's all gone to hell like this. Hopefully it can still be salvaged."

"You said you kept the other Jennifer's secrets. Did you just mean this situation, or were their others?"

"If I answer that either way, I'm breaking her confidence."

She nodded and turned away to look into the dark. Neither of us spoke for a long time. At last Jenny caught me yawning and said, "If you'd like, you can stretch out in the back. I can drive a wagon."

"That's okay." I urged the horses to a faster pace. They snorted their disapproval but obeyed. I doubt they were used to working this late, either. "We're close, if the map was right."

She nudged me in the ribs. "You won't be much of a bodyguard if you're too sleepy to hold your sword. Go get some rest, I'll be fine. I promise to scream if I need you."

She had a point, and I really was having trouble keeping my eyes open. So I crawled into the back of the wagon and used her bag for a pillow. I put the sword beside me and snapped the hilt into my cast. In my dreams, I fought with Agravaine while Marcus Drake sat in judgment and the two Jennifers, one on either side of him, watched and laughed.

TWO things woke me. One was the realization that, with all the other insanity I'd found in Blithe Ward, I hadn't mentioned the dust cloud to Spears. If those were soldiers on the move, he'd run right into them. Of course, he was their commanding officer, second only to King Marcus, so there should be no danger. As long as they were Grand Bruan troops.

The other was the awareness that we'd stopped.

It was still mostly dark, although the horizon ahead had begun to lighten. We were no longer in the forest. I sat up and saw Jenny on the wagon seat, absolutely still, facing ahead. One of the horses whinnied impatiently.

"What's wrong?" I asked thickly. My mouth tasted as if a badger had bedded down in it.

"That *idiot*," she hissed.

I climbed onto the seat beside her. "Which idiot?"

"Cameron Kern." She nodded ahead of us.

We were atop a slight rise that gave a wonderful view of the rolling countryside below, all tinted gray in the dawn. Short stone fences marked off plots and pastures, and a small cottage lay about a mile away. Beside it rose a barn, and on the barn's sloping roof were painted the words, visible in the predawn light even at this distance, SEE THE CRYSTAL CAVE.

"I can't believe he would *do* that," she fumed.

"Do what?"

"That he would"—she sputtered in her fury before she got out the word—"*advertise*."

I shook my head to wake up and found a sack of water in the basket. I splashed some on my face and said, "So what is the Crystal Cave?"

"It's where Cameron always told everyone he was going to retire. To live secretly, quietly, in peace away from the world. No more kings and knights seeking his advice and counsel." Her sarcasm grew stronger as she spoke. "And now he's announcing its presence to everyone."

I blinked a few times and yawned. "Does that change anything?"

"No," she said, dejected. "It's just disappointing."

She whistled at the horses and we started down the hill. As the sun rose, we passed two more barns with the same message. I'd never seen that before, but if you were trying to drum up business, it was a great idea.

We met a local family on their way to market with a cart full of produce. I asked if they knew anything about the Crystal Cave.

"Oh, sure," the farmer told us. "The guy who runs it, Cammy, comes by every so often to buy some vegetables. He always gives us tokens for a free visit."

"What kind of place is it?"

"It's pretty neat," a little boy about ten said.

"Was anyone asking you?" his father snapped. "I know you have manners, boy, I've spent your whole life beating them into you. Don't speak until spoken to."

"Oh, it's okay," I said, although the kid didn't look very intimidated by this threat. I asked the boy, "Have you been there?"

The kid looked at his father until the man said in exasperation, "All right, tell him."

"Yeah," the kid began, so quickly it was as if the words had been piling up behind his lips. "He can do magic tricks, and he sings all the songs about King Marcus. They say there's dragons in the forest where he lives. They protect him from the bad guys."

"There are no more bad guys," his father said. "Marcus chased them back across the sea. We live in a peaceful kingdom now."

I thought of Mary lying dead beneath Nodlon Castle. I said nothing.

"It's got this whole model of Motlace, the king's main castle, all made out of crystal," the boy continued. "It covers the whole floor of the cave, and if you peek in the windows, you can see little scenes of the king and queen and all the Knights of the Double Tarn."

"It really is something," the father agreed. "I can't imagine having the patience to do it myself."

"Does Cammy live there alone?"

"You sure ask a lot of questions," the little boy asked.

"That's how I find things out."

"What kinds of things?"

"All kinds."

"Like what?"

"Like that you're a really curious little kid."

His father smacked the back of his son's head. "With the manners of a damn billy goat. Stop pestering people."

Throughout, Jenny remained silent, the brim of her hat pulled low ostensibly against the rising sun. She tapped her fingers impatiently on the back of the wagon seat. I thanked the farmer and his son, and we clattered off in opposite directions.

We followed signs down a narrow road to a clearing in front of an immense rock outcropping. At its base was the dome-shaped cave mouth shaded by an awning. Nearby stood a small stone cottage. Smoke curled from the chimney, and in the dawn lamps glowed through the windows. Seems somebody got up early.

I stopped the horses with an extra-loud "Whoa," so that Kern would know we'd arrived. "Stay here for a minute," I told Jenny as I hopped down. Just as I reached the cottage door, it opened.

A portly man with thick, wavy gray hair and a beard that covered his cheeks almost to his eyes peered out at me. He was clad in a baggy, multicolored tunic that hung almost down to his knees. He wore no pants or shoes. He held a long-stemmed pipe in one hand, and I saw he was missing most of his right middle finger; all that was left was a stump out to the first joint. The tapestries at Nodlon had captured his likeness, but they gave him more reserved dignity than the man before me possessed.

I smelled burning giggleweed; rather than getting up early, he seemed to have forgotten to put out the lamps the night before. Giggleweed did that to people.

"Hey, man," he said genially. "I'm afraid you're too early for a tour today, but come back closer to noon and we'll be open for business. Here." He flipped a coin-like token at me. "Tour's on the house. Peace."

"We're not here for the tour," I said, and ungracefully caught the token with my left hand. "We're from Blithe Ward. Elliot Spears sent us. I'm Eddie LaCrosse."

"Hello, Cameron," Jenny called from the wagon.

The big man squinted his red-veined eyes toward her. His expression changed instantly from benign curiosity to guarded acknowledgment, and a lot of his haziness vanished. "Dark Jenny. Last person I expected to see on my doorstep first thing in the morning."

She took off her cap and shook her long hair free. "I'm sorry to impose on you, Cameron, but I need a place to stay for a while. Elliot was called to Nodlon Castle; he should be back to pick me up within a week at the most."

"You mean a place to hide," Kern said.

"If you prefer."

Kern puffed on his pipe and regarded her with the skepticism one might give a wild horse that seemed suddenly resigned to the bit. "And why should I get my feet muddy in your swamp again?"

"Because your hands are still dirty from the last time," she fired back.

He remained motionless except for the smoke that swirled around his head. I politely kept my distance; as tired as I was, the last thing I needed was a contact high. After a long moment he replied, "Well, then, I guess I should be a more gracious host. Come in."

Inside the little cottage a low fire smoldered in the hearth and something simmered in a pot hung below the mantel. It rekindled my gnawing hunger. Neat shelves sported dozens of little knickknacks, and obscure vellum books lined one wall. Two lutes and a hurdy-gurdy leaned against a chair. A closed door indicated a private bedroom or study.

I dropped Jenny's bag near the door and gratefully slipped the scabbard from my back. I had to kick a woman's discarded shift aside to prop the sword against the wall. Other articles of clothing, the residue of past meals, and general clutter covered most of the flat surfaces. Kern's magic apparently didn't extend to housekeeping.

Kern said, "Whoa, man. You seem to be injured."

"Yeah." The cast felt looser around my wrist as I held it up.

He leaned close and squinted at it. "One of the royal healers did this. You mentioned Nodlon Castle; is this Iris Gladstone's work?"

I nodded.

"She's a good healer." With a wink he added, "Bit of a looker, too, or at least she used to be."

"So how have you been, Cameron?" Jenny asked as she came inside.

He shrugged. "It's a lot quieter here than at court."

"I'll bet." She ran her fingers through her hair in an unsuccessful attempt to tame it. "Do you hear from court much?"

He shook his head. "Not a word. Marcus and I have nothing to say to each other."

The door to the other room suddenly opened. I reached for my sword but checked myself when I saw the new arrival. Despite the manners drilled into me as a boy, I confess I stared.

It was a beautiful young girl with wavy golden hair and big blue eyes. But she was a giant, almost as tall as Marcus Drake. Yet she was built perfectly to scale, so that she took your breath away even as you worried she might step on you. She wore a too short towel tied under her arms and nothing else, which gave a clear view of many tattoos. She gasped when she saw us, tried to pull the towel in ways it wouldn't go, and cried, "Whoops!"

"Hey, baby," Kern said. "We've got some guests. Didn't you hear the wagon?"

She looked out the window and giggled. "Gosh, there *is* a wagon out there, isn't there? Wow . . ." Clearly Kern wasn't the only smoker in the house.

"It's okay," Kern said. "Amelia, this is Mr. LaCrosse. And this is Jenny."

The girl looked down at Jenny with the practiced eye of one used to evaluating rivals. "Jenny," she repeated. "You look familiar."

"She gets that a lot," Kern said quickly. "She has a generic kind of face."

"I'm an old friend of Cameron's. I need somewhere to stay for a few days, and I knew he wouldn't mind."

"No, he's a very kind man." Amelia's eyes flashed to Kern. "Cammy, may I speak with you for a moment?"

He sighed, followed her into the bedroom, and closed the door. Over the crackling fire, I heard their muffled, insistent voices. To Jenny I said, "That's not his daughter, I take it."

"No. Young enough to be, but no. He's always liked his girls . . . impressionable."

At last the door opened, and Amelia emerged in a robe cinched at her slender waist. Her voice was calm and reasonable now, and her smile gracious. "We just needed to discuss some things in private. I'm sorry I jumped to conclusions before. You both can stay as long as needed. Anything we have is yours."

"Thanks, but I'll be leaving," I said. "My job was just to get her here."

"Well, you're certainly welcome as long as you'd like." Amelia turned to Jenny. "If you'd like to join me, we have a hot spring in one of the caves. I was on my way over there. It's a great way to relax after a long trip, or"—Amelia glanced at Kern with a lascivious little smile—"a long night."

To my surprise, Jenny nodded. "That would be very nice. Thank you."

"Good. I'll get you a towel, and we'll leave the men to talk." Amelia gave Cameron a quick kiss as she went back into the bedroom, and he patted her behind through the robe.

chapter TWENTY-ONE

Kern closed the door after the two women left and gestured to a chair. "Had to explain that Jenny wasn't an old girlfriend. Amelia's a bit territorial. Sit down, man, stay for a spell." He chuckled. "That's a wizard joke. But seriously, you look like you could use some low time before you rush off."

I started to demur, but the cushions looked too comfortable to resist. When I sat, I sank so deeply that I feared I'd fallen into a trap. But Kern plopped into his old chair and put his feet up on a battered ottoman.

He held the pipe in my direction. "Do you partake of the weed?"

"No, thanks. My head's naturally fuzzy most of the time."

He laughed. "Without the fuzz, I might jump off that big rock out there and land splat in front of the cave." He picked up one of the lutes and noodled idly on it. "Memories can slip up on you if you're not careful."

"You seem happy now."

"What, because of Amelia? Oh, she does her part, that's for certain. Would you believe she was considered a hideous freak in her home village? Just because she was tall. The boys made fun of her and wouldn't be seen with her in public, although plenty of them snuck off with her in the dark. I found her crying by a lake, about to slit her wrists with her father's sword." He puffed some more. "She responds to kindness like a mistreated dog. And I don't mean that the way it sounds. Once I convinced her my affection was genuine, she became the most loyal partner you can imagine. I won't do anything to jeopardize that."

He took another long drag from his pipe. "And she introduced me to giggleweed. Cheaper than ale, and I can grow my own stock. No fermenting needed, just a dry place to hang the leaves."

"Good for you both, then."

His eyes grew more unfocused. "But as bright and shiny as she is, she's no match for the real darkness. I've got a lifetime of it, and if my head clears too much, it all comes back."

It occurred to me that, given my own darkness, I might be looking at myself in thirty years. Before I could follow that thought too far, Kern said, "So how did you get mixed up with Dark Jenny?"

"Why do you call her that?"

"Because she's afraid of the light."

I told him the story, again leaving out the personal bits with Iris. At the last moment, I also left out that the queen was a moon priestess. I had no reason to keep it a secret, but I'd learned not to ignore those sudden cosmic hints. Kern listened with half-lidded eyes and gradually stopped playing, so that when I finished, I was afraid he'd fallen asleep. But then he said, with surprising venom for one so apparently mellow, *"Megan."* He struck the strings so that they punctuated it with a sharp jangle.

I jumped and said, "I beg your pardon?"

"Megan Drake. She's behind this. She's pulling Ted Medraft's strings. Elliot knows it, he just doesn't like to gossip."

"The king's sister? I thought she was banished."

Kern smiled. "The strings are attached to her apron, and they stretch a long way. She's Medraft's mother."

"So Dread Ted is the king's nephew?" I said, trying to sound as if I didn't already know.

He cackled. "Yes. And Thomas Gillian may be his father, which is proof that a good man always has at least one bad decision in him. She wanted him to marry her and tried to rope him into it, but once he got to know her, he ran like the wind. A hoot, isn't it? You need a chart just to keep track of it all." Kern took a long draw from the giggleweed pipe, let the smoke out through his lips, and drew it into his nose.

When he made no comment for a long time, I risked asking, "Did you leave the king's service because of all this?"

"The king knows why I left. And I know. That's enough."

"Was it because of the switch with the Jennys?" I pressed.

He began to pick the strings again. "No. That was even my idea. Marc knows nothing about it, and if he ever found out, he might execute us all. But it's all his fault anyway. I warned him ahead of time that Jenny, the one you brought here that he first fell in love with, wouldn't make a suitable queen. She gets stage fright. She gets *audience* fright. Her backbone has the consistency of a boiled noodle."

That seemed an unduly harsh assessment of the woman I'd got to know on the ride here, but I didn't point it out.

"Jennifer, though, she has a spine. She'll look you in the eye and tell you what she thinks, which is what a king needs in a queen. When I learned of her existence, and of the difference in the two sisters, I met with them and Elliot and made them swear to secrecy. Elliot left to bring Jenny to the wedding and instead brought Jennifer. No one knows the truth except the four of us."

"Are you sure?"

Kern frowned again, shook his head, and put the lute aside. "You know, you're right. Someone has to know. Someone's trying to provoke this into coming out. Show that Marcus is such a fool he never noticed the switch."

"Who would gain by it?"

"I don't think this is about monetary gain. This has the smell of personal grudge. Which leads me back to Megan Drake, the bitch. And witch."

"Could she have arranged the poisoning at Nodlon?"

"Good God, she could arrange snow in July."

"Because she's a moon priestess and knows magic?"

He sat up suddenly and thrust one long, big-knuckled finger in my face. I saw the bristly white hairs growing from the creases. "Magic? Don't tell me you believe in that nonsense?"

"I have an open mind."

"Be careful your brains don't fall out, then. It's got nothing to do with magic, anyway. She's a goddamned zealot,

that's what she is. Drake banished her religion from the kingdom, and she wouldn't go along with it, so he banished her as
well. Now she wants to bring his kingdom down to prove that
her high-and-mighty moon goddess won't take that kind of
insult. She'd leave a trail of corpses from the south shore to
the north if it helped her cause."

Now I was glad I'd kept the queen's religion to myself.
I wished my source for this other information wasn't a
giggleweed-addled old man living in the middle of the woods,
because suddenly a lot of things made sense. Charging the
queen with murder might very well bring out her secret
status as a moon priestess: in the hearing before the trial by
combat, anyone of sufficient rank could ask anything. If Kern
was right, Megan Drake would most certainly have someone
positioned to raise the issue publicly. Even if the queen de-
nied it, the seed would be planted, and if the king himself was
shown to be married to a moon priestess, then he could not
very well enforce an edict against it. Especially if it also came
out that his queen wasn't who everyone thought she was. It
was a double layer of potential treason, and kingdoms had
crumbled for far less.

"Everyone calls *you* a wizard," I pointed out.

"Of course they do, because everyone is a *moron*. You
know why they think I know magic? Because I understand
cause and effect. And first principles. And a whole lot of
other simple rules that explain pretty much everything, but
that the general population is too willfully stupid to comprehend. Pay attention, really pay attention, and there aren't many
secrets." He pointed the pipe stem at me. "Like you. You know
what I know about you?"

I gestured he should tell me.

"You're from Arentia. You were once in the military. You normally wear a beard."

"I could see how you'd pick up all that."

"Wait, I'm just getting warmed up. You lost the love of your life at a young age, and you feel responsible for it. You have a large sense of fairness, a real taste for violence, and a weakness for lost causes." He grinned smugly. "How'd I do?"

I said nothing and kept my face as neutral as the sudden surge of outrage, annoyance, fright, and shame allowed. If this wasn't magic, it was close enough.

He picked up the other lute, but did not play. "I know Megan Drake is behind this because I paid attention to her, too. And for a lot longer than I've known you. I know what her mind is like, and I know what's in her heart. I don't need magic to know that, it's simple observation, seeing what people *do* as opposed to what they *say*. Marc takes people at their word, and that's why he . . ."

Kern stopped, looked surprised at his own vehemence, and sat back in the chair. He exhaled slowly and began to play a soft, minor-key tune.

I knew I could be verbally poking a sleeping bear when I prompted, "'Why he' does what?"

"Nothing, man," Kern said, his eyes closed. "I spoke out of turn. Marc and I know why Marc and I don't talk. No one else needs to. Water under the bridge, smoke up the chimney, sands through the hourglass."

I wanted to shake the old man until he told me, but first I'd have to escape from the chair. "That's okay," I said. But it wasn't.

Before I could really pursue it, the door opened and Amelia entered again, dominating the room with both her size and her beauty. She was clad in nothing but her tattoos and the steaming water beading on her skin. Her hair was slicked back and lay in a loose braid down her spine. "We need some wine," she said, not giving either of us a glance.

She knelt beside the wine rack, picked out a bottle, and left, but not before giving Kern a kiss that would curl a bald man's hair. As she closed the door, she glanced at me, giggled like a child, and winked. It reminded me to close my mouth.

There was a long moment of silence.

Finally Kern shook his head and whistled appreciatively. "Wow. A man's got to die of something, right? What were we talking about?"

This was my chance. "Marc's judgment of people. Or lack thereof."

Kern looked puzzled. "Really? I was talking about that?"

"You were. You said because I knew about the two Jennys, I should know everything."

He picked up his pipe and puffed away. The room's air looked like fog over a swamp, and I had the overwhelming urge for something baked and sweet. It took all my strength to concentrate. At last he said, "Marc was fifteen when he won the crown, you know. That's pretty young. He was a brilliant tactician and warrior, but a man's judgment isn't fully formed by that age."

"That's true."

"He did something wrong. And then to cover it up, he did something evil."

"We all make mistakes."

"No, this was no mere mistake, this was . . ." Kern trailed off again into his memories. I tried prompting him, but he ignored me. When he finally spoke again, it made me jump. "Say . . . you haven't seen the Crystal Cave, have you?"

I shook my head.

He got to his feet, wiped the lute strings with a cloth, and gently put it aside. He extended a hand to help me out of the chair. "Come on, then. See a man's life's work."

I leaned against the doorjamb for a moment while my head stopped spinning. I didn't realize how fuzzed-up I'd become until it began to dissipate. The clean air outside felt like ice water in my lungs, and I sucked it in until my chest hurt. Give me good old drunkenness any day.

A cobblestone path led from the cottage to the mouth of the cave. The individual rocks were pressed deep into the ground, indicating a lot of back-and-forth traffic. In the bright morning sun I saw lots of other other bare spots and paths; the Crystal Cave must do bang-up business.

"Beautiful day, isn't it?" Kern said with a satisfied sigh. "Come on, youngster."

Kern's bare feet smacked on the stones. As I followed, I looked around at the shadows within the thick forest, suddenly struck by how many places were suitable for an ambush. It seemed unlikely that Agravaine and his pals could have tracked us, though. We'd been on well-traveled roads with a wagon identical to hundreds of others on the same byways, and we'd gone hours without seeing anyone else. With no distinctive trail or witnesses, we should be completely safe. Unless they knew where to look.

"You know," I said to Kern, "I met a boy who said you have dragons in the woods around here."

He laughed. "Hot steam shoots up from the ground in a couple of places. Same thing that heats the spring in the cave. Makes a hell of a noise. I might've let on that they were dragons, though. It keeps a certain kind of person from trying to sneak in here and make mischief."

A wooden gate blocked the cave entrance, its lock dangling from a chain. Kern opened it and called out, "Hey, girls, it's just us!" A giggle of acknowledgment rang faintly from the depths.

Kern took a lamp from a hook, struck a flint, and lit the wick. It cast a golden glow that sparked off the wall's quartz deposits. "I found this place when I was a boy," he said wistfully. "I bought it as soon as I could and for four decades never told a soul. Chased two bands of squatters out of it over the years before I finally built my cottage and moved in permanently. It's the last place I want to see when the light finally fades for good." He closed the gate behind us and locked it.

"You have the key?" I asked. He had no apparent pockets on his tunic.

"I'm the world's greatest wizard, I don't need a key." He snapped his fingers and the big lock popped open. He snapped it shut again and we headed deeper into the cave.

"When I left court," he said as we walked, "I decided I'd create my dream here, out of rock that wouldn't equivocate or resist when I tried to polish it."

"Like Marcus?"

He didn't respond.

More faint giggles and splashing reached us. The floor was relatively level, going horizontally into the rock instead of downward. The ceiling was a high arch, the stalactites safely out of range. "It's just up ahead," Kern said, pointing with the lamp.

A wooden partition closed off the tunnel; one end went flush to the wall, while the other left a gap you could step around. The words YOU'VE FOUND IT! THE CRYSTAL CAVE were painted on the wood in big, looping letters, decorated with flowers and butterflies.

He stopped. "Wait," he whispered, and closed his eyes. I was about to ask what he'd heard when I realized he was praying. His lips barely moved, but he stood formally straight. Then he sighed, turned to me, and smiled. "Every time I come in here, I thank the spirits of the cave for their hospitality."

"I thought you didn't believe in magic."

"I never said *that,* son. I said I didn't need to use it to do the things most people consider magical." Then he gestured that I should precede him around the barrier.

I admit, I was skeptical. I'd seen gimmicky things like this before, and they never failed to be tawdry, vaguely depressing experiences. Such as the Mermaid of Agoya, who was just an old woman with deformed feet trying to be sexy in nothing but strategically placed seashells. I stepped around the partition and stood in the darkness, waiting for Kern to bring the light.

And, boy, did he bring it.

A miniature city of impossible detail rose from the cavern floor. The tallest building didn't quite reach my chest with its delicate, impossibly thin spires. Since it was built from the same rock as the cavern, it sparkled with the same reflected light, helped by the black paint that covered the cave walls and ceilings.

At the center stood the walls of a huge, square fortification. Within these, taller than anything else, rose a beautiful castle with tiny banners flying from its towers. Inside the real building, I knew, lay the fabled meeting chamber of the Knights of the Double Tarn, unseen by anyone not part of their brotherhood with the lone exception of Cameron Kern. I wondered, if I peered into this model, if I would see a facsimile of the real one.

"Motlace," Kern said proudly. "As I always saw it. The real city is considerably less . . ."

"Sparkly?"

"Clean," he said with a laugh. "I left out the mud and manure."

"It's . . . something," I said, truly at a loss for words. I knelt and looked at the nearest building, a tiny livery stable at the city's edge. I realized that, rather than being an etched surface, its walls were made of tiny stone-chip planks stuck together with glue. Even the ropes dangling from the hitching posts were not made of thread, but rather tiny stone beads fitted and glued to resemble ropes. The illusion was uncanny. It would not have surprised me had a little blacksmith no taller than my thumb emerged and waved up at us.

"This is what I tried to create through Marcus," Kern said. His voice was no longer amused, but had grown sad and weary; for the first time he sounded like an old man. "We had everything we needed at our fingertips. And it almost happened, too. A bit more focus, a frog's hair more courage, and it wouldn't be just an old man's toy. But the real world won't stand for such beauty." He sighed with weariness and defeat. "That's really why I left. I wanted to create something beautiful, but the ugliness always wins."

I stood, still awed by the creation before me. "How long did this take?"

"It doesn't really matter. At least I created my paradise somewhere, and people can see it and appreciate it."

"Has Marcus ever been to see it?"

"No," Kern almost spat. "He's not interested in seeing more proof of his failure."

"Most people consider Grand Bruan a stunning success."

"Compared to an acorn, a sapling is a giant. But it's nothing like a full grown oak."

"You know, Mr. Kern," I said diplomatically, "you keep dropping these hints and comments, so I feel I have to ask. What exactly did Marcus do that was so bad?"

Kern sagged, and his eyes grew wet. He closed them tight. "I can't tell you, son. You're right, I want to tell you, I want to tell *everyone*. Nothing, not rock or metal or the dirt of your grave, is as heavy as a genuine secret." He wiped the lone tear that escaped his eyes and smiled. "I'd hoped you would figure it out for yourself, you know. You're a smart one, I can tell. Maybe smarter than I was at your age. You know all the players and all the pieces."

I scowled. I didn't need a giggled-up old man criticizing

my professional skills. "Maybe I'm not as smart as you think I am."

"Do you play anything?" he asked out of the blue. "Any musical instrument, I mean."

I was a worse musician than I was a horseman. "No."

"Learn. Pick something, learn to play it. Best thing in the world for staying sharp. Your brain will thank you one day." He had an idea and slapped my shoulder. "Come on, I'll give you your first lesson."

"No, that's okay, really." I held up my cast. "See?"

"Ah, come on, that's nothing. I'll have you playing 'The Smiter and the Smote' before dinner."

I tried to change the subject. "Shouldn't we check on Jenny and Amelia?"

He threw back his head and hollered, "Jenny and Amelia!"

The cry echoed until its response—a lilting "Wha-at?"—drowned it out.

"Just checking on you," Kern bellowed.

"Fine as wine," Amelia replied.

Kern turned to me. "There's no way into the cave but this one, and I pity anyone who riles up Amelia." He waggled his eyebrows. "Unless you want to join them? Amelia and I share everything. *Everything*," he repeated with a wink.

"That's okay," I said quickly, hoping the unwanted mental image would soon fade. With a forced smile I added, "You know, I've always wanted to play the lute."

BACK in the cottage, Kern relit his pipe and I again demurred a puff. He handed me one of the two lutes. "Okay, first get used to the weight." His eyes narrowed. "Hey, you've held one before."

"I've tried." The knuckles on my good hand tingled in anticipation of the whacks I used to get from my music tutor.

He plucked a few notes. "Try that."

I leaned against the wall; there was no way I could play trapped in those chair cushions. I imitated him, hitting the right notes but with no rhythm. It had nothing to do with the cast.

He winced. "Try again."

I did.

"It sounds like a chicken caught between two millstones," he said.

"I do have a bad hand."

"Maybe your ear needs a cast, too." With that he gave up on me and began plucking the strings. He sang in a surprisingly strong, youthful voice.

Riding my steed,
Giggling the weed,
Shining knight, you better watch your quest.
Bandits ahead, dragons behind,
And you know that lady just crossed my mind. . . .

With no warning the door burst open and Amelia and Jenny staggered inside. Both were damp, drunk, and cackling in delight at some joke. Amelia's robe was open, and the towel around Jenny threatened to fall away at any moment. I wondered if she'd notice.

Amelia filled the room with her larger-than-life feminine

presence. She held up the now empty wine bottle she'd claimed before and announced, "We're dangerously close to sobering up. And *nobody* wants that."

Kern grinned, his pipe clenched in his teeth. "Help yourself, ladies."

Amelia bowed, her sizable, unrestrained bosom jiggling with the motion. "Why, thank you, kind sir."

Jenny was unsteady on her feet and heavy-lidded. She regarded me with a damp, measuring gaze that told me she'd left her inhibitions back in the cave. "Well, hello," she said throatily. "You want to pick up where that kiss last night left off?"

"Ah-*HA*!" Amelia cried as she found the bottle she sought. She stood, wrenched the cork out with her teeth, and spit it into the fire. She turned up the bottle and took a long, sloppy swallow. The liquid spilled down the sides of her mouth, trailed down her neck, and dovetailed into her cleavage. She extended the bottle toward Jenny.

Jenny reached for it, then said suddenly, "I need to sit down." The words were thick and heavy; evidently she wasn't used to real drinking.

Amelia put her arm around the other woman's bare shoulders and held her up. "We're going to lie down," Amelia said. "Anyone care to join us?" She looked directly, blatantly, at me.

"I don't think that's a good idea," I said.

Amelia shrugged and turned to Kern. "What about you, Cammy?"

"You know I'm always up for adventure."

"Just a minute," I said. I took Jenny's face in my hands. Her eyes were red and watery and her mouth hung slack. Her hangover would be vicious. "How drunk are you?"

"Not so drunk I need a babysitter," she slurred.

"Do you want to go with them?" I pressed, nodding at the other two. "You don't have to, you know."

"Why not? Might be fun. Something I'd never do at Blithe Ward." Her home castle's name barely escaped her thickened tongue.

Amelia led her into the bedroom. The tall woman looked at me over the top of Jenny's head and licked her lips as the door closed.

Kern stood and stretched. "Sure you won't join us?" he asked, as casually as if inviting me to go fishing.

"She's drunk. They're both drunk."

"Oh, don't be such a square peg. You sound like that hypocrite Marcus. No one's making anyone do anything."

"That won't make her feel better when she sobers up."

"Join us, then, and make sure she has nothing to regret." He winked, and I really wanted to punch him.

Kern went into the bedroom. Through the open door I glimpsed four bare female feet at the end of the bed, one set significantly larger than the other. Then the door closed.

I immediately went outside; I damn sure didn't want to overhear anything. The horses raised their heads from the trough. They were still hitched to the wagon so I let them loose to graze in the clearing. I climbed onto the wagon's seat. The sun was almost directly overhead, and I put on Jenny's discarded hat against it.

Kern said I knew all the players and the pieces. So I sorted them in my mind. If Megan Drake was truly stage-managing things from off the island to avenge both her mother and her sisterhood, as well as take out the lover who once jilted her, she had to have agents in the king's inner circle. Her son, Ted Medraft, was one, but he was nowhere near Nodlon when Sam Patrice died. Medraft pulled Agravaine's strings, though, and Agravaine had been there. Yet how could he have done it? If he'd been around the apples, someone would have seen him. So if *he* did it, he'd have to use an agent as well. That was a lot of fingers pulling a lot of strings, and the puppets could easily get tangled.

This all assumed Marcus was the ultimate target, and that it wasn't just a simple murder plot gone wrong.

And how did the absurdity of two identical Jennifers, one light and one dark, fit in? And what if this was all about the Jennifers and had nothing to do with Marcus?

No, that didn't work, either. They hadn't tried to hurt or kill Jennifer, they'd tried to publicly embarrass her, something that could've been accomplished much more easily by revealing the prenuptial switcheroo. So that secret, so far, was still safe. So it had to be a plot to get at the king through his queen.

But wait: Megan Drake was a moon priestess, just like the queen. I knew nothing of their order's rules, but this kind of betrayal seemed uncharacteristic of the ones I'd known elsewhere. Unless—that word cropped up a lot—Megan Drake had gone against her sisterhood in her quest for revenge.

And beneath all this confusion, literally, was the unmarked body of an innocent young woman who'd been beaten to pieces hours before. Among my various chains of improbabilities, that was my lone impossibility.

Unless . . .

And I got it. Again literally, it had been right in front of me all along. At one point even close enough to touch.

Then I heard the whinny and rattle of approaching riders.

chapter TWENTY-THREE

Through the trees I saw movement on the road that led only here: three men on horseback. In a moment they'd reach the clearing, and I sat in plain view. I had no time to make it to the cottage, where my sword still leaned against the wall, so I threw myself flat in the bed of the wagon. I pulled the hat over my face and crossed my ankles so that if they did see me, they might think I was some sleeping farmer. Since I still wore expensive, if dusty and wrinkled, court clothes, it was one of my weaker disguises.

None of the riders spoke as they approached. Their spurs jingled, and leather armor creaked. I expected to hear Tom Gillian's voice saying I'd missed my deadline, and he was here to collect my head. I hoped I'd have time to explain.

One of the three dismounted, groaned as if he'd been in the saddle a long time, and said, "Now what?"

A familiar distorted voice replied, "Sped out. Ib dey try anything, kill dem."

I felt a huge rush of relief that it wasn't Gillian. I hadn't realized how truly scared of him I was until then.

"But Kern's a wizard," said a voice I now recognized as Cador's. "He probably already knows we're coming. He probably knows *why* we're coming."

"Don' be a candy ass," Agravaine snapped. "He's juss an obe man. He's gop as much 'magic' as I hab in my ass."

Hoel, the one who'd dismounted, yelled, "Hey, Cameron Kern! Come out in the name of King Marcus Drake, and bring the man LaCrosse with you!"

I risked lifting the hat's brim. I couldn't see them over the side of the wagon.

When there was no reply, Agravaine said, "Ty abain."

"Cameron Kern, this is Sir Vincent Hoel of the Knights of the Double Tarn! I order you and LaCrosse to appear in the name of the king!"

At last the cottage door squeaked open. Cador gasped, "Shit!"

"The cave isn't open today," Amelia said. Her sheer presence froze the three knights in their tracks. "Hold on and I'll get you free tokens for your trouble."

Another pair of boots hit the ground. Careful not to make the wagon squeak, I rose enough to see that Agravaine now stood beside Hoel, both of them in front of Amelia. Agravaine looked even more squat and dwarfish with her towering over him, her robe cinched tight against her showstopping form.

"Whez Kamera Kerr?" Agravaine demanded.

She scratched the side of her head and frowned, as if thinking was a real effort. "Who?"

"Kerr, Kamera Kerr!"

"I can't understand you," she said sincerely.

With no warning he punched her. Hard. In the face, just as I'd punched him. He had to raise on tiptoe to do it. It knocked her back into the house, and I heard her big body thud to the floor.

Hoel and Cador laughed. "Damn, that's a big bitch," Cador said.

"Get between *those* legs, she'd snap you in half," agreed Hoel. "You can have her first."

"Only if she's tied down safe," Cador said, laughing.

"Kerr!" Agravaine yelled again. "Geb your ass oub heb!"

They still hadn't noticed me. Kern stepped past Amelia and emerged into the sunlight completely naked, his portly body as white as his hair. It had the desired effect of catching the three knights off guard. "David Agravaine," Kern said flatly, fists on his hips. "Still punching women, I see."

"Shut ub. Where is he?"

He scowled. "What's the matter with your nose?"

"Fubbett my nobe. Where is dat son of a bid?"

He glanced over his shoulder, where Amelia sat catching the blood from her nose with a pillow. "'Bid'? What is a 'bid'?"

Agravaine was almost hopping with anger now, and he whipped out his sword with a furious flourish. "Donb you fub with me, Kerr!"

Kern laughed and crossed his arms above his belly. "I'm sorry, first you punch an unarmed woman, then you draw a sword on a naked man? You've always been crazy, Agravaine, but now you're really losing it."

Agravaine swung the sword at Kern's head, but the old man simply leaned back to dodge it. The momentum made Agravaine spin in place and almost fall. Cador chuckled.

Kern risked a glance in my direction. He was clearly buying time for me to stage a rescue. I wished I had his confidence in my abilities.

I looked around the wagon bed for anything that might help. I saw an old apple core and carefully picked it up. If I could add to the confusion, I might be able to contribute something useful. But I'd have to use my left hand. I lined up on Cador, the only one still in the saddle, and threw the apple as hard as I could at the horse's rump.

The horse immediately tried to rear and spun in place as Cador fought for control. "Whoa!" he cried. "What the hell?"

Everyone turned to me, and I had only a moment to think. In my Lord Huckleberry voice I said, "What is the meaning of all this ballyhoo? Can't a man take his morning nap in peace?"

Agravaine and Hoel exchanged a puzzled look. As I hoped, they didn't recognize me at first without my beard. I hopped daintily from the wagon, tucked my cast behind my back, and brushed at the dust on my clothes with my good hand. "My goodness, men hitting women, old men in the altogether, and three Knights of the Double Tarn in the midst of it? King Marcus will not be pleased, I assure you. Oh, it will drive him to a royal tizzy!"

Kern played it perfectly, drawing their attention back to him as I minced closer. He said, "I'm going back to bed, Agravaine, after I tend to my girlfriend's nose. If you want to talk like a human being, come back tomorrow without your goon squad."

"Don't you turn your back on me!" Agravaine screeched. His sword flashed in the sun as he raised it over his head.

I grabbed the hilt of Hoel's sword with my left hand and snatched it from its scabbard. Before he knew it, I'd transferred it to my right and snapped it into the cast. I closed my fingers around it; they hurt a little, but not as much as the day before. I swung it low at the backs of Hoel's legs as he turned and felt it bite through the muscles and tendons of his nearest calf. He screamed and fell.

Then a lot happened quickly.

Agravaine spun in midswing, finally realized who I was, and came at me spitting like a rabid wolverine. I could imagine how terrifying he was in battle. Still, he was out of control and I wasn't. I parried his wild blow and grabbed his hair with my good hand. I brought his face down and my knee up, and they met with a satisfying thud.

As he fell, I spun toward the still-mounted Cador. He'd drawn his sword but his nerve failed him. Hoel's ongoing high-pitched screams helped a little, I'm sure. He threw his sword away, turned the horse, and spurred it toward the road.

He never made it. As he rode along the edge of the clearing, something rumbled and roared in the forest. A blast of steam shot from the ground diagonally across his path. If Kern hadn't told me its source, I'd have thought it was a dragon, too. Cador's already skittish horse reared again.

Then there was a loud twang, and an arrow struck deep between Cador's shoulder blades. He fell, arms and legs wide, and his horse fled. I turned and saw Amelia standing with a bow in the cottage doorway. Her face was streaked with blood, but her expression was calm. When I looked back, Cador hadn't moved; I knew he never would again.

Agravaine rose on all fours. My knee had split the skin between his eyebrows and blood ran down either side of his ruined nose like red tears.

"You're deb now," he hissed wetly. "You kibbed a Knibe of de Dubba Tawn."

Kern grabbed Agravaine by the back of the neck and yanked him to his feet. The cords on the old man's forearm stood out as he dug in his fingers; the giggleweed softness was gone. He held him so high only Agravaine's toes reached the ground. "Dave, you little pissant, you really should learn some manners. And don't pretend you're doing any of this out of loyalty to Marcus. Now tell me who sent you here and why."

Agravaine said nothing. The red streaks on his face, along with the purple-and-yellow lump where his nose used to be, made him look like a war-painted savage. His breath hissed through his teeth.

Without releasing him, Kern bent and picked up the knight's dropped sword. He put the blade against Agravaine's throat. "You punched my girlfriend in the face, Dave. I'm not feeling charitable. Answer me."

For a moment everyone was silent except for Hoel and his high-pitched whimpering. I'd seen enough men hamstrung in battle to have an idea of the pain, and I wished I'd done it to Agravaine, too. I flexed my fingers around the sword hilt: even with the cast, my grip felt strong and solid.

"What's all the shouting about?" a new sleepy voice said.

Jenny stood beside Amelia in the doorway. She wore a robe that dragged the ground and clearly belonged to the taller woman. Jenny looked giggleweed-addled and confused. "What happened? Who are these people?"

Agravaine made a sound unlike anything I'd ever heard, a kind of childish, disappointed whine distorted by his broken nose. He legs went limp, and his dead weight dropped from Kern's grasp. He landed on his knees and lowered his head at once.

"Your Majesty," he whispered.

Jenny blinked a few times, looked at him, and said, "I'm sorry . . . do I know you?"

"Go back inside," I said an instant too late.

With a wet shriek of rage, Agravaine exploded from his crouch and sprang at her so quickly none of us could stop him. He yanked a dagger from his belt and drove it into Jenny's midsection with enough force to knock her back into the doorjamb.

Amelia grabbed him by the collar and shoved him away. He held on to his knife as he flew back; it left an arc of blood through the air. He landed on his butt and slid in the grass. He slapped the ground and screamed, *"You know me now, you bid?"* like a little boy having a tantrum. *"Do you?"*

Amelia caught Jenny as she fell. Jenny's eyes were open wide and she stared down at the wound, which had just begun to bleed. Amelia slapped her hand over it and said with reasonable calm, "Cammy!"

Agravaine was still screeching, *"Do you know me? Do you know me?"* He switched his grip on the knife and started to get to his feet.

He never got the chance. I whacked him in the side of the head with my bad hand, using the weight of cast and sword for added impact. He fell back flat, and I straddled his chest. With my good hand I snatched the knife away and tossed it out of reach.

"I stuck it in her," he hissed with a crazed smile. "Did you see that? I gabe it to her good."

His hateful bloody grin caused something I'd thought long extinguished in me to flare back to life. I raised Hoel's sword above my head and repeatedly pounded Agravaine's face with the heavy pommel. My voice rose to an unintelligible screech of rage and fury. I saw in Dave Agravaine every bullying, smug, ignorant soldier I'd ever met. Or ever been.

I stopped when the cast on my hand cracked and fell away, except for a cup-shaped piece pinned between my palm and sword hilt. I sat there breathing, which seemed at the moment to take all my strength. I wasn't sure how long I'd been hitting him, but not only was Agravaine dead, his face was pounded to unrecognizable red mush with pieces of white bone around the edges.

I'd felt like this before in the heat of battle, but always at a professional distance; this was the first time I recalled this level of rage directed at someone for personal reasons. I stared at the ruin of Agravaine's face; one lifeless eyeball suddenly popped up from the blood pooled over its socket. I almost threw up.

Instead I got to my feet. "Always pay the insurance," I hissed to myself, and decapitated Agravaine for good measure. Watching his head roll over while his body stayed in place felt better than it had any right to feel.

The smell hit me then. I choked down another surge of bile. I'd forgotten the coppery, raw-meat odor of violent death.

Hoel sat on the ground clutching his injured leg, his fingers soaked with blood. He stared at me as if I were some supernatural monster. Now *that* was something: my battle rage had scared a Knight of the Double Tarn.

I pointed the sword, *his* sword, the pommel still dripping Agravaine's blood, at him. *"You."*

His words tumbled out as he tried to scoot away. "Wait, it was all Dave's doing, we were just following orders, we didn't know the queen would be here—"

"Shut up," I said. I wasn't sure it was audible, but it must've been because Hoel did it.

I felt a droplet of Agravaine's blood drip from my sword hand to the grass. My arm did not waver. "I have," I said quietly, "some questions for you."

"I think they can wait," Kern said from the cottage door.

y bad hand, even without its cast, felt plenty strong. I tied Hoel's wrists to one of the wagon wheels, his back against the spokes. When he protested that the ropes were too tight, I tightened them. Then I put a tourniquet around his injured calf. I stuck his sword, the hilt still dripping Agravaine's blood, into the ground between his legs. He couldn't reach it, of course, but I wanted him to try. He shouted desperate, high-pitched curses after me.

Kern had carried Jenny into the cottage bedroom. Amelia sat in the living room, a bloody rag to her nose. She looked up at me as I closed the front door to muffle Hoel's cries. Without a word she handed me another rag to wipe the blood from my hands.

"Are you okay?" I asked, hoping I sounded reasonably normal. The rage still quivered just below my sternum.

She nodded. "It's just a bloody nose. Had lots of 'em. The little fucker blindsided me, that's all."

"He liked hitting women."

"Wish I'd had the chance to hit him back. But it didn't break my heart to watch you do it." She paused, checked the blood on the rag, and returned it to her face. "Is the man I shot . . . ?"

"He's dead."

She blinked numbly a few times. "Wow. I've hurt people before, but I never killed anyone." She looked up at me. "How am I supposed to feel about it?"

"Any way you feel is the right way."

"How do *you* feel about it?"

"If you have to kill a snake, kill it once and for all."

She paused, seeming to search inside herself, and said at last, "I don't feel . . . anything."

"That's okay, too." I touched her cheek with the back of my good hand. She smiled and leaned into my caress.

I went into the bedroom. Jenny lay on the bed, robe open, sheets strategically covering her demure parts. Her side was bare, and the freshly stitched cut oozed blood as Kern wiped it. Thankfully he'd also put on his multicolored gown again. "That should scab up quickly," he said. "But you'll need to stay still until it knits good and strong."

I smelled something sour and familiar. Jenny moaned and tossed her head, eyes closed. If she'd heard Kern, she gave no sign.

"How is she?" I asked.

"I don't know, there's something wrong. It's a nasty cut, sure, but nothing more than that. It hit a rib, so it didn't reach anything vital. A few stitches, some poultices to keep it from getting inflamed, and she should be fine. Yet look at her."

Kern was right. She was pale, sweating, and seemed to have trouble breathing. Her eyes opened and flickered about in fear. She had trouble focusing. "What do you mean?" she gasped in a weak, trembling voice. "What's wrong with me?"

"Nothing, honey, we'll figure it out." Kern's nose wrinkled. "Although I can't place that smell."

I could. I felt a mix of horror and impotent rage as I lifted one of the bloody rags used to clean the wound and sniffed. "Shatternight. He coated his knife with shatternight."

"What's that?" Jenny asked urgently.

Kern leaned down, sniffed the wound, then looked at me with a mix of respect and fear. "How the hell did you know that?"

"It's what somebody used on that knight back at Nodlon."

"I've been poisoned?" she asked more urgently.

"The dose couldn't have been very strong," Kern said to me. "Exposed to the air, it would've started to weaken almost immediately."

I dropped the rag. "How strong does it need to be?"

"*Stop ignoring me!*" she screamed.

Kern tenderly brushed damp hair from her face and smiled his best paternal smile. "I'm sorry, you're right. We shouldn't talk about you like you're not here. One of men's worst tendencies toward women, I'm afraid. Yes, it's a kind of poison. I've dealt with it before, and I know exactly what to do."

"Will I die?" she asked in a small voice.

His smile faded, but his tone remained gentle. "We all do. Now I want you to rest, and let that cut air out. I'm going to fix up some medicine to make you feel much better. It'll only take a jiffy, if your friend here helps." He nodded at me.

"Of course," I said.

"I'll send Amelia in to keep you company. Call if you need us." I followed Kern from the bedroom, lacking the heart to look back at Jenny. Kern was careful to close the door.

"Amelia," he called quietly, and she jumped to her feet. Her nose had stopped bleeding but was beginning to swell. "I need you to stay with Jenny. I've got to mix some medicine in the shed. I'll be back shortly."

"Will she be okay?" Amelia asked.

Kern said nothing. Which, of course, was an answer.

We went out the back door to a little shack only a few steps away. Inside was a well-stocked apothecary, its shelves filled with bottles, jars, and boxes. A table loaded with various mixing devices occupied most of the open floor space. Kern turned a handle mounted on the wall, and a section of the roof opened to admit light. Then he closed the door behind us.

Between him and the table, I had little room to move. I stood with my back against the door and said, "There's nothing you can do for her, is there?"

"No," he said as he thumbed through a thick, battered book of drawings and strange scripts. "Once shatternight gets into the blood, that's it. If she'd swallowed it, there might be something I could do, but this way . . . no."

I nodded. "At least it's not a heavy dose."

His head snapped up and he glared at me. "A heavy dose would be quick and merciful. How long did it take your knight to die?"

"A couple of minutes."

"This will keep her in agony for hours, maybe days. You think that's better?"

I knew his anger wasn't really directed at me. "She's not in agony now."

"No. She's in shock, and the poison is still spreading. But the pain will start soon." He used a feather to mark his place in the book, then looked down at a large mortar filled with brownish powder. He stroked his long beard, deep in thought.

The confines of the place did not help me stay calm. "There has to be *something* we can do," I insisted.

"I can hasten her end."

"No. She's crucial to stopping what's going on at Nodlon."

He looked at me, his eyes perfectly clear for the first time. "What *is* going on at Nodlon?"

I hadn't verbalized my idea yet, and I figured at this point Kern had earned my trust. So I said, "Originally a simple plan to make the queen look bad. She's got enemies, as I'm sure you know. And because of your switch on their wedding day, a lot of people think she and Elliot Spears are cuckolding King Marcus."

"*Cuckold*," Kern said with a chuckle. "Always liked that word. Sounds like *cock hold*, which is what it usually is. A woman gets a hold on a man's cock, literally and symbolically."

"Yeah, well, the Knights of the Double Tarn think Queen Jennifer has a hold on Elliot's spear, which makes them distrust her. Someone wants to capitalize on that, so they made it look like she tried to kill Thomas Gillian as a warning to the other knights to stop gossiping."

Kern nodded. "All that makes sense. But you haven't told me *why*."

"I'd hoped you would figure it out for yourself, you know," I shot back. "You're a smart one, I can tell."

He said nothing.

"When I met Queen Jennifer," I continued, "she compared herself to a ring setting and said Marcus was the jewel. It's hard to make a jewel look bad on its own, but you can put it in a bad setting and it'll look cheap and tawdry. *That's* why she was framed. But it only halfway worked because I was there. The Double Tarn knights believe the queen's responsible, but the nobles think *I* did it. They're too shrewd to go against the queen when there's a handy scapegoat dropped right in their laps. So whoever's behind it has to make another move." *If they haven't already,* I thought as I recalled the dust cloud.

"Whoever's behind it," Kern repeated. "And just who is that?"

"I'm not sure yet. One person can't be doing all the dirty work, but Bob Kay insists it's still the work of one hand."

"Megan Drake, just like I told you," Kern said. "Bob's always had a thing for her. Not a romantic one, but he sees her behind every misfortune. He probably thinks she makes all the bad weather. And he may be right, she's a brilliant young woman."

"Young? I thought she was older than Marcus."

"Everyone's young to me. And, yes, she's a couple of years older, so she'd be . . . let me think . . . around thirty-five by now."

"What does she look like?"

"Average. You wouldn't look at her twice if you met her. Probably wouldn't remember her the next time you saw her."

"And she's in exile?"

"Oh, yes. And every knight memorizes her portrait because in Grand Bruan, she's to be killed on sight."

"That's harsh for a princess, isn't it?"

"It's not harsh for a traitor."

I nodded. Everything was pulling together, except for one final element: motive. "Bob says she hates Marcus because his father raped their mother. Is that true?"

"That he did it? Yes."

"But is it why she hates Marcus?"

"You'll have to ask her."

It was one more evasive answer than my patience could stand. I slammed my right hand on the table so hard all the glassware jumped. "I'm asking you," I said quietly.

Kern tried to hold my gaze, but couldn't. He picked up a pestle and began to grind the powder in the mortar. "If I tell you, you can't—"

"No strings. This island has yanked my chain enough, and I'm about to yank back."

He looked down and his long white hair fell to either side of his face as he spoke. "Has anyone mentioned a man named Kindermord to you?"

"The name's come up a few times. Who is he?"

Kern's voice was numb, flat, and matter-of-fact. What he told me was horrifying, and disgusting, and made perfect sense. It was the motive that explained everything. He concluded, "Choosing the lesser evil is still choosing evil."

We stood in silence. The weight of his revelation demanded that moment of respect. At last I said, "An army was headed to Nodlon. Medraft was in Astolat ahead of it. That means I have to get Jenny to Nodlon fast."

"Why? What can she do?"

"She's the wild card. I don't think the murderer even knows she exists. With her, I can show that the queen is innocent of treason."

"Won't Elliot prove that?"

"By strength of arms, yes. But I'll prove it for real."

"And prove the king a fool."

I shook my head. "No. All I have to do is show that Spears has a wife who looks like the queen, which means Jennifer had no motive for killing Patrice, or trying to kill Gillian."

That was all true. But an equally big motivation was so that she could see Elliot one last time before she died. It might make up a little for my failing to protect her. At least I could tell myself that I did *something*.

Kern looked at me steadily. "It's unlikely she'll make it there alive. Even if you left right now."

"We *are* leaving right now, or at least as soon as possible. And she'll make it. I just need some Cameron Kern magic."

"Magic," he practically spat. "You mean those deceptions of the ordinary and the obvious that morons *call* magic."

"Whatever they are, I believe you can use them to help me. And her."

A scream of bone-deep agony, even muffled by walls and distance, made us both jump. Kern said, "I can't save her. Do you know how shatternight works? It dissolves the nerves, from the tips up. So the longer it works, the more painful it gets. It's like boiling inside. If it reaches the big nerves, the ones in the spine . . ." He shook his head. "I can't imagine enduring it."

"What *can* you do?"

He opened the book, removed the feather place-marker, and turned some more pages. "I can *almost* kill her. I can mix something that will slow down her body's processes, which will also slow the shatternight. She'll appear dead to all intents and purposes, but when you give her the antidote, she'll wake up. Unfortunately, she'll be no better off, and her life will run out then just as it would now. But it would give you time to get to Nodlon."

Another groan reached us. There was a knock on the shed door and a distraught Amelia said, "Cammy? She's hurting so bad, I don't know what to do."

"Just hang on," the old man said. "I'm mixing something right now." To me he said, "I'll also give you something to send her on her way, if you think it's the right time."

"That's not my call, it's hers."

"She may not be able to make it."

"I still can't make it for her."

"Then I hope you like watching pain."

I clenched my fists. Then it suddenly registered that I *could* clench my fists. I looked down at my right hand, and while it was still black-and-blue, the swelling was totally gone. I'd even pounded the table with it and felt no pain. I held it up to the light. "The hell?" I whispered.

"You broke your cast. Need a new one?"

I was still puzzled. "No, I . . . guess I don't."

"You know, that's one thing those moon priestesses can do that I could never figure out. They can make a bone knit in a fraction of the time it should take. They call it magic. But there's no such thing, is there?"

The weight of this final revelation made me suddenly very tired. I leaned back against the door and closed my eyes. So there it was: I'd known no one when I came to Grand Bruan, and it appeared that was still true.

In a little while Kern held up two small bottles. One was open, the other corked and sealed with wax. The liquid inside the open one was clear, the other deep forest green. He said, "You wanted magic? I give you the power to raise the dead."

I said nothing. I was way past irony.

He shook the bottles so the liquid in them sparkled. "I'll give this to her now," he said about the clear one. "The other is for when you want her to come out of it."

I took the sealed bottle and put it in my jacket's inner pocket. The nice thing about expensive clothes was that they were loaded with little compartments like that. "And you're sure this will work?"

He glared at me in annoyance. "Fuck, no. I've never done

this before. I don't have a goddamned lifetime's accumulation of apothecarian knowledge."

"I was just asking."

"Well, you got your answer, didn't you?" he muttered as he put away the various ingredients. He'd been through a lot, too, I reminded myself.

We went back into the cottage. Amelia sat on the bed beside Jenny and held her hand. The stitched wound no longer oozed blood, but Jenny was still bathed in sweat, and her knuckles were white where she gripped Amelia's hand.

The tall girl stood and pried herself free from Jenny's grip. Kern knelt beside the bed, touched Jenny's forehead and neck, then leaned down to listen to her breathing.

Amelia sniffled next to me. I would've put my arm around her shoulders to comfort her, but I couldn't gracefully reach that high.

"Jenny," Kern said softly. "Can you hear me?"

She opened her eyes and looked wildly around, terror in her face like a little girl's. I'd never felt so helpless in my life. She said, "My fingers and toes feel like they're burning."

"I know," Kern said. "It's the poison from the knife that cut you."

"Am I going to die?" she whimpered. "Please, tell me."

"I can't say for certain," Kern said. "But . . . probably."

Her eyes welled with tears. "How soon?" she asked in a tiny voice.

He forced himself to meet her gaze. "I don't know. But not long."

She turned her head and cried silently into her pillow.

Amelia, also crying, sat on the opposite side of the bed and stroked her hair.

Abruptly Jenny tried to sit up. "I have to see Elliot one last time. Can you send for him?"

"I've got a better idea," I said. "I'll take you to him."

She looked at me with the hope of a man in the desert wondering if the oasis is a mirage. "You will? You promise?"

"I promise." For her sake I managed a no-big-deal smile, as if I took dying women to find their husbands every day and twice on holidays.

Kern handed Amelia the bottle. To Jenny he said, "Drink this. It'll help you sleep. Amelia will stay with you. And when you wake up, you'll be with Elliot."

Amelia put the bottle to Jenny's lips and she drank it in one swallow. Almost at once her face visibly relaxed, and her heaving chest began to slow down. Her eyes slowly closed.

"I'll get her dressed," Amelia said. "You men wait somewhere else."

Kern nodded toward the door and I followed him out once more, this time into the sitting room. He lit his pipe and took several furious puffs, pacing in the small space like a bull in an outhouse. Once again I found myself backed up to the closed door. Through it I heard Hoel's continued cries of pain and outrage.

"That little peckerhead son of a bitch Agravaine," Kern snarled, his words accompanied by blasts of smoke. "They say poison is a woman's way, did you know that? That's probably why he used it. Kill them with their own weapon of choice. Even a total stranger."

"He thought she was the queen," I said. "He didn't know about the switch."

Kern looked up at the ceiling and blew a thin, narrow column of smoke at it. "It didn't matter. For Dave, if a woman wasn't on her back or her knees, she was out of line. He killed his own mother, did you know that? Caught her in bed with another man."

"Another man besides her husband, or besides Agravaine?"

Kern touched his nose to say I'd caught the crucial detail.

"Did he kill her with poison, too?"

"No, he chopped her head off. Medraft used his influence to keep him from hanging for it." Kern laughed coldly. "It was the beginning of a beautiful friendship."

I felt the poetic justice of what I'd done to him. "He won't be hurting any more women."

Kern looked at me from the corner of his eye. "No, and he won't give you any more information, either. Think maybe you acted too rashly?"

The roomful of smoke was beginning to mellow me out, and I didn't want that. "I'll regret things when I'm your age. If you'll excuse me, I'm going to go talk to the survivor for a moment."

Hoel stopped moaning and glared up at me as I emerged from the cottage. The sun had moved past its zenith, and he was not in the shade. His sweaty skin was pale from blood loss, and his exposed hands were purple. His sword, still stuck in the earth between his legs, reflected a vertical bar of light on his face.

I ignored him, walked a few steps away, and took a long,

deep breath. Partly it was to clear out the giggleweed, partly to annoy Hoel. It did both.

"I can't feel my fingers, you asshole," he hissed, recovering a bit of his soldier's bravado. "Loosen the goddamn knots. I'm not telling you squat until you do."

I took in the scene of pastoral carnage. The two dead men lay where they'd fallen. A crow perched on Agravaine's chest and pecked at the stump of his neck. The remaining pair of military horses grazed placidly alongside the ones from my wagon. Where the grass was taller, it waved in the gentle breeze.

"You hear me?" Hoel's struggles made the wagon creak. "I'm a Knight of the goddamn Double Tarn, you can't intimidate me."

I picked up Agravaine's severed head by the hair, with its smashed and ruined face, and plopped it beside the sword in front of Hoel. "Your friend had an attitude with me, too. Look at him now."

Hoel sneered up at me. "I remember him being taller."

I slapped him so hard his head slammed against a wheel spoke. Fear mixed with his hatred when he glared back at me. "You're a big man with someone who can't fight back. Untie me, then we'll see how tough you are."

"I am going to ask you questions," I said carefully. My chest was so tight with fury the words came out as a wheeze. "Answer them, and you'll live through this day."

"And if I don't?" he sneered mockingly.

I pushed his bruise-colored pinkie back until it snapped. His hands weren't as numb as he thought. His scream startled a flock of birds from the nearby trees.

"Nine more fingers and ten more toes," I said. "Plus a mouthful of teeth and a couple of balls. I sure do hope you keep trying not to be intimidated. Now: who sent you here?"

He glanced at the severed head. "Look, we just followed Agravaine. He outranks us, we have to do what he says."

"Like when you ambushed me in that courtyard at Nodlon?"

Hoel nodded and tried to laugh. "We were just delivering another love poem from General Medraft to the queen, we didn't even know you'd be there. We just had standing orders that if we saw you again, to make sure you didn't cause any more trouble."

"Standing orders from who?"

He tried to hold it back, but when I reached for his hand again, he broke. "A woman. I don't know who. I never saw her face. She had on a cloak, but you could tell she was a woman."

"What did she say?"

"I didn't hear." I reached for another finger and he added quickly, "No, seriously, she never spoke to me or Cador. She only talked to Agravaine."

"I thought he hated women. But he took orders from them?"

"She didn't give the orders, she just relayed them from Medraft. At least, that's what I figured."

"Why did Medraft send him secret orders?"

Hoel laughed. "The general had Agravaine convinced he'd be seneschal when Medraft took the crown. I didn't believe it, but I figured I might get some advancement if I went along."

"So Medraft *is* planning a coup."

Hoel nodded. "Agravaine said Medraft knew something the king would never want to get out publicly. He was sure he'd even abdicate to keep it quiet. Medraft just had to wait for the right moment."

"What was it?"

"The moment?"

"The *secret*."

Hoel shook his head. "I don't know. Really. As far as I know, Medraft never told Agravaine, either." Hoel nodded toward the cottage. "I guess it was about that woman inside. That isn't really Queen Jennifer, is it?"

"Depends on who you ask," I said. But it confirmed what Kern had told me. That act of perversion and violence had started a whole chain of events long before I got to this wretched little island, but I'd be goddamned if I wasn't the one who was going to stop it. And make sure the murderers involved paid. If I survived that long-ago whorehouse massacre for anything, it was for things like this. "Does Medraft have troops?"

"Yeah. He's been bringing in mercenaries and soldiers from the Spatelo islands. They've been smarting ever since Marcus ran them out."

"What about the rest of the Knights of the Double Tarn?"

"They're outnumbered and out of practice. But they're all with Marcus, no question."

"Except you three loyal men at arms."

He looked down and said nothing. I wondered how truly loyal the other knights would be if they knew what Marcus had done. I realized that's exactly what Medraft was counting on. He knew nothing about the switched Jennifers, which meant I had a hole card. If I could figure out when to play it.

"Next question," I said. "What exactly were you supposed to do with Spears and me when you found us?"

He swallowed nervously. "We, ah . . . were supposed to make sure Elliot didn't show up to defend the queen."

"You three losers against him?"

"We weren't going to *fight* him, we were going to tell him the king had moved the trial to Motlace."

"And me?"

"We were supposed to, ah . . . eliminate you. Then bring your head back to Nodlon."

"How did you know to find me here?"

Again that nervous swallow. "We made one of the stable-boys tell us. Agravaine spoke his language."

I knew which stable boy they meant. "He was a little kid."

Hoel looked desperately guilty and fearful. "I know."

"You killed him, didn't you?"

"Cador did," Hoel said quickly. "Agravaine held him."

"And you just stood there and watched."

Hoel's words spewed forth in an attempt to save his life. "I was just following orders, I didn't have a choice, I'm a soldier. You were a soldier once, weren't you? I can tell. We have to do what we're told, even if it's awful. A soldier who goes against his orders is a traitor, right? *Right?*"

Despite my best efforts, I recalled that eager little boy's bright face. "Was it quick?"

Hoel knew what I meant. He didn't answer.

I slowly drew his sword from the ground, its hilt and pommel still gummy with Agravaine's drying blood. Dirt stuck to the blood at the tip. The horror on Hoel's face as the blade rose above him filled me with my own icy joy.

"I have an order for you." I gripped the hilt with both hands.

Hoel swallowed. "Anything."

I smiled. "Go to hell." Then I split his skull down to the bridge of his nose. It took a long time for his corpse to stop twitching.

"That was for you, Jack," I added, even though no one was alive to hear. I hoped wherever he was, the boy could now rest easy.

chapter TWENTY-SIX

I left Hoel's sword outside by his body and went into the cottage. Kern was gone, and the bedroom door was closed. I took off my jacket, went into the kitchen, and found a bucket of water and some soap. Washing my hands did nothing about the blood splattered on my clothes, but I couldn't help that. I also washed my face and wet down my hair. My beard was starting to grow back. It had been three days since I had a bath, and I could smell it even if no one else could.

My movements stirred up the dust, which sparkled in the light coming through the window. I watched it for a long time; the only sounds were the birds and insects outside, and Amelia's muffled crying.

Man, I was tired. Down to the bone. The last time I'd slept decently was before Sam Patrice's death . . . three days ago? Had it only been that long? Since then I'd grabbed a few hours here and there, but not enough to call any of it *rest*. Certainly not last night, bouncing in that wagon.

My shoulders and wrists still felt the impact of the blow that killed Hoel. Splitting a skull wasn't easy, and I was lucky the sword was both heavy and sharp. I looked at my formerly broken hand again, marveling at the flexibility despite the purple blotch over the knuckles. I tried not to think about what it meant.

At last I knocked softly on the bedroom door and went inside. Kern stood at the foot of the bed smoking his pipe, while Amelia knelt and brushed Jenny's hair. The tall woman hummed a nursery-rhyme song, her voice cracking.

Somewhere she'd found a demure white dress that fit the smaller woman. With her eyes closed and hands crossed on her chest, Jenny did indeed look like a corpse. If she was breathing, it didn't show, and the giggleweed masked any lingering shatternight odor.

"She was so sweet," Amelia said, interrupting her nontune. "She just wanted to live with her man in peace. She never wanted to be someone important." Amelia's face contorted and she began to cry anew. Her nose ran, the snot pinkish with dried blood, and she wiped it carelessly on her sleeve. "Why did this have to happen?"

"If I could answer that, honey, we wouldn't be living in the middle of the woods," Kern answered. He turned his red eyes on me and said, "She'll stay like this for three days or so. Then it'll wear off on its own. To bring her out of it before then, wave the fumes from that sealed bottle under her nose."

I nodded.

Kern waved his pipe at my bloody tunic. "Would you like some fresh clothes?"

"Do you have anything with less than five colors?"

He smiled. "I left all those behind when I quit my job at court."

"I'll pass, then."

I watched Amelia's brush make its way through Jenny's hair. She really *did* look like Queen Jennifer with her features immobile and relaxed. Then I had an idea. I was too tired to judge if it was good or bad. I said, "Amelia, do you have any jewelry?"

The question caused her face to scrunch with effort. Her nose, puffy and starting to bruise, did not join the scrunch. She said guardedly, "A little. Odds and ends. Why?"

"Is it sparkly stuff?"

She looked more confused. "Some of it."

"I need you to use it to make Jenny look regal. I want people to think she *is* Queen Jennifer." I turned to Kern. "Do you have any wooden planks?"

"Some."

I patted him on the arm. "Good. We have some carpentry to do. Come on."

IT was nearly dark before we finished. I'd long since accepted that I'd get no sleep this night, either.

First we cleaned up the mess. We carried the bodies of the three knights far into the cave and dumped them down a crevice so deep we never heard them hit bottom. I used bent nails to attach one of their discarded swords under the wagon's seat, one along the inside edge of the bed behind me, and one on the bottom of the wagon. It was only overkill if I didn't need them. Then Cameron showed me his available lumber and we got to work. It was a simple project, and there were two of us, so it didn't take long.

As the sun set behind the trees, Amelia carried Jenny out to the wagon. I'd hitched up my original two horses; the knights' mounts ran when I tried to catch them and didn't look suited to such mundane work anyway. The horses from Spears's stable were well rested and fed now, so they'd do fine.

Amelia had also done well. In addition to the white gown, the false corpse now wore a tiara, long earrings, and a wide necklace. All were gaudy and weren't really the jewels they pretended to be. But they worked: Jenny looked angelic and almost magical in them, a sleeping princess awaiting true love's kiss. If only.

When she saw what waited in the wagon bed, Amelia froze. "No."

"Amelia," Kern said gently.

"No, Cammy, that's a *coffin*."

"I need to take people off guard," I said. "A man hauling a coffin gets automatic respect and right of way. And if anyone looks inside, they'll think it's the queen, which should be a surprise that buys me some more time."

"She's *not dead*," Amelia insisted. "What if she wakes up inside there?"

"She won't," Kern said with certainty.

Amelia looked at him. "Cammy—"

"She wants to see Elliot," I interrupted. I didn't have the patience for long explanations. "There's an army between us and them that we have to get through. This is the only way that'll happen." At least, the only way I could think of in my sleep-deprived state, but I saw no need to mention that.

Amelia continued to look at Kern. He said nothing.

At last the tall woman stepped to the side of the wagon and slowly lowered Jenny into the box we'd built for her. She arranged the unconscious woman's hands on her chest, stroked her hair a final time, and softly kissed her. Backlit by the setting sun through the trees, a lone tear fell from Amelia's cheek to Jenny's lips as she stood.

"Good-bye, Dark Jenny," Amelia said softly.

Then Kern and I put the lid on the coffin.

I only used two big nails, enough to hold it in place. I didn't want it to be airtight, and if I needed to open it, I'd bet it would be quickly.

Chattering birds settled into the trees for the evening. It would be full night soon. As I put the scabbard Spears gave me across my back, I said to Kern, "I haven't asked because I hoped you'd offer, but I could use your help."

"You've had my help."

I climbed onto the wagon seat. "I mean at Nodlon. Come with me."

He put up his hands. "No. I'm happy here. I'm *staying* here."

"If Ted Medraft gets the crown—"

"He'll never bother me."

"How do you know?"

Kern smiled and waggled his eyebrows. "Because I'm Cameron the Wizard, and I know all."

I smiled wryly. "If you're so all-knowing, then what's the shortest way to Nodlon from here?"

"I've got a map for you." Kern handed me a rolled parchment. "This takes you back to the main road. You'll come out just to the east of a little crossroads town called Astolat. After that it's a straight shot."

I took the reins and was about to snap them when Kern put his hand on my leg and motioned for me to lean down. It was hard to do with the scabbard holding my spine straight. He said quietly, "Because I'm so all-knowing, I'm going to give you some advice. If I were still at court, I'd call it a prophecy and use lots of bells and whistles to scare you shitless, but under the circumstances I'll skip all that. Are you ready?"

I just looked at him, too tired for a snappy comeback.

He checked that Amelia was out of earshot. She stood in the cottage door, long arms wrapped around herself. Kern said quietly, "Remember I said you had a taste for violence? You need to keep in mind that every man you kill was once somebody's little baby and had a mother who probably loved him. I'm not saying you shouldn't kill people; some people *do* need killing. But you should never enjoy it, because if you do, you've killed part of yourself that won't ever grow back. And I don't think you've got many of those to spare."

I still said nothing. He'd watched me kill Agravaine and seen the results of my discussion with Hoel, so I suppose he felt he understood me. Maybe he did.

He patted my stubbly cheek, then stepped aside. I snapped the reins, the wagon made a wide turn around the clearing, and we headed back to Nodlon.

chapter TWENTY-SEVEN

The route led across farm country, along roads and trails most used at harvest time. Since that was several weeks away, they were overgrown and in need of repair; it was rough going. I couldn't believe the constant jostling didn't wake Jenny, but apparently Kern's "magic" was as good as he said. I deliberately put his "prophecy" out of my mind.

The weather also didn't cooperate as it had the night before. It was cloudy and therefore much darker, especially when we passed beneath the trees. I wondered if it would've been faster to go back the way I'd come; then I wondered if Kern sent us this way because it *was*. This wasn't paranoia; by then I was sure no one on Grand Bruan did anything for the obvious or stated reasons.

As Kern promised, though, we came out just to the east of Astolat and turned west toward it, and Nodlon beyond.

Before that, though, I stopped and checked the coffin. Jenny had not moved, although the ride had disheveled her a bit. I straightened her clothes, rearranged her hair, and replaced the lid. I wondered if she was somehow aware of my presence, so I was careful not to touch anything untoward. The memory of that one kiss, whatever its real purpose, remained vivid. Too vivid.

An orange glow illuminated the clouds past Astolat, the distinctive reflection from a large fire. It was too close to be Nodlon Castle, and too far away to be the town. I didn't recall anything in between big enough to make so large a blaze. But, since I was headed toward it anyway, it seemed useless to waste time pondering it. I'd find out soon enough.

Astolat was eerily quiet and still. No light showed in any windows, and none of the chimneys produced any smoke. A dog or wolf ran silently across the road without looking in my direction; it was the only sign of life. Granted it was the middle of the night, but usually there'd be *something*, such as a crying baby or a couple fighting. There was nothing.

This was extremely creepy. I didn't speed the horses, but I drew the sword from my back and put it on the seat beside me. The empty scabbard was flexible enough I could finally slump a bit, although I was so tense I didn't.

I passed the Crack'd Mirror, where I'd encountered Ted Medraft; its door stood open, and inside was solid darkness. No hearth fire or lamp glowed anywhere. I'd never known a tavern to close and leave its door unlocked. Something had happened here and either left no trace or the traces were hidden by the night.

As soon as we left town the road became a shambles of

broken and missing stones. It hadn't been like this yesterday, so something massive must've come through. I recalled the size of the dust cloud I'd seen to the north; it looked as if this was where the troops turned west, straight toward Nodlon just as I'd feared.

I kept the horses moving as fast as they would; on the broken stones, the wagon rattled so hard I feared my eyes might shake loose. Luckily the horses were in as big a hurry to leave the ghost town as I was.

THE trees closed in over the road. They had tall, straight trunks so that when everything lined up, you could see quite a way through the forest. Through the trees, on the far side of the woods, I saw several distant fires; the glow on the clouds wasn't from one big blaze, but from a scattering of smaller ones. They were too large for hearth blazes, but it was past midsummer and not yet first harvest. What would people be celebrating with bonfires?

I got my first hint of what had happened when the horses, growing progressively more nervous, finally stopped in the middle of the road and stomped in place. Nothing I did or said convinced them to move. Their whinnies were loud in the silence, and I realized no insects were singing.

I grabbed my sword when I spotted the large, dark shape on the road ahead. I watched it long enough to be reasonably sure it wasn't moving. I got down from the wagon and approached. It was a dead horse and, still halfway in the saddle, its equally deceased rider. In the orange half-light I counted four arrows stuck in his torso and a half dozen more in the horse.

I knelt to look over the victim. His clothes marked him as a farmer, and his face showed him to be barely out of boyhood. I pulled an arrow from the horse and studied it as much as the light allowed. It wasn't expensive or fancy but simple, utilitarian, and lethal.

Ten arrows is a good-size volley, which spoke of an awful lot of archers. I knew at once who had done this: the kind of soldiers who get paid to fight whoever they're told is their enemy that day, and who think nothing about leaving a trail of dead civilians for no good reason except fun. Mercenaries, as I'd once been.

I recalled Ted Medraft's presence in Astolat just before the troops from the north arrived. It was clear who put the gold in their pockets. Hoel had told me the truth.

I saw three more fires through the forest. They made sense now: farms or homesteads, looted and burned by men who had no one to fight. Medraft left a scorched trail reflected in the lowering clouds all the way to Nodlon.

There was no question of moving the dead horse, so I led the wagon team around it, giving as much leeway as I could. Then I climbed back on the seat and urged the horses on as fast as my rattling bones could stand it. I envied Jenny her oblivion.

As I got closer to Nodlon, I passed more burning farmhouses and bodies in the road. I'd been wrong: this wasn't just professional killers blowing off steam, it was a battle tactic designed to terrify the civilian population into keeping its distance. The bodies were deliberately left on the road where they'd be found. After twenty years' peace under King Marcus, the citizens were completely unprepared for this level of brutality.

Ahead of me a light moved on the side of the road, arcing back and forth in the air. As I got closer, I made out a torch waving to get my attention.

Again I drew my sword and put it on the wagon seat beside me. I had no shield, so if they had arrows, I'd be a pincushion. I stopped the wagon fifty feet away and called, "Who's there?"

"I've got an injured Knight of the Double Tarn here," a woman's voice said. "Can you help me?"

I crouched as much as I could to make a smaller target. "How'd he get injured?"

"How do you think? Those dirty bastards who came through here cut him up and left him for dead."

"Who is he?"

"Says his name is Kay."

Well, *hell*. I jumped from the wagon and cautiously approached the torch. The old woman holding it had limp white hair and clothes that had never been new. "Where is he?"

She warningly pointed the torch in my direction. "Not so fast. How do I know you're not one of them?"

"How do I know you've really got an injured knight?"

She pondered this, then raised the torch. "I reckon at this point it doesn't matter. I've got nothing left anyway. Come on."

I followed her down into the shallow, dry ditch. The torchlight reflected off armor that moved a little as we approached. A sword waved a weak warning in our direction.

"It's okay," the woman said. "It's me. I've brought help."

Bob Kay lay on his side, a bloody makeshift bandage around his neck. His face shone with sweat and his breathing was louder than the crackling torch. He lowered the sword but kept his hand around the hilt.

I knelt beside him. "Bob, it's me, Eddie."

It took him a moment to focus on me, and another moment for recognition to hit. "LaCrosse?"

"Yeah."

"What happened?" His voice was thin and raspy.

"Isn't that my line?"

He grabbed the front of my tunic with his empty hand and pulled me close. "Elliot never showed up, you bastard. You betrayed us."

"The hell I did," I said, and slapped his hand away. I was too tired to endure insults. He fell forward, and if I hadn't caught him, he would've landed on his face. I pushed him back onto his side and said, "I got to Blithe Ward and delivered the message. He should've been at Nodlon yesterday morning."

Kay's eyes closed and his head sagged. "Then they got him, too. I went to find him under a flag of truce, and as soon as I got out of sight of Nodlon, they jumped me." He sighed despairingly. "Without Elliot . . ."

"Is Ted Medraft behind all this? Did he bring in an army of mercenaries?"

Kay nodded, then winced at the movement and gingerly clutched his neck. "All those months he was supposed to be protecting our northern coast from raiders, he's been hiring them instead. He's got Marcus pinned at Nodlon. Brilliant move, tactically speaking. At Motlace, Medraft never could've forced a confrontation, but Nodlon's not set up to endure a siege." Kay coughed painfully. "How that little pig turd and his mother managed to pull all this together . . ."

"How bad is your neck?"

He shrugged. "Hurts like a bastard. Hard to breathe. But it can't be too bad if I'm not dead yet." He raised up on his elbows. "Polly here fixed me up. She's got a sure hand."

The white-haired woman shrugged. "I've had three husbands. They all tended to get into scrapes."

I leaned close to Kay. "Listen, I know what's happened and why. But we have to get to Nodlon before the real fight starts, and before Marcus does anything he can't undo. And I have a secret weapon."

"You've been busy," Kay rasped. "Sorry for doubting you. Hard to know who to trust anymore on this fucking island."

I nodded. "Ain't it the truth."

He saw the sword in its scabbard across my back. "That looks like one of Elliot's."

"I told you I found him."

"Yeah. There was a time a whole division's worth of men couldn't have stopped him from getting to Jennifer. I guess we all slow down when we get older."

Kay was a big man, and it wasn't easy moving him out of the ditch; he was weak and couldn't really help. Polly and I got him onto the road, and they waited while I brought the wagon closer.

Both of them stared at the coffin. "What the hell is that?" Polly asked.

"*Who* the hell is that?" Kay rephrased.

"Just a favor I'm doing for someone," I said.

"Is that your secret weapon?" Kay muttered as he struggled up onto the seat. I didn't answer.

"What about me?" Polly said. "You going to leave an old lady by the side of the road?"

"We're heading literally into the middle of a battle," I said. "Hopefully we'll get there before it actually starts, but I can't guarantee it. You sure you want to come?"

She gestured around her with the torch. "There's not a standing farmhouse or a living person within ten miles of this road. I won't be much better off."

"You'll have to ride in the back."

She scraped the torch across the road stones and extinguished it in a shower of sparks. Then she jumped over the tailgate with surprising nimbleness. "It's not the first time I've ridden with a coffin. Who's in it?"

I didn't answer. I made sure Kay wouldn't fall off, then urged the horses on their way. We headed west into the blazing clouds toward Nodlon Castle.

chapter TWENTY-EIGHT

Kay was too weak, and Polly apparently disinclined, so we rode without talking. I kept tabs on the old woman out of the corner of my eye; I knew exactly what her game was. But she just watched the fires, her expression unreadable.

The road became an obstacle course of bodies, both human and livestock. The nauseating death smell grew stronger as well. At one point I had to stop and drag an overlapping pile of corpses aside to make room for the wagon. They were tied together at the wrists and weren't all adults. They'd been marched here and then executed; the family dog, no doubt loyally tagging along, was on the bottom.

When I returned to the wagon, Polly said flatly, "What a mess."

"You think?" I said, and snapped the reins before she could reply.

* * *

AT last the rising sun burned through the cloud cover and showed the full extent of the damage. Homes were reduced to their stone parts. Fields smoldered, bodies lay everywhere, and livestock stood numbly, not sure whether to flee or graze. Buzzards began to appear in the sky as wolves skittered for the shadows. The worst part was the utter silence: there seemed to be no wounded, only the dead.

"That son of a bitch," Kay muttered. "That son of a *bitch*. This was never supposed to happen again. We *promised* the people it wouldn't, and they trusted us. They made this a country, not just an island." His rage, even muted by his injury, was fearsome.

"Why would he do this?" Polly asked from the back, as calmly as if discussing a pot roast.

"Because he enjoys it, the son of a bitch," Kay said. "As a kid he liked to cut the legs off birds and watch them try to land."

I remembered the adolescent Medraft I'd encountered. This is exactly how I'd have guessed he'd grow up. But as I came to appreciate the scale of it, it no longer made sense as a tactic. "If he's planning a coup, then he must believe that all this will be his soon. Why destroy it?"

"I don't know," Kay growled. "You can be sure there's a plan, though. Courtesy of the poison-titted bitch that suckled him."

"That's somebody's mother you're talking about," Polly said, her words echoing Kern's warning. "If he's a grown man, his mother can't make him do anything."

Kay turned to snap a reply, having to swivel his whole body

due to his neck. Instead he exclaimed, "Holy shit, that's a coffin!"

Polly snorted. "Nothing gets past him, does it?"

Kay's anger vanished in his confusion. "Seriously, La-Crosse, that's a coffin. Has it been there all this time?"

"Yeah," I said.

Kay's face no longer shone with sweat; his fever must've broken. "Did you tell me about it before?"

"I mentioned it."

"I guess I was really out of it. Who's in it?"

"I'm doing a favor for a friend."

"The favor involves taking a coffin to Nodlon? At a time like this?"

"Yes." I jerked my head slightly toward Polly.

She saw it, though, and said, "He means he won't talk about it in front of me because he doesn't know if he can trust me. Fine, I only stayed with a total stranger in a ditch for hours and risked my life flagging down help for him. That's all."

Kay leaned close and asked quietly, "Is it anyone I know?"

"No."

He sighed with relief. "Then never mind. I have a feeling I'll be attending plenty of funerals soon enough."

Or just one, I thought but didn't say.

WE topped a small hill. At the bottom, four horsemen blocked the road at a place where the forest gave way to open, wild meadows. There'd be no sneaking past them.

Two of them noticed us as we looked down at them. They wore mismatched metal and leather armor scavenged from past battles and had the arrogant posture of men used to

pushing people around. Even without it, the bodies littering
the nearby ground, the empty "confiscated" wagons parked
in a neat row, and the riderless horses tied to available tree
branches told the story. Nobody got through this roadblock.
But we would, because I wasn't walking away from this now.
Sure, I'd earned my money and kept my word, but if I didn't
avenge the innocent blood, no one would. And that was a
contract with my conscience.

The other two guards stood in the meadow near a solitary
tree. They shared a longbow and took turns firing shafts into
a corpse that hung by its ankles from a branch. At this ridiculously close range the arrows went almost entirely through
the body. The two archers laughed as the most recent shot
made the corpse swing in a shallow arc.

As she took in the tableau, Polly said, "Shit."

"Well put," I agreed.

"I'll handle this," Kay said, and forced himself to sit up
straight.

I put my hand warningly on his arm. "These aren't Knights
of the Double Tarn."

"They're under Medraft, and I outrank him."

"I don't think you do today."

We had no choice but to continue down the hill toward
them. I stopped the wagon when one of the men stepped in
front of us and raised his hand. He was missing the tip of his
nose. "That's far enough, shit-kicker. By the king's order, this
road is closed."

Kay said raggedly, "I'm Robert Kay, King Marcus Drake's
seneschal and General Medraft's commanding officer. I'm
on my way to Nodlon, so move aside."

The second man, tall and skinny with ears that stuck out like open closet doors, said, "Tough titty, old man. You ain't getting there on this road." He rubbed the neck of the nearest horse. "Nice team, though. Strong. Make good army horses."

Nose-tip walked around the wagon. He gestured at the coffin and said, "Hey, who's the worm farm?"

"My mother," I said. "She died six months ago. I'm moving her to be buried by my father."

He scowled. "You dug her up?"

I shrugged. "It's what she wanted."

"You stupid country fucks," he said. The two men laughed. I guess my expensive clothes, spattered with dried blood and coated in trail dust, no longer gave me away.

By now the archers had noticed us, too. I said, "So what's the toll?"

"Toll?" Closet-ears said.

"Yeah, you know. The toll to use the road."

The two exchanged looks and snickered. "So you got money to pay a toll?" Nose-tip asked.

"Show it to us," Closet-ears added.

I held up my money bag and shook it so it rattled.

"Whoo-ee, we got us a rich boy here," Closet-ears said. "Jingles like the bells on a whore's ankle."

"You know," I said wearily, "there's no reason to be an asshole about this. I'm willing to pay to get past you."

"He called us assholes, didn't he?" Nose-tip said.

Closet-ears shoved him playfully. "I think he just meant you."

"Really? Well, in that case, I think I'll just take all the money as an insult fee."

I said, "Tell you what: I'll shoot you for it."

Closet-ears and Nose-tip exchanged a look. Closet-ears said, "Huh?"

I pointed at the archers, who had stopped their contest and now intently watched us. "One arrow each, me and your best man. You pick the distance and target. If I make a better shot, you let us through. If I don't . . ." I trailed off with a shrug.

Closet-ears called out, "Hey, Raven! This guy wants to shoot against you!"

The one called Raven, tall and about thirty years old, walked over with the bow. He looked at me carefully, evaluating both my skill and my status as a threat. I did my best to hide both, which—given my unwashed hair, disheveled clothes, and unshaven face—wasn't hard. "What do you know about shooting?" he said at last. "Poaching the king's deer in the winter?"

"Only one way to find out," I said.

He thought it over for a minute, then gestured I should get down. I did. When I began slipping off my scabbard, two swords appeared at my throat. I finished much more slowly. The blades went away, but their owners watched me minutely.

I followed Raven, Closet-ears, and the fourth man over to the swinging corpse. Nose-tip stayed by the wagon, nonchalant but certainly alert.

We stopped twenty paces from the tree. Closet-ears rushed over and gave the corpse a shove. It began to swing, dislodging two crows who'd swooped in for a snack. The body was a well-dressed middle-aged man's; his purplish face was still frozen in its dying look of surprise. Raven pulled an arrow from the quiver and nocked it. "Can you do this?" he said smugly, then fired. The arrow pierced the swaying palm of the dead man's right hand. His compatriots laughed.

I took the offered bow and arrow. I was a fair shot, but certainly not in Raven's league. Then again, what I really planned to shoot was closer and not moving. If I got the chance.

I tested the bow's tension. It was considerable. "Too much for you?" Raven asked with a cackle.

I nocked the arrow and smiled. "Just getting a feel for it."

I turned sideways to the target just as I'd been taught, raised the bow, and drew the string. I kept my elbow up, the way my dad had always showed me. My knuckles reminded me that they'd been broken just a few days ago, but they did the job. I felt my thumb against my cheek and knew the string was as taut as it was going to get.

Then I pivoted and shot Raven from an arrow's length away. The shaft passed right through the soft tissue of his neck and thudded into Closet-ears' chest behind him.

I dropped the bow, grabbed Raven as he started to collapse, and drew his sword. I rushed at the remaining man, who got his own blade out in time to knock aside my jab. He was young and heavily muscled, and he grinned once he realized he was in a fight he understood.

We exchanged enough blows for me to know he was too good for me to fight him this way, so I pretended to lose my sword—not that hard—and when he raised his own to bring it down on my skull, I rushed under his arm and knocked him to the ground. I sat on his chest just as I'd done with Agravaine, only this time I was a complete professional. I hit him once in the hollow of his throat with the edge of my hand, and when his eyes bulged and he clutched his neck, I pulled his own dagger from his belt and used my weight to drive the blade through his secondhand leather armor into his heart.

He died with a wet, bubbling cry. He may once have been someone's child, as Kern said, but he gave up that humanity the first time he killed someone and laughed. And unlike me, fate never gave him a chance to earn it back.

I took a moment to catch my breath. Sometimes experience was better than youth, but youth could recover faster. I ran back to the wagon, where Kay slumped across the seat. Nose-tip lay moaning on the ground with Kay's sword in his belly. Stabbing him had taken all the wounded knight's strength.

Nose-tip looked up at me. "Finish it, then," he gasped.

I pulled the sword from his stomach. Blood and organs surged forth, and he clutched them with both hands as he curled into a ball. "Finish it yourself," I said. Kern would be proud that I resisted the urge to kick him in the head.

I tossed Kay's sword into the wagon and helped the wounded knight sit up. He opened his eyes and said, "Did you get the others?"

"Yeah, I got 'em."

He grinned, which turned into a scowl of pain. "You'd make a fine Knight of the Double Tarn. Sorry I could only handle one."

"You did your part." Then I realized Polly was gone. I looked around, but saw no sign of her on the road, in the fields, or in the forests. I hadn't counted the horses, so I couldn't tell if one was missing.

That annoyed me. I had plans for her. I made a quick check

of the coffin, which hadn't been tampered with. Then I propped Bob back on his side of the seat and we resumed our trip to Nodlon, leaving Nose-tip still writhing on the road. Three crows hopped nearby in anticipation.

t noon I again stopped the wagon at the top of a hill. Kay had fallen asleep, and the sudden halt didn't wake him. I checked his pulse; it was weak but steady.

The view below and ahead would've made a great tapestry. In the background stood Nodlon Castle, perched starkly on its cliff against the sea and sky. Sun sparkled along the top of the walls, where men in armor patrolled the parapets. Flags fluttered in the breeze, and white gulls flew in place against the wind.

The land just outside the walls was empty. I'd seen it crowded with vendors and merchants just days before, but they were long gone now, leaving only bare spots in the grass where they'd previously camped.

Beyond this open space, closer to us, men and horses in armor formed a defensive crescent around the castle. They'd established a line with spears, shields, and barricades, but their strength wasn't deep. If the line broke, there were no reinforcements to fill it.

Next came another crescent of open land, except for two things. One was a fifteen-foot pole protruding from a pile of wood. It was the stake where the queen would be burned if found guilty of her crimes. The other was a large tent set up just beside the road.

The tent's walls rippled in the wind, and several Knights of the Double Tarn stood guard outside it. It flew a large white flag of truce. The rival commanders would meet there to negotiate prior to engaging in battle; each would give the other the chance to surrender. *That* was where I needed to be.

Between me and that destination was the vast camp of Medraft's enormous mercenary army.

Unlike the orderly billets of government-sponsored troops, the mercenaries' tents were a hodgepodge of sizes, styles, and personalizations. Men sat around campfires polishing armor, sharpening weapons, and drinking to excess. Pages and water boys ran among them, and screams occasionally punctuated the steady clatter. I estimated five thousand men; the knights in Nodlon, even counting the trainees, might manage a sixth of that. Currently Medraft's men hadn't even established a real perimeter to face their opponents; they were content to rest after their march and let their sheer presence do the work.

My horses tossed their heads nervously. I wanted to do the same, but I'd look silly.

The road went down the hill through the mercenaries, past the white tent, and into the castle. In places the stones were shattered so badly that it became merely a muddy path littered with rock shards. Like the landscape it passed through, the mercenaries had deliberately destroyed the road to prevent its use.

Kay stirred beside me. He yawned, winced at the pain it sent through his neck, and looked around in confusion. It only took a moment for him to orient himself, though. "We made it," he said. "Did you have any more trouble?"

"No. But this could make up for it."

He grimly surveyed the scene. "It's like the last twenty years never happened," he said at last. The horror, regret, and dismay in his voice was heartbreaking. "We're back to the way we were."

"It's not too late. If we can get down there before the sword-clanging starts, we can stop this."

"What *is* going on? Do you know who killed Sam Patrice?"

"Yes," I said with certainty. "I'll tell you when we're all in the same place at the same time."

"All who?"

"Everyone involved."

He sat back and closed his eyes. "Sounds like one of those damn mummer shows." In a faux upper-crust twitter he said, "'I suppose you wonder why I've asked you all here.' I hate those things."

"You'll like this one," I assured him.

FIRST, though, I had to get through the army. No one had paid any attention to us so far; they assumed that if we were here, we were supposed to be. Certainly I looked only marginally more presentable than most of the mercenaries, and the bloody bandage around Kay's neck helped him blend in as well. But the drive to the white-flagged parley tent was a long one, and the chances we'd make it without being challenged were pretty slim. It seemed smarter to make the first move myself.

I started the wagon down the road slowly, watching the soldiers who passed nearby until I saw the kind of man I wanted. I called out, "Hey! Pissant!"

A young man with a vague suggestion of a beard on his chin turned, saw us, and pointed questioningly at himself. "Yes, you!" I snarled. "Get your ass over here when I call you."

He threaded through the crowd until he reached us. He was bare-chested, his hair and body wet from recent washing. This must be his first campaign if he still worried about hygiene. He also wore no weapon, a sure sign of a novice. When I was a mercenary, I never went anywhere unarmed. I said, "Get up here and drive this thing." I stepped over the back of the seat into the wagon bed.

He looked at me blankly. "Do I know you?"

I used the voice that, in my day, made new recruits wet their pants. I caught Kay's admiring glance out of the corner of my eye. "Your ass will get to know my boot really well if you keep giving me lip. Now get up here and drive!"

The bare-chested young man quickly climbed up and took the reins.

"What's your name?" I demanded.

"Ollie. I'm with—"

"I didn't ask for your goddamned life story, did I? Or would you rather I keep calling you "pissant," because that's fine with me." He stared at me, and I added, "Are you a moron? Let's go! This coffin's supposed to be at the parley tent three hours ago!"

He yelled at the horses, and they started forward so abruptly I nearly tumbled out of the wagon. Kay covered his mouth so Ollie wouldn't see him laugh.

WE got halfway through the camp before someone finally stopped us. A tall, wide-shouldered man with a missing eye and a permanent scowl stepped right in our path with no apparent doubt the horses would stop for him. They did.

"What the hell is this?" he asked, and pointed at the coffin.

"It's a coffin, what do you think?" Ollie said before I could answer. I realized with a start that he was imitating my own tough-guy voice. Now *I* struggled not to laugh.

The tall man did not. He narrowed his good eye and said, "Do you know who I am?"

Ollie's braggadocio broke like a paper-thin dam. "Yes, Captain Ivy, I'm sorry, sir."

Ivy chewed his lip thoughtfully, looked at Kay and me and the coffin, then said, "Somebody better tell me the story about this or we'll add three more corpses to the fire."

"Sure," I said. "General Medraft sent for this coffin personally. It's something he wants to show King Marcus."

Ivy walked slowly around the wagon. Others began to stop what they were doing and watch. If we drew too much attention, we'd never get away. Ivy reached the back of the wagon and patted the coffin lid. "Open it."

"I don't think you want to do that," I said. I tried to project superiority, but didn't do a very good job of it. Ivy was way too sure of himself.

"I think I do," Ivy said, and smiled the way a wolf does when it finds an unattended fawn.

I looked around suspiciously, then motioned Ivy in close. He put his hand on his dagger as he leaned over the tailgate. I said quietly, "*I* don't even know who's in here. I met the general in Astolat before the rest of the army got there, and he told me go get this and bring it straight here. He said if anyone asked questions about it, I was supposed to make sure they never asked any more."

I put in enough truth about Medraft's activities in the last few days that I hoped my story sounded legitimate. Ivy's expression didn't change, but after a moment he nodded. "All right. But wait a minute."

He looked around at the small crowd of watchers. "Jameson, you and . . . yeah, you and Barker. Get on this wagon and go with this guy. Do what he says." Ivy turned back to me. "Give the general my regards."

"I will," I said. The irony threatened to choke me.

Jameson and Barker hopped into the back with me. Both were lean, long-muscled types with numerous white and pink scars on their bare arms. Jameson wore a necklace of mismatched baubles taken after battles. If he lived long enough, he'd realize that it was far scarier not to have the need to display trophies. Barker had a blank, dim expression and his hair fell in his eyes. His fingers tapped constantly; either he had more energy than he needed, or he took something to keep him alert. His bangs kept me from seeing if his pupils were affected.

The camp smells assailing me—sweat, mud, urine, burning meat, and metal—brought back memories I'd hoped to repress until my old age. And the worst part was, not all of them were unpleasant. When I saw two men laughing over their tankards as they sat beside a fire, I remembered the hours I'd spent doing the same thing, telling bullshit stories and calling bullshit on other people's. After all, we'd faced death together, and even though it was just a job, it bonded us with shared experience. In the thick of battle the paid soldier took as many risks as the noble knights, and often more since we got bonuses based on results.

There was a difference, though, and it was crucial: we fought to fight, the knights fought to win. If they defeated us, the war ended. If we defeated them, we'd just hire out for the next war somewhere else. How well they did depended on how desperately they wanted the victory, and that usually came down to leadership. How well we did depended simply on how much we needed our pay.

There were the freaks on both sides, of course: men (and occasionally women) who enjoyed any excuse for killing. They were easy to spot, tough to stop, and ultimately did everyone a favor by attracting attention while the rest of us did our jobs. Their kills were usually less than you'd think, because after a while no one would engage them. They spent the latter part of the battle striding among corpses looking for someone to fight.

Following the battles were the celebrations. We always had plenty to drink, and plenty of willing (or not) girls. There were boys for the ones who went that way as well. And unlike regular soldiers, we celebrated whether we won or lost.

Without meaning to, I'd grown wistful and nostalgic over

this period of my life. Which is why the universe had to balance things out by ensuring that I glanced to the side at just the right moment. "Stop," I told Ollie.

He did so without question. I hopped out of the wagon.

"You need us?" Jameson asked.

"No," I said.

Three crude tents circled a small fire, and weapons lay scattered about. The only person visible was a naked boy of about ten, who lay on his side. His wrists and ankles were tied to a stake. He looked up at me blankly, already numb from the horror he'd endured.

Willing. Or not. Yeah.

I drew my sword and cut the ropes. The boy slowly sat, his head down. "Get out of here," I said. "Run toward the castle."

He rubbed his wrists and shook his head.

I grabbed him by the hair and yanked him upright. "Did you hear me? Get going!"

"No," he said hoarsely. "My mom's in there." He pointed to one of the tents.

"LaCrosse," Kay said warningly, over the blood thundering in my head. I ignored it and tossed the tent flap aside.

There *was* a woman in the tent, at the moment its only occupant. She was naked as well and tied to the tent's central pole. I cut her loose.

She sat up and turned hateful, rage-filled eyes on me. "Where's my son?" she hissed.

"Outside. He wouldn't leave without you." I tossed her a blanket. "Go get him and run toward the castle. They'll take you in."

"They're the ones who *did* this," she snarled as she pulled the blanket around her shoulders. "King Marcus gave them permission."

Aha. Now the destruction made sense. "Is that what they told you?"

She nodded.

I pulled her to her feet, more roughly than I probably should have. "The Knights of the Double Tarn are out there ready to defend the castle against these bastards. Think about that. Then take your son and run to them. Unless you like the way you're being treated?"

I thought for a moment she might spit on me, but instead she rushed out. Through the open flap I saw her grab the boy by the wrist and drag him behind her. She dropped the blanket for the sake of speed and ran toward what I sincerely hoped was rescue.

As I stepped from the tent, its owner returned to camp. He saw me, then his captives fleeing in the distance. He was shorter and broader than me, like Agravaine but without the madness in his eyes. He was plenty pissed, though.

"Who the fuck are you?" he demanded. "That bitch was mine!"

Without a word I drove my sword into his belly. I ripped it upward as I removed it. I returned the sword to its scabbard as I walked away and climbed onto the wagon seat without watching him fall.

"What the hell was that all about?" Barker demanded.

"Yeah, that was somebody's prize," Jameson added. "We get to keep whatever we—"

I looked at them. Whatever they saw in my face silenced them. "Go," I told Ollie. My nostalgia curdled in my belly.

"And make it fast," Kay said. He nodded toward several men riding down the hill toward us, led by Ivy. I suppose he'd checked me out.

I grabbed the reins from Ollie and kicked him from the wagon. Kay drew his sword and put the tip at Jameson's throat. Barker froze as well, too confused to make any move. I snapped the reins and shouted at the horses. We sprang forward and headed downhill at a full gallop. Ollie shouted curses after us.

Now it was a simple race. Either we got through the mercenary camp and into the open, or we didn't. After all the secrets and ambiguities, it was nice to have things be so simple for a change.

I threw back my head and laughed.

chapter THIRTY

I glanced back. Ivy and his men were also at a full gallop, gesturing for others to stop us. You'd have to be foolish to jump in front of a wide-open team going downhill, but fools in armor were common. And if one did try, the resulting collision would no doubt trip the horses and send us ass-over-teakettle across the grass.

As we neared the bottom of the hill and the mercenary army's indistinct front line, men with swords ran up to either side of the road. They lunged and swung wildly as we shot past. The blades clattered against the sides of the wagon and managed to cut one of the reins. I saw red slashes on the horses' flanks as well and felt the wet spray of horse blood and sweat flying back at me.

Then we were in the open. I looked back and saw Ivy and his friends slow down and stop. Without orders they wouldn't follow us into the neutral no-man's-land and risk precipitating the battle. They yelled insults, and a couple of badly aimed arrows whizzed overhead. I pulled on the remaining reins and slowed the wagon to a trot. The horses, terrified and injured, fought me at first but then obeyed.

Ahead across the field, the Knights of the Double Tarn outside the white parley tent shuffled in their heavy armor as they watched us approach. No light fancy-dress metal for them today. The sun reflected in blinding hot spots from it. I hated wearing full armor; I knew just how uncomfortable it would be on a day like this. But the men here, and in the defensive line beyond, and on the castle walls, held their positions in stoic silence. Most of them might lack experience, but at least they'd had training.

"You all right?" I called back to Kay.

"Fine, but we lost one of our strong backs."

I looked back. Barker lay on the bed beside the coffin, nearly decapitated by a passing sword. Jameson's own throat was shallowly sliced in places where the tip of Kay's sword had bounced against his skin.

When we got close to the tent, I saw a round figure in bright lavender bouncing in frustration before the knights. It was Chauncey DeGrandis, lord of the manor, trying in vain to assert his lord-dom.

"But I *demand* to see the king!" he shrieked, his voice high like a woman's. "This is *my* castle! Those are *my* supplies you're hoarding!"

Two knights stepped around DeGrandis and into my path, swords drawn. A third leveled a crossbow at us. I stopped the wagon and showed my hands so they wouldn't feel threatened.

One of them raised his visor, exposing his sweat-drenched face. He was one of the older veterans. "That's it, friend, stop right there. Keep your hands where I can see them, all of you. Now what's the meaning of this commotion?"

I did as ordered. Kay sat up straight and said, "It's me."

The knights all snapped to attention with a mass metallic click. I was so tired this struck me as ridiculously funny, and I began to giggle. Kay shook his head.

DeGrandis whirled on us like one of those vicious little dogs some women have instead of children. He pointed at me and said, "That's him! That's the killer! Arrest him at once! *At once,* I say!"

No one paid him any mind. "Sir Robert," the knight who'd stopped us said. "Your neck—do you need a physician?"

"Get me a drink and we'll see if it leaks," Kay said. Two knights covered Jameson with their swords, and Kay climbed stiffly from the wagon. "First I need to know who's inside that tent."

"King Marcus, Queen Jennifer, and Sir Thomas Gillian." The veteran nodded at DeGrandis. "And this guy, if we'd let him."

"Where's Medraft?"

"He's not here yet. He wanted to meet at sunrise but hasn't shown up. The king is . . . annoyed."

"I bet. Get DeGrandis back inside the castle."

"But—," the purple man started to complain.

"Throw a pork roast at him if he won't shut up," Kay added.

Two of the knights took DeGrandis by the arms and pulled him bodily away. They visibly strained to support his bulk.

He kept his legs straight so that his heels left tracks in the grass, disturbing a big mottled snake as they raked over it. "But this is my castle! *Mine!*"

I turned to Jameson. "All right, bring that coffin into the tent."

He looked at the knights, then at me. He finally understood he'd been had. "I can't carry it by myself."

"Try," I said flatly, and one of the knights prodded him.

It was awkward, but he did manage to get his arms around the box and lift it. I knew Jenny wasn't heavy, and the coffin was made of light, thin wood. Kay led the way inside the tent, followed by Jameson. I brought up the rear.

It was dim and stuffy beneath the heavy canvas. In winter this kind of insulation would be luxurious, and on a normal summer day the tent's sides would be open to let in the breeze. But this was a prebattle conference between opposing commanders, so privacy trumped comfort. It took a long moment for my eyes to pick out the figures from the furniture.

A large rug covered the grass, and a small, round table with four chairs was set up in the middle of it. Benches waited along the sides for those of insufficient rank to sit at the table.

King Marcus Drake, in full regalia including crown and scepter, turned in midpace with a swirl of his fur-edged official cape. He wore the same huge sword, the legendary Belacrux, at his waist. His deep blue tunic was sweaty around his neck and under his arms. "Bob!" he shouted in a mix of relief and anger. "Where's Elliot?"

"Elliot's not coming," Kay said as he dropped to one knee. I thought at first he'd collapsed, but then realized he was just greeting his king. "I'm sorry, Marc. I barely got out of sight of the castle before I got jumped. I never had a chance to look for Elliot."

"What?" the queen gasped. She stood on the opposite side of the table, in a simple dress devoid of any ornamentation. She wore the same kind of manacles Kay had put on me, with the chain slack but definitely present. "Is he . . . dead?"

I looked at her. Her face shone, and strands of hair stuck to her cheeks. The resemblance was absolutely staggering: if I didn't know Jenny was in the box, I'd think she stood before me. No wonder it fooled Marcus.

"I don't know," Kay said, using one of the chairs to get to his feet. "But there's just so many of them, I can't see how even he could get through."

Gillian stood quietly at ease near the tent's wall. He wore a uniform but no armor. "That is unfortunate."

The sight of him, after all the time I'd spent dreading his appearance, annoyed me. "Yeah, well, at least you didn't have to come chasing after me. I came back, like I said I would."

He looked puzzled. "I beg your pardon?"

Kay laughed. It was a tight, harsh, barking sound, and everyone in the tent turned to him. He fought what appeared to be the giggles and said, "Hell, Eddie, I made that up. You really think we send the Knights of the Double Tarn out as roving assassins?" Kay shuddered as he struggled not to laugh, one hand pressed to the wound at his neck.

I stared at him. I was exhausted, pissed off, and no longer impressed by the world's happiest kingdom. Then I used my arm to rake the royal finery from the table. The dishes, utensils, and crystal goblets hit the ground in a loud clatter, and Jennifer jumped back.

"What are you doing?" she cried.

I turned to Jameson. "Put the coffin on the table."

He didn't move, frozen in place by the outsize presence of King Marcus Drake. His mouth hung open in wonder.

"Do it!" I barked.

He did so, then dropped to his knees before Drake. The king looked at the mercenary, then at me. "Who *is* this man? And what is that coffin doing here?"

I nudged Jameson with my foot. When he looked up fearfully, I said softly, "Run." He was out of the tent like a crossbow bolt.

I took a deep breath and wiped the sweat from my eyes. Gillian said quietly, "This conduct does merit an explanation, Mr. LaCrosse."

"And it'll get one," I said, "as soon as all the players are here." By now Medraft would know someone had broken through his lines bearing a coffin, and he'd have to come check it out. Then I could finish this.

A hand the size of a dinner plate grabbed my shoulder and spun me around, and again I found myself face-to-chest with Marcus Drake. He glared down at me like a storm cloud about to spit forth lightning. "I really don't have the time or the patience for showboating today, Mr. LaCrosse. I'm facing an insurrection."

I slapped his hand away. "You better have time for it." I stood on tiptoe, leaned close, and spoke so softly only he could hear. "I know about Kindermord."

Even in the tent's dim light I saw him turn red, then white. He stepped away from me without a word.

Jennifer put one hand gingerly on the coffin. The manacle

chain scraped lightly against the wood. "Is Elliot in there?" she asked me, her voice shaking. "Is that what you told Marc? Please, I have to know."

"Not unless we cut him off at the knees to make him fit," I said. It was cruel, but I was out of patience.

One of the knights standing guard called, "Someone's coming, sire!"

Kay peeked outside. "Medraft," he spat.

Cheers from the direction of the mercenaries grew louder. Armored horses approached and rattled to a halt outside. The tent flap was flung aside and two mercenaries entered, their eyes darting around to scope out any threat. They wore reasonably clean clothes and their hair was slicked down and neatly parted, like children forced to attend a civic function. It didn't make them look any friendlier.

They stepped to either side of the opening. One held the flap while the other gestured for someone outside to enter.

It was "Dread Ted" Medraft. He wore his Double Tarn knight show armor and stood stiff and proud. A boy carried the end of his bloodred cape so it wouldn't drag on the ground. Two more spit-polished mercenaries followed him in; the four soldiers took up positions at each of the corners.

Medraft frowned a bit at the coffin, but only momentarily. "Queen Jennifer, Sir Thomas," he said coolly. His gaze finally settled on Marcus. "King Marcus." No bowing or kneeling, not even a nod. "Or rather, Uncle Marc."

Marcus said nothing. Gillian stepped between the two men and said, "General Medraft, you're a traitor to your kingdom, and possibly to me. I challenge you to defend yourself."

He swung a glove to slap the younger man, but Medraft

blocked it with his forearm. "Don't be an idiot, Tommy. I don't know for sure if I'm your bastard or not, but this is not between you and I. It's about our lovely queen, and her attempted murder of one of our fellow knights. I'm here to see a trial by combat. Now where, I wonder, is the queen's champion?"

"Not so fast," I said, loud enough to get everyone's attention. This was the crowd I'd been waiting for. "Before anybody challenges anybody to anything, I have a story to tell you. You all know pieces of it, but only one person here knows it all."

"You, I suppose," Queen Jennifer said scornfully.

"Actually, no. But someone here does."

Then I spun, pulled my sword, and grabbed the boy who'd been holding Medraft's cape. I yanked him into the open, kicked his feet out from under him, and put the tip of my sword beneath his chin. I bent back his wrist to immobilize him. He lay still, flat on his back.

In drawing my sword I'd inadvertently slashed the tent's roof. A shaft of sunlight fell on the boy's face. I saw no fear, only rage and frustration.

"I think," I said coolly, "you should introduce yourself."

The tavern had grown chilly as I told my story. No one had stoked the fire, and it had died to almost nothing. My mouth was dry from all the talking, and my winter-chapped lips were starting to crack. I picked up my mug.

The crowd leaned in closer as if I might whisper the next part of the story. In the dead silence I heard the wind whistling outside. I'd never had so many eager faces turned my way, and it was kind of funny. The last of my ale bit at the raw spots on my lips, but it felt great going down my parched throat.

"And?" Gary finally prompted. I could see his breath.

"Yeah," Sharky added. "Who was the boy? Is he Kinder-mord?"

I held up my hand. "I'll get to it."

The room groaned its collective disapproval. Even Liz

rolled her eyes. I winked at her and grinned. "Somebody better get the fire going again before we all freeze to death," I added.

"So did you know then who did it, Mr. LaCrosse?" Sharky's daughter Minnow asked.

"Who did *what*?" said Emmett the fur trader. "Is this still about that knight who died?"

"That's the thing, it never really was," I assured him. "And I didn't know everything, but I knew most of it. By the time I got to the tent, I knew who did it, and why, and how. Although there was still one big surprise left."

"What was the secret Kern told you?" asked Mrs. Talbot, my landlady. She knitted winter tunics on the side, and her current project had grown considerably since I started my story.

"How did Marcus and Medraft really die?" Drucker the gambler demanded. "I mean, I know they *did* die that day, all the songs say so. Right?"

"And who is Kindermord?" Sharky said, sticking tenaciously to his question.

"I'll get to it all, I promise." Angelina put my fresh drink down on the counter so hard a third of it bounced up and splattered the wood. I picked it up and sipped it before adding, "So . . . has anyone figured it out yet?"

"Figured out *what*?" Gary demanded.

"Would it help if I told you I already met both the murderer of Sam Patrice *and* the mastermind of everything else before I left Nodlon Castle to go to Blithe Ward?" I said.

"What?" Callie said. "Why didn't you tell us?"

"Because I didn't know it myself at the time."

"The ballads all say it was Ted Medraft," she insisted. "He killed Marcus because he couldn't have Jennifer, but Marcus gave him a moral blow before he died."

"You mean a *mortal* blow, honey," Liz gently corrected.

"*I* bet it was that girl Iris," Angelina said.

"No, I will say that," I said, unable to keep the sadness from my voice. "It wasn't Iris."

"What gave it away?" Ralph demanded.

"The one absolutely impossible thing that happened," I said.

"Finding two identical Jennifers?" Gary guessed.

"No. That was unlikely, but it wasn't impossible."

Liz snapped her fingers and said, "Your hand healing so fast?"

"No. Although that *was* a clue. But it wasn't impossible."

"That stupid Lord Huckleberry thing actually working?" Angelina said.

I laughed. "I can see why you'd think so, but no."

Their eager faces now looked blank, and they exchanged puzzled glances.

"So the woman you called Dark Jenny is who's in the coffin outside," Angelina said without her usual disdain. Even she was now caught up in my story.

"No, don't jump ahead of me." I stood to stretch, and hands grabbed me to hold me in place, along with cries of protest.

"Hey, hey," Liz said, slapping the hands away. "Don't be rude, now. He'll finish it." She smiled at me the way a crocodile smiles at a calf drinking from the river. "Or at least he will if he knows what's good for him."

"I will, I promise. I just need to go upstairs for a minute and look at my notes again. This was complicated, and I want to make sure I get it all correct. It'll give everyone a chance to get fresh drinks. Not on me this time, though."

They grudgingly parted to let me visit my office. This time Liz followed, and I didn't protest. She closed the outer door after I lit the lamp and said, "You don't need to check your notes."

I sank into my chair. "No."

She perched on the edge of my desk and crossed her legs. "You're just not sure if you want to tell the whole story."

I took her hand. "How did you get this smart?"

"I'm not smart, I just know you. There's something you don't want everyone to know, and you're trying to think of a way to finish the story without including it."

I shrug-nodded. The danger of a smart girlfriend was that you couldn't easily fool her.

She leaned down to look in my eyes. The lamplight made her impossibly lovely. "Then tell *me*. I'll help you decide."

"I can't tell just you, they're waiting."

She got right in my face. "Let them. You don't owe them. For that matter, you don't owe me. But I would like to find out what happened, and I know you'd like to finish telling the story. So tell me, leave in everything, and then decide if you want to tell them."

After the kiss I said, "I'm sorry you had to hear about Iris."

"Long time ago," she said dismissively.

"You sure?"

"Positive."

I got my office bottle from my desk and poured us each a

drink. As we touched mugs, the impatient voices downstairs grew louder.

"Better make it quick," she said.

I agreed.

6 o to hell," the boy snarled as if he might bite me. Spittle collected at the corners of his mouth.

"Probably," I agreed. "But not today."

I moved the tip of my sword to his forehead and flicked it at his hairline. His hair came off, and Jennifer shrieked. Then she, and everyone else, realized it was just a wig. Long dark hair was pinned flat to his scalp.

I'm not sure I'd ever had a more dangerous captive. I moved the sword's tip to the front of his tunic, keeping the pressure on his bent wrist. "If you want to retain your modesty, you'd better be more cooperative."

The hatred in his eyes didn't change. But his face did, rippling and becoming more feminine as we all watched. It only took a moment before someone, in this case Marcus, exclaimed the obvious.

"Megan!"

To this day I'm not entirely sure how she did it. Common sense says it was simply a supreme actor's skill, combined with a moon priestess's knowledge of substances and the kind of hatred only the righteous can feel. But it could very well have been some kind of magical glamour, because her true face bore no resemblance to that of the boy she'd just pretended to be. She was a woman near forty, neither beautiful nor homely, but as Cameron Kern had originally said, someone you wouldn't look at twice. The perfect template for any disguise.

"Megan Drake," Bob Kay whispered in wonder.

"And Polly, the old lady by the road who patched you up," I said. "And Elaine at the Astolat tavern, who had all her teeth. And Rebecca, the queen's attendant."

"What?" Jennifer gasped. I could imagine her terror now.

Megan smiled. Her face changed again, to that of Rebecca. "Right under your nose, Marcus," she said in Rebecca's voice. "And you say there's no magic in Grand Bruan."

"And one more. Not a made-up identity this time, but a nice young serving girl named Mary who wore her prettiest dress to serve the queen." I kept the sword at her throat. "Add a few cosmetic bruises and no one could tell the difference. Especially with the real girl out of the way in the sewer."

"Let my mother go," Medraft said calmly. It was the kind of calm that made weak men flee.

"I'd sooner kiss a scorpion," I said. "Why don't you take your sword out—slowly—and give it to Bob. Then tell your men to get out."

He might've been discussing his boot laces. "And if I don't?"

I nicked Megan Drake's cheek. She gasped but didn't cry out. "Let's see your goddamned glamour hide that."

"Oh, my friend," Medraft said even more quietly, "that's a debt to be paid." But he took out his sword and placed it on the table beside the coffin with such deliberateness that it didn't make a sound. He nodded at his bodyguards, and they departed.

"Get his sword, Bob," I said. "Then tie this woman to a chair. Keep her hands where we can see them."

He did, using strips torn from the tablecloth, and I kept my sword at her throat until she was secure. I said to her, "If you say anything out of line, I'll gag you. If you try anything funny, I'll kill you. I mean it."

"I believe you," she said simply.

Now it was just me and a tent full of tense men and women trapped between two armies itching to go to battle for the fate of a kingdom. No pressure. I put away my sword and said, "I suppose you wonder why I've asked you all here."

Despite everything, Bob Kay loudly choked down a laugh.

"It's because I'm going to tell you a story," I continued. "If I get something wrong, I apologize. I wasn't there for some of it. But the broad strokes will be right.

"I'll start with what I know for certain. A few days ago, a poisoned apple ended up on a tray in the queen's possession. It was intended for Thomas Gillian. Before it got to him, though, a serving girl named Mary held it, and a new knight named Sam Patrice snatched it by mistake. He died in front of everyone in Nodlon. Some folks said the queen was responsible, some said I was. Neither was the case. I think we all know now who was behind it."

Gillian said to Megan, "You wanted to *kill* me?"

"No, I—"

"Not a word," I snapped at her. To Gillian I said, "Yes, she wanted to kill you, but that wasn't the main point. And once it all went south, three groups got involved, all working at cross-purposes. One was the nobility, desperate to exonerate the queen in order to preserve the status quo. They decided *I* was guilty. The second was the Knights of the Double Tarn, long suspicious of the queen's fidelity, and convinced *she* was guilty. The third was the king's exiled sister, her son, and a trio of disloyal knights trying to salvage their original plan."

No one said anything.

"My presence was what really screwed things up," I continued. "The attack had been aimed at Gillian, but Patrice, another knight, would do almost as well. And if I hadn't rushed to try and help Patrice, it might've still worked. Let that be a lesson about no good deed going unpunished. Then, when I started actually investigating things, the original plan had to be abandoned and covered up. That's when the second murder happened. The serving girl who held the poisoned apples was quietly killed and dumped in the drainage tunnel beneath the castle."

"She was?" Kay said in surprise. "We questioned her."

"No, we didn't. She was already dead. We questioned Megan here. She painted on some fake injuries and a lot of acting and fooled us both. She put the blame back on Jennifer by convincing us Agravaine tried to protect the queen. After all, why would a knight beat up a lowly kitchen girl if she didn't know something important? And we fell for it."

"How do you know all this?" Drake said coldly.

"Because when I found Mary's body *after* we'd supposedly talked to her, there wasn't a mark on her face. Not a scratch. Which was impossible. The only explanation was that we hadn't questioned Mary at all. And once I figured that out, I realized how closely Mary, and Rebecca, and Elaine all resembled each other. Same height, same size. So when I met Polly, I knew exactly who she was."

I let that sink in. Megan sat with her chin up, her eyes focused on nothing.

"So the queen was charged with treason, and once again my presence gummed things up," I continued. "Kay sent me to fetch Elliot Spears, which Megan wanted to avoid at all costs; after all, Spears was unbeatable on the field, and a victory would end the plan once and for all. Megan left Nodlon ahead of me and made it to Astolat, where she planned to meet her son and explain the new situation. He, meanwhile, had amassed an army that would arrive at Nodlon just in time to witness the queen's conviction and execution, catching King Marcus at his weakest point.

"When I got to Astolat before Medraft, she disguised herself as a poor tavern whore and tried to get me into a back room. Luckily I didn't fall for it, but I did see Medraft arrive, and the dust from his approaching troops.

"I got away and made it to Blithe Ward. Elliot set off for Nodlon, while I got another task: deliver something important to a safe hiding place. Thanks to Dave Agravaine and his pals, I failed at that." I grabbed Megan's chin and forced her to look up at me. "And that *pisses me off,* Princess."

"I'll shed a tear when I'm old," she said.

I released her contemptuously and resumed my story. "But I did kill Agravaine and his pals. They missed their rendez-vous, so Megan assumed Elliot had dealt with them. She disguised herself as Polly and waited to intercept Elliot on his way to Nodlon. She had a wounded Bob Kay to use as bait. It says a lot about her that she didn't trust an entire army of battle-hardened killers to deal with one man and felt the need to do it herself. But instead of Elliot arriving, *I* did, and she tagged along to learn what had happened. She probably would've killed me then, except she didn't know who was in the coffin. When we got close to Nodlon, she disappeared. Until now."

My fury rose as I looked at her again. "I knew it was you last night. I should've just killed you on the spot. Be glad I didn't." *Be glad,* I thought, *that Cameron Kern made me second-guess my instincts.*

Drake stepped between Megan and me, towering over us with his considerable regal presence. He touched her cheek, smearing the blood from my cut. "*You* should be glad you didn't, Mr. LaCrosse," he said quietly. "She's still a princess of the realm, and we'll settle this according to our codes of law. Untie her, Bob."

"I'm not done," I snarled, my temper barely under control. "We haven't gotten to Kindermord yet."

"This is not the place to discuss that," Drake said in the same soft voice.

"Oh, I think it is," Bob Kay said. Loudly.

Everyone looked at him.

"I've been hearing that name for years," he continued. "I overheard you and Kern talking about him, right before Kern stomped out of court. Every time I asked you who it was, you blew me off."

"It's never been the right time," Drake said, as calm as if discussing which fork to use for his salad.

"*Fuck* the right time!" Kay shouted. He gestured with the sword. "Do you know what your precious nephew's army has done? They've massacred everyone in their path. Men, women, children, even the goddamned farm animals!"

Marcus turned to Medraft. "Is this *true*?"

Medraft had no problem meeting the king's gaze. "Shock-and-awe is a well-known tactic, Uncle Marc. With the queen compromised, someone has to step in and keep order."

"Then your coup has already failed," Drake said. "The people will never trust you now."

"Sure they will," Kay spat. "Because he made sure the survivors knew it was all done in the name of good King Marcus Drake."

"They'd never believe that," Drake said.

"They will when they see the bodies," Medraft said coolly.

Drake turned away from Medraft. I couldn't see his face, but I saw Medraft smile. It was the most contemptuous expression I'd ever seen.

"So please, Eddie, tell us about this goddamned Kinder-mord," Kay finished. "Who the hell *is* he?"

"A secret identity," I said. "Megan's not the only Drake who pretends to be other people." I looked at her. "Right?"

"You told me not to speak," she said sullenly.

"Megan here has always been good at acting," I said. "And she's always hated her half brother for something his father allegedly did."

"Allegedly?" Megan spat. The veins in her neck stood out as she strained against her bonds. "My mother would never have willingly let him touch her. She was a priestess and a sworn wife, not some tavern whore! She deserved respect and admiration, not the brutality of some robber knight who happened to win a joust. None of you here even *knew* her!"

"She still carries a grudge, as you can see," I said. "It must've been awful back then, watching the seed of her mother's degradation claim the throne of Grand Bruan. So she played the ultimate trick on him, one night after a battle when the local girls were giving their all to the victorious forces of King Marcus."

I paused for effect, and to muster the resolve to say out loud something that had been kept secret for two decades. I wasn't sure who to look at when I said it, so like Megan Drake I just stared into nothing.

"In disguise, she seduced her own brother. And she got pregnant from it. Her own living, breathing trump card to play at the right moment in the future."

The tent was silent. Drake neither moved nor visibly reacted. The only noise came from outside: wind, clanking armor, distant voices.

At last a lone voice spoke. "So what are you saying?" Medraft asked in careful, measured words.

I'd thought there were no more surprises in this twisted tale, but I was wrong. Kern had told me only he, the king, and Megan knew about the seduction, but I'd assumed Megan had told Medraft, since he was both her son and her instrument of revenge. I'd guessed wrong.

When I didn't answer, Gillian spoke to Megan. "Yes, what exactly is he telling us?"

"It means," I said to Medraft, "your uncle is also your father."

Here was a tangled family knot, all right. Everyone in the tent except me was bound by blood at some level: mothers and sons, husbands and wives, brothers and sisters. And the fate of the kingdom was bound up in it as well.

"Cameron Kern found out the truth," I continued, as much to break the painful silence as to finish the story. "He knew Megan had gone to the moon priestess settlement in Smithwick to have the baby. This was before the edict that kicked them off the island. He told Marcus, hoping that the new king would make peace with his sister before word got out about what had happened. He arranged for Marcus to slip away, disguised as a merchant named Kindermord. But Marcus was still young, proud, and terrified his newly unified nation would find out the truth about him. So he panicked.

"One morning the good people of Smithwick awoke to find the moon priestess compound on fire. No one survived; oddly, no one even screamed or tried to escape, as if they were dead before the fire even started. Women, pregnant mothers, newborn babies, small children all died. Including, it was hoped, the king's sister and her son. But they somehow got away."

The tension made the air feel like thick gravy. At last a

lone, small voice spoke. Queen Jennifer said, "Marc, is this true?"

A tremor went through the big man. He never got the chance to answer because at that moment one of the knights outside called out, "It's Spears! Elliot Spears is coming!"

lliot's alive!" Jennifer exclaimed.

"You said he was dead," Drake said to Kay.

"*You* said he was dead," Kay said to me.

I was too surprised to reply.

"Clearly none of you know the great Elliot Spears," Medraft said ironically. "He can *never* die."

"Don't take your eyes off her," I told Bob. He nodded, Medraft's sword still in his hand, and stood behind Megan Drake. He placed the blade flat on her shoulder, its edge against her neck. She glared javelins at me.

I held back the tent flap so we could all see. Rattling down the hill the same way I'd come was a wooden hay cart pulled by a lone horse. The driver was indeed Elliot Spears, his tattered clothes revealing bandaged wounds even at this distance. In the cart were the bodies of at least half a dozen men, their limbs flopping as the rough wheels traversed the battered road. Unlike me, no one moved to block *his* path. A wave trailed and spread from him through the army, as the men realized who he was and stood to get a better view.

Spears stopped the cart beside my wagon. He winced as he stepped to the ground and looked back at the mercenary army. If he'd yelled, "Boo!" half of them would've fainted.

Spears saw me in the tent opening. "Mr. LaCrosse. I'm glad to see you safe. Things were more difficult than I expected. I got sidetracked."

"You don't know the half of it," I said.

"Elliot!" Drake cried as he strode from the tent. The two men embraced. I had a sudden flash of the question that every small boy on Grand Bruan must ask at some point: in a fight between these two great warriors, who would win?

"I can't tell you how happy I am to have you here," Drake continued.

"Since the pyre remains unlit, I assume I've arrived in time to fight for the queen's honor." Spears nodded at the mercenaries. "But what is all this?"

"Guess," Drake said.

"Medraft," Spears spat.

"Good to see you, too, General Spears," Medraft said as he sauntered from the tent. "We thought you weren't coming. The queen's guilt or innocence is now in your capable hands."

The look Spears gave the younger man could've melted rock. "Yes, despite your best efforts, I am here. Next time send better assassins."

"*My* best efforts?" Medraft shot back. "I'm only interested in justice. If the queen's integrity is compromised, then it's a threat to the whole kingdom. My army is here simply to maintain order." He nodded at the corpses in the cart. "I have no idea who those men are. Or rather, were."

Spears ignored him and looked at me. "Did you do as I asked?"

The look in his eye reminded me of those dogs that appear blasé and indolent until their master orders them to attack. I had no idea what would happen when he learned of Jenny's fate. It wasn't inconceivable that he'd blame—and take it out on—me. I said, "Yes."

Spears turned to Drake. "Then when do we begin the battle and clear out this trash?"

"We were just passing the time by discussing some events of the past," Medraft said. "Family stories I'd never heard before. They were quite compelling."

"No one was speaking to you," Spears snapped. "Enjoy the sensation of your head on your shoulders while you can."

Gillian emerged from the tent behind Drake. He said softly, "You're a rather large target, Your Majesty, for an archer out to make a name for himself."

I think at that moment Drake would've preferred wading naked into the opposing army to going back into that tent, but he nodded and led the way. I dropped the flap when we were all back inside.

Spears stopped dead. "Why is that coffin here?"

Protocol saved me from having to answer. "Elliot," Queen Jennifer said with relief; at the sound of her voice Spears immediately dropped to one knee and lowered his head.

"Forgive my rudeness, Your Majesty," he said. "I am your servant."

She offered her hand, and he kissed it, ignoring the cuffs around her wrists. "No forgiveness is necessary now that you're here."

Spears rose with a groan, favoring his right knee. Then he saw the woman tied to the chair, with Kay diligently guarding her. "Megan Drake," he said coldly. "I thought I sensed your vile hand in all this. If she is to be executed, Your Majesty, I beg the swinging of the blade."

"Go back to your own country, foreigner," Megan snapped.

"This is my country more than it will ever be yours," he fired back.

"I'm not sure any of us can claim the moral high ground here," Medraft said. "Mr. LaCrosse has been sharing some pretty interesting family secrets."

Spears frowned at me. "Such as?"

Oh boy. Nowhere to go but forward. "I was about to explain that there would've been no opportunity for this plot if there hadn't been gossip about the queen and you, Elliot. I can say with total certainty that it was unfounded. The queen was not unfaithful. The proof"—my mouth had gone dry— "is in that coffin."

Everyone looked at the box. Elliot froze, then with a cry of anguish pushed me aside and wrenched off the coffin's lid. He held it and stared at the apparent body of his Dark Jenny, the love for which he'd risked both his life and his honor.

"Elliot—," I began.

"*Silence!*" he yelled.

I didn't know what to do or say. I didn't know what would happen.

Queen Jennifer stepped forward, looked inside the coffin, and gasped.

Drake's eyes opened wide.

Megan strained to see.

Gillian and Bob Kay exchanged a confused look.

Spears made a strangled sound and stepped away from the coffin. Again there was that terrible instant where he seemed to grow larger and broader, as if his muscles could expand at will. Suddenly Marcus Drake did not seem like the biggest man in the tent.

The moment felt like the one between a flash of lightning and the crash of thunder.

I raised my hands for calm and said, "Nobody jump to conclusions. It's not what it looks like."

Spears *roared*. It's the only way to describe the sound he made. It mingled fury, agony, and outrage. He swung the coffin lid as if it weighed nothing. Even in the tent's impossibly confined space, he missed everyone but his target, Ted Medraft. "*You* did this!"

The wood cracked lengthwise from the impact against the side of Medraft's head. The would-be usurper spun in place and dropped without a sound.

"Teddy!" Megan cried, and strained with all her strength against the bonds holding her. Kay firmly held the chair. "That's my son, you foreign bastard!"

Spears looked down at the two halves of the broken lid, one in each hand.

Gillian stepped forward and put a hand on Spears's arm. Calmly he said, "Elliot, please—"

At the instant of contact Spears spun around with one half of the lid in his right hand like a blade. The broken, jagged edge slashed across Gillian's exposed throat, and for a moment I saw a ghastly cross-section of blood vessels, muscles, and windpipe.

Gillian's eyes opened wide and his hands rose to his neck. His fingers found the edge of the gash just as the blood started to surge forth. He fell back into the tent wall, clutched at the canvas, and slid to the ground. He died almost at once.

Queen Jennifer shrieked.

The sound snapped Spears back to reality. He looked down at the two halves of the coffin lid and threw them to the rug as if he didn't remember where they came from.

"I'm not dead yet, Mom," Medraft said woozily. Blood coursed down the side of his face, but he managed to get to his feet. He smiled and said drily, "The heir to the throne of Grand Bruan still lives."

That got Spears's attention. To Drake he said, "What does he mean by that?"

Medraft looked down at Gillian and shook his head. "Poor Tommy," he said flatly. Then he gingerly touched the gash under his hair. "Apparently not only is King Marc my uncle—"

"Stop!" Queen Jennifer said. Her voice had an assertiveness I hadn't heard before, and it got everyone's attention. She looked at us with an authority that easily overwhelmed her plain dress and shackles. "Just . . . stop, all right? All we've heard are wild accusations, with no proof. Including this woman in the coffin, whoever she is." I caught her momentary look of pleading desperation toward Spears. *Please go along.*

Please don't give away the truth. "It's clearly just more of Megan's attempts to drive wedges between us, just like the absurd charge against me."

Spears looked at his hands as if they'd been acting on their own, then shook his head. "No, Your Majesty. It's time to be truthful."

"Oh, God, not more truth," Kay muttered.

Spears turned to Drake. The king had not moved during the quick fight, and now he stared dully at Gillian's corpse. I could well imagine he felt overwhelmed. It took a moment for him to realize Spears wanted his attention.

"Your Majesty, I must speak. The queen is innocent of the charges against her, as I'm sure you realize. She and I have never been intimate. But I *have* been party to treason and betrayal. I ask no mercy for myself, just that you look mercifully on my fellow conspirators."

The words took a long time to register on Drake. "I'm sorry, Elliot, you said . . . what?"

It was my last chance to salvage something here. I said loudly, "Elliot, before you say anything else, please give me a moment."

Avoiding any sudden movements, I went around Spears and bent over the coffin. He grabbed my arm in a grip like a blacksmith's tongs and jerked me back. "Do not touch her," he commanded.

The pain revived my own temper. Who the hell were any of these fucked-up, low-down maniacs to tell me anything? I twisted free and snarled, "Or what? You'll cut my throat, too?"

His gaze slid to Gillian, and he swallowed hard. "My apologies. I am . . . wrought."

"Yeah," I said. I unstoppered Kern's second bottle and waved it under Jenny's nose. I didn't catch any odor from it, but almost at once her eyes popped open and she looked around disoriented.

I heard a sharp intake of breath behind me. I turned, but it wasn't Spears. Marcus had turned white as a sheet, and his eyes were bigger than I'd ever seen them.

"Elliot?" Dark Jenny asked hoarsely.

Spears pushed me aside so hard that if Drake hadn't caught me, I might've gone right through the tent wall. He swept her from the box and crushed her to him. "Jenny!" he cried with relief. "Oh, my God, I was so frightened, you don't know!"

He kissed her furiously. Drake stared in confusion, Bob Kay looked puzzled, and even Megan Drake seemed taken aback. Medraft ignored the whole thing, more interested in his bleeding scalp.

They broke the kiss. Jenny touched Spears's face with her fingertips and said, "Oh, my love, I wish this were the happy ending you deserve, but I don't have long. I was poisoned. I'll die soon. Cameron and Mr. LaCrosse fixed it so I could see you one last time."

"What?" Spears said numbly.

"I am dying," she said carefully. "Nothing can stop it. I want your face to be the last thing I see."

Spears now looked as blasted as Drake. Both men had taken their share of blows today. "How . . . how long?"

"I don't know." She closed her eyes and winced at a fresh wave of pain. "Not long, I suspect."

"Then we're leaving," he said, and turned toward the exit. "You will not die in this loathsome company."

"Wait!" she said, and looked around until she found Drake. "Your Majesty . . . dear Marc . . . I hope you understand. Elliot never betrayed you. I did, and my sister, but not him. He was your best and bravest, true to the end."

Drake said nothing. What could he say?

"You switched," Megan said almost in delight. "That fat bastard Kern helped you. You *switched*."

Spears turned to Megan. "I have broken my oath and slain a fellow knight, one who served his king with loyalty and valor. I am no longer worthy of my title. But if I find that you still breathe when she does not . . . ." He didn't finish the sentence, but carried Jenny out of the tent. A moment later we heard the hay cart clatter off. And as far as anyone knows, neither of them were ever seen or heard from again.

The tent was silent.

Finally Bob Kay spoke for us all. "Well, what the hell do we do *now*?"

"Obviously the king can't continue to rule Grand Bruan," Medraft said calmly, daubing at the blood on his face with a corner of his cape. "I don't know exactly what just happened with the queen and her apparent twin, but clearly the king doesn't, either. And once word of my parentage gets out—and it will—no one will look at him the same way again."

We all watched Drake. He remained silent. He hadn't physically shrunk, but his presence no longer dominated. He was like an image on glass, so insubstantial you could see through him if the light was right.

Medraft grinned as he continued, "Publicly I'm still his nephew, and the closest he's got to a legitimate heir. People will accept that. Not to mention I've got him outmanned five to one. Don't I . . . *Dad?*"

"You are a heartless monster," Queen Jennifer said.

"Oh, you tease," Medraft said mockingly. To Drake he said, "And I'll take her off your hands as well as the crown. It'll make the transition go more smoothly. No one else needs to know about that other woman in the box."

Drake just stared at him dully, mouth slightly open, no longer in the same place as the rest of us.

Jennifer stood protectively in front of Drake and hissed, "You will *never* touch me. And you will never be king of Grand Bruan."

"But he's my son," Drake said numbly, those four words giving long-sought legitimacy to everything Medraft, and his mother, wanted.

I don't know if my next act came from anger, exhaustion, moral outrage, or simply because I was fed up with everything to do with this stupid island. But I nudged Jennifer aside, stepped in front of Drake, looked him in the eye, and slapped him as hard as I could with my miraculously healed hand.

"Listen to yourself!" I yelled. "Act like a goddamn king, will you? So what if you made mistakes and did horrible things? There's an island full of people out there counting on you! You don't *get* to crap out!"

He stared at me.

I couldn't stop if I wanted to. I yanked Belacrux from its scabbard at his waist and waved it at him, barely registering its weight. "When you pulled this out of that goddamned tree, you knew you couldn't put it back! You signed up for the ride, now suit up and *get to work*!" I grabbed his wrist and pressed the sword's hilt into his palm. His fingers closed around it with no conviction.

Man, was I rolling now. "So what if you're outnumbered? You're fucking King Marcus Drake, and those are the god-damn Knights of the Double Tarn! You lead them up that hill, I guarantee three-fourths of those jackasses will turn and run at their first sight of you."

Drake stared at me, blinked as if waking from a dream, and said slowly, "You know . . . you're right."

He turned on his heel and with one thrust of his huge sword ran Medraft through.

Megan's scream will haunt my nightmares forever. *Every man was once someone's little baby and had a mother who probably loved him.*

For a moment father and son looked into each other's eyes. I wondered what common things they saw. Then Medraft slid off Belacrux's heavy blade to the floor of the tent.

"Teddy!" Megan wailed.

"Shut up," Drake snapped calmly. "Bob, put her in irons and have three men guard her. And gag her, too: her words are as dangerous as any man's sword."

"My pleasure," Kay said, and wrapped a strip of the table-cloth around her head, covering her mouth. She sobbed through it.

Drake knelt beside Gillian. A red arterial spray marked the tent wall where he'd fallen, and blood soaked the rug beneath him. "Sorry, Tommy," he murmured. "You were a good knight."

Then Drake turned to Jennifer. He produced a key and

unlocked the manacles at her wrists. They fell to the ground between them. He said, "When this is over, I expect an explanation as to why you changed places with the girl I fell in love with all those years ago." When Jennifer opened her mouth to speak, he said, "I'm not threatening you. You've been the best queen a king could ask for. Whatever else you've done, we can discuss in private, husband to wife. When this is finished." He grabbed her forcefully around the waist, pulled her close, and passionately kissed her.

Still holding her, he tossed back the tent flap and called to the nearest sentry knight, "General Medraft has killed General Gillian, and I've executed him for it. Get a funeral detail together. And summon the rest of my staff."

Then louder, in a voice that could make burning men proud to run into a fire, he cried, "And pass the word to prepare for battle!"

A cheer went up from the knights and spread through the ranks. In moments it became a chant: *"Drake! Drake! Drake!"*

The king dropped the flap, released his queen, and turned to me. "Thank you, Mr. LaCrosse. You've shown me my duty to my people and saved Grand Bruan. Is there anything I can grant you to show my gratitude?"

"Twenty-five gold pieces a day," I said with a little smile. "Plus expenses."

chapter

THIRTY-FOUR

The group clustered around me in the tavern stared in disbelief. The air was thick with the smell of burning wood from the restoked fire, spilled ale, and sweaty bodies. Outside the wind futilely sought entrance, and no doubt blew snow over the coffin.

Finally Angelina said, speaking for them all, "That's *it*?"

"That's it," I said.

"But . . . King Marcus *died* that day," Emmett, the fur trader, said. "There *was* a civil war. The island is a wasteland now."

"That's true."

"You mean Drake and Medraft didn't die at each other's hand, and Drake wasn't carried off to a magical castle by his sister and all the other secret moon priestesses?" Callie blurted.

"Nope."

She put her hands on her hips in outrage. "Then all Tony's ballads about him are *wrong*?"

"They're songs, sweetie, not news," Liz gently pointed out.

"Then how did Drake die?" Minnow Shavers asked.

"You know the old saying 'If it was a snake, it would've bit me'?" I said. "It *was* a snake. It *did* bite him."

"He died of a *snakebite*?" Gary Bunson practically shouted in disbelief.

I nodded. "Walking through the grass to mount his horse and lead the Knights of the Double Tarn into battle. It happened right after I left. There was no antidote to the poison. So you can see why the minstrels might need to spice it up a little."

I met Liz's steady gaze and saw her slight smile. This was exactly the reaction I told her I'd get if I told the truth. People don't want their heroes brought low by random, capricious fate. They want bold deaths, courageous sacrifices, bravery in the face of certain doom. They want the ballads and broadsheets.

I imagine the heroes wanted that as well.

Liz, of course, knew the true end of the story. Not that I'd lied about anything: what I told them is what really happened. But I left out a part that was too personal to narrate to a roomful of people. Only Liz had heard it, and she agreed that I could keep it to myself.

GILLIAN and Medraft were carried away for burial, and Megan Drake was dragged off to the dungeon. She met my gaze for a long moment as they took her out. I expected to see hatred, but there was only anguish. I guess "mother" came before "priestess" and "avenger."

When Drake's staff showed up to plan their attack, I slipped from the tent, exhausted and barely upright. Everywhere men in armor clattered to their tasks, and their sudden activity caused Medraft's mercenaries to prepare for battle as well, even without their commander. I leaned on my wagon and put my head down on my arms, grateful for a chance to close my eyes. I seemed to be the only still thing within miles.

Until I felt a light hand on my shoulder and a familiar voice said, "Eddie? Is that you?"

I raised my head. Iris Gladstone, in her white coat and carrying her bag, smiled at me. "I can't tell you," she said, "how happy I am to see you in one piece." She stepped toward me, lips already pursed for a welcoming kiss.

I put a hand out to stop her. "I'm too tired to slap you. But for the sake of this conversation, let's pretend I did."

She tossed her black bangs from her eyes and said, "What for, exactly?"

"Let's see. There's helping Megan Drake try to overthrow the kingdom to avenge her family honor, just because you and she share a religion. There's keeping me occupied so Megan could get to Astolat first and warn her son about how things had changed."

Iris looked down at the grass and chewed her lip thoughtfully. I could see she was deciding whether to confirm my accusations or try to deny them. She chose the honorable path, at least.

"It was more than just 'keeping you occupied,'" she said. "A lot more. You know that."

"Not enough more. But whatever. The real thing I'd like to slap you for is that you helped hide the murder of a young girl who did nothing but hold the wrong plate of apples at the wrong time."

She looked at me unapologetically. "Then go ahead and slap me. In fact, use the hand I fixed for you."

"Yes, you fixed my hand. By using moon-priestess magic at the same time you were calling it 'superstitious hocus-pocus.' A nice touch."

"You call it magic. What if it's just a science that you men just can't comprehend?"

"Same difference to me. So how many of you are on this island?"

She smiled with no warmth. "You think I'd tell you?"

I shook my head. "I really don't care, Iris. I've known a few moon priestesses, and none of them were as nutty as your bunch seems to be. Maybe it's just because you were taking orders from a lunatic like Megan Drake. But it's not my country, and not my problem. All I want to do is go somewhere else. Anywhere else."

She stepped closer and spoke with the urgency of the converted. "There's more at stake here than just Marcus Drake's pride, Eddie. The moon goddess doesn't insist on blind obedience. Megan Drake has her reasons, and I have mine. And if that girl had to be sacrificed so women all over this island can worship the moon goddess freely, then even though I regret it, I believe her death served a good cause."

"Did anybody *ask* her?"

She lowered her head and said nothing.

"Did you get your hands dirty and actually kill her, or just look the other way?"

Still nothing.

"I have one last question for you, then. You knew I'd been asked to get Elliot Spears. Why didn't you just kill me instead of stalling me so Megan could get out of Nodlon first?"

Iris peered up from beneath her bangs, and for an instant there was that jolt again, the one that said she and I were bound to connect. The memories of our night together rushed back with an urgency I didn't anticipate and hope I hid. I wouldn't count on it, though.

"Because I like you, Eddie. I couldn't stand Agravaine, even though he had his uses, and I appreciated you for what you did, and why. I decided on my own that you were worth saving." She bit her lip slightly. "You still have time to show me I made the right decision."

I laughed. Not the funny kind of laughing.

"Laugh if you want," she said. "In six months, this island could be a paradise where women are free to do as they please."

"Baby, in six months this island will be ankle deep in blood."

"Don't call me 'baby,'" she snapped. "I am a grown woman and a doctor."

"Yeah, you're also something else." But before I could tell her what, Bob Kay came out of the tent and joined us.

To Iris he said, "I hate to bother you, but could you take a look at my neck? I don't think it's too serious, but I'm not a doctor."

"Apparently neither am I," Iris said to him, but looking at me.

He looked from one of us to the other. "Am I missing something?"

I couldn't turn her in. She could've killed me and didn't. I owed her. But just this once.

"No, you're not missing anything, Bob," I said. "She'll fix you up." The last glimpse I had of her was following Bob Kay into the tent. She did not look back.

I climbed onto the wagon's seat, turned the horses toward the hill, and departed through the mercenary camp. The bustling swords-for-hire were too distracted by the Knights of the Double Tarn's visible battle preparations below to pay me any mind. I rode straight to Lady Astamore and gave her my report on her husband. Then I took the first ship leaving port and never set foot on that damned island again.

I don't know if including that bit would've made my listeners any happier, but they sure seemed cross with the ending they got. "That's the worst story I've ever heard," Sharky Shavers said. "And I work on the river, so I hear nothing but fish stories."

"Hey, I didn't *want* to tell it," I said. "You guys insisted."

"And he *did* buy a round of drinks," Liz pointed out. "So be nice."

"*I* liked it, Mr. LaCrosse," Callie said. "Except for the ending."

"Thank you." When I turned to put down my mug, I looked up at Angelina. "What did you think, Angie?"

She said nothing for a moment. Then, in a voice trembling with emotion, she said, "Ever since I heard about it, I always wanted to go to a place like Grand Bruan. I wanted to live under that kind of ruler, in that kind of kingdom. I wanted to believe there was a place where power was used for good to keep the weak safe." Her eyes shone with tears she fought mightily to restrain. "Thanks for setting the record straight for me, Eddie. We'll call it even on your tab. Callie, get your ass up here and pour some drinks." Angelina turned and rushed into the kitchen.

We all fell silent, and no one looked at anyone else. Liz silently took my hand. Callie went behind the bar and began refilling mugs.

At last Gary Bunson said, "Not to be a critic, but you still haven't told us who's in the coffin."

"Dark Jenny," Emmet said.

"Marcus Drake?" Callie asked almost hopefully.

"Elliot Spears," Minnow suggested.

"The real Queen Jennifer," Mrs. Talbot said.

"Nope," I said.

"Then who?" Gary demanded.

"Not *who*," I said. "*What*."

I t was spring before we made the trip.

"Are you sure it's around here?" Liz asked.

"You read the directions, too," I said.

"I'm not sure the directions can be trusted. Consider the source."

"The source brought me a sword in a coffin in the middle of winter and asked me to return it to its home. Seems counterproductive to give me the wrong map."

It was a lovely day on Grand Bruan, and the trees—the ones that hadn't been burned down—were in the last stages of budding out. Birds sang in the branches, and wildflowers bloomed. Bees and insects frolicked. If you ignored the abandoned towns, destroyed farms, empty roads, and occasional skeletons, it was a beautiful place.

It had not been easy getting here. No boats other than

raiders and treasure hunters made the trip. No reliable information about the political situation reached the mainland.
The consensus was that the island had devolved back into
warring clans and factions, and you crossed borders at your
own considerable risk. The heroes of Marcus Drake's reign
were either dead or missing.

Yet here I was. Or rather, here *we* were, because Liz ada-
mantly refused to let me go by myself. She claimed it was a
combination of curiosity and loyalty, although I think a little
jealousy might've been involved. Liz wanted to make sure Iris
Gladstone didn't get another shot at me. In any sense.

Then again, perhaps that was just my male pride. Liz wasn't
the jealous type.

So we found a small ship willing to drop us off and return
in a week to pick us up. The captain came recommended by
Sharky Shavers, so I was reasonably sure we wouldn't be ma-
rooned.

We landed with our horses, our bags, and our treasure
from the coffin, which I'd carefully disguised as just another
sword. I had no desire to visit Nodlon or Blithe Ward, but
Cameron Kern's cottage was abandoned when we found it
and had been for some time. There was a grave beside it, but
the marker had been destroyed so I wasn't sure if it was Kern,
Amelia, or someone else entirely. The entrance to the Crystal
Cave was blocked by a rockfall. Even that dream had been
destroyed.

The note Megan Drake gave me that snowy day in Neceda
told me where to find the tree where young Marcus first
drew Belacrux and claimed the Grand Bruan throne. The
trail through the forest was overgrown now but still visible; I

was more worried about a possible ambush by bandits than losing our way. And, of course, I kept an eye out for any snakes. But bandits only operated where there were likely victims, and this part of the forest held none. Only ghosts wandered here, and they carried no gold.

A square monument stone said UPON THIS SPOT KING MARCUS DRAKE STOOD TO WITHDRAW BELACRUX FROM THE ANCIENT OAK. Scrawled over this was graffiti that suggested Marcus Drake go have sex with himself.

The tree it marked was much larger than any of the others we'd seen in the forest: its trunk was a good twenty feet in diameter, and its branches rose higher than those of any other trees around it. They were gnarled with age, but their leaves were fresh and vibrant.

Carvings of distorted faces marked the four cardinal directions on the trunk. One large root bore a worn spot where generations of pretenders to the throne had stepped when they tried to claim Belacrux for themselves. I wondered just how many warlords, minor nobles, criminals, and commoners had placed a foot on that root, wrapped their hands around the sword's hilt, and pulled with all their might. Then I wondered how Kern had arranged it so only Marcus could actually do it.

Liz stood with her arms folded, taking it all in. "So it all started here."

"No, it started when Drake's father and Megan's mother got together. It just went public here."

"Why did she take the same name, I wonder?"

"Who?"

"Megan Drake. If she and King Marcus had different fathers, why did they have the same surname?"

"I'll tell you a bigger irony. She *also* had sex with the island's king, under circumstances that could be considered rape, except she was the rapist. I wonder if she ever thought she might be retracing her mother's footsteps in reverse?"

"That's a very male perspective."

"And it always will be."

I withdrew Belacrux from my saddle scabbard. I felt its weight in my shoulder and lower back. It was its own best disguise: the world imagined it as bejeweled and spotless, so no one thought twice about a large, clearly battered weapon.

It shone in a shaft of sunlight filtering through the branches, the nicks on the blade flashing like sparks. I remembered the winter day when I'd retrieved it from the coffin and brought it into Angelina's. When I raised it so the firelight blazed along the blade, my audience collectively gasped, and Callie put their thoughts into a single heartfelt word: *"Wow."*

I'd resisted the urge to polish and sharpen it, as well as to keep it for myself. Someone might recognize it: Grand Bruan refugees had now spread throughout the world. Really, though, deep down I knew that Megan's request was its only possible fate, even if complying with it meant considerable risk.

From what you told Marcus that day in the tent, I know you understood the dream, her note said, *and why it failed. Maybe the next dreamer who draws this thing can make the dream come true. For everyone.*

Liz stood on tiptoe and examined the tree. "I think it goes here," she said, and slid her fingers into a vertical slit roughly the width of the blade.

Then with a shriek she jumped back, waving at the cloud that surged forth. "Bees! *Bees!*"

I helped her swat them away and we fell laughing to the grass on the other side of the clearing. We waited until the angry insects calmed down, then I snuck up and put the tip of the sword into the opening. I pushed it in and ran back in case more bees appeared. But none did.

"Well, that's it," Liz said.

"Not quite. I still have to check it."

"Check it?"

"Yeah, you know."

She shook her head. "Boys."

I put my foot on the root where so many others had stood, wrapped my hand around the hilt, and pulled. Hard.

The sword that had moments before slid in like butter now refused to budge.

I shifted my grip and braced one foot on the tree's trunk for leverage.

"That's cheating," Liz observed.

I tried again. The sword remained immobile.

I rejoined Liz and put my arm around her shoulders. The wind ruffling the branches made the sun dance around the sword like little fairies of light. It must've looked like this when Marcus Drake first approached it as a boy, guided by Cameron Kern toward a destiny that had consumed him. Now it awaited the next Marcus Drake, who would hopefully be older, smarter, and better able to resist his own darkness.

The future king, once again.

Or something like that.

Turn the page for a preview of

𝔚𝔞𝔨𝔢 𝔬𝔣 𝔱𝔥𝔢 𝔅𝔩𝔬𝔬𝔡𝔶 𝔄𝔫𝔤𝔢𝔩

ALEX BLEDSOE

Available in July 2012
from Tom Doherty Associates

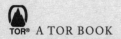 A TOR BOOK

Shawano was six days' ride from Watchorn. For a guy looking for a pirate, I was spending an awful lot of time in the saddle.

Two nights we stayed at inns, but the rest we camped along the way. The third night I spotted another fire behind us, and crept back to check it out. Granted, it could have been anyone who happened to be going the same way, but the hackles on my neck told me otherwise. By the time I got there, the fire was out and the camp abandoned. Whoever it was didn't show themselves again.

The prison outside Mosinee, capital city of Shawano, was known as "the pirates' graveyard," because if a pirate was captured and not executed, he ended up here. After a few weeks in this facility, most pirates would welcome being hanged, their tarred corpses displayed as a warning. The prison was smack in the middle of a stretch of desert, isolated by a range of low mountains. On the other side of these slopes stretched miles of verdant countryside leading down to Mosinee and the ocean. Here, though, there was nothing but heat, dryness, and death. For a man of the sea, there could be no closer approximation to hell.

Only one road led to the pirates' graveyard, and it ran straight across the open desert. This made sense tactically, since no one could approach without being seen. I'd picked up a wide-brimmed straw hat for the occasion, but this early in the morning, it wasn't needed. Some weird weather inversion had drawn moisture across the mountains and bathed the area in a heavy mist. It wouldn't last, but while it did, the temperature was almost pleasant.

Queen Remy of Mosinee led the international coalition that supported and funded the Anti-Freebootery Guild. Her goal was to make it more lucrative for these sea bandits to turn honest than to keep raiding ships, and it worked for a lot of them. I didn't know the exact circumstances that turned Jane from pirate to pirate hunter, but she became as legendary fighting on the right side as she had on the wrong. I also didn't know what had caused her to leave the sea entirely and turn landbound sword jockey, but I could accept that none of it was my business. She never asked where I'd come from, either.

The prison walls were twenty feet high, with guards stationed at each corner. The only thing that rose higher was a single round tower, stretching into the mist so that we couldn't see the top. Jane looked up at the tower and sighed wistfully.

"Sentimental about prison?" I teased.

"About my old job. Rody Hawk was the toughest son of a

bitch I ever crossed blades with. When they sent me out to find him, I almost peed my pants, both because I was excited and because it scared me to death. For the first three weeks I hunted him, I was afraid he might be a ghost, the way he'd appear and disappear, like he was taunting me. Which he was."

She'd shared many stories of the man known as "the Sea Hawk" on our ride. If only a fraction of them were true, I was very glad he was locked up. "He knew you were after him?"

"He knew *everything* about me," she said distantly, then came back to the moment. "He was a mean bastard anyway, but he got much worse when he heard I was after him. Like he was trying to pack in all the evil he could while he still had time."

"Really?" I said. Jane wasn't above a little self-aggrandizement, but something in her tone told me she wasn't doing that here. Her intensity sounded almost religious.

"Yeah. I found one ship he'd hit, a little merchant vessel carrying settlers along with a cargo of rum. He killed the crew, then tied all the civilian men together around the mast. He hung the women and children by their ankles and drilled tiny little holes in their foreheads, so they'd rain blood down on their husbands and fathers. We heard the screams across the water before we even sighted the sails." She shook her head. "Not many of the hanging ones lived. And a lot of the men forced to watch died by their own hand before we reached port."

"I'm glad you finally caught him," I agreed. We were close enough now to see the archers along the wall, and the long curves of their bows. They watched us with the silent composure of men secure in their profession.

Jane said, "Do you know what the hardest thing about catching him was, though?"

"What?"

"Leaving him alive when I had him under my sword."

I knew that feeling for sure. The fact that she *did* leave him alive reinforced my opinion of her. "And now where do they keep him?"

She pointed at the tower. "Up there. Permanently. No way in, no way out, and no visitors until he tells where his treasure's hidden, or dies."

"Then how do we talk to him?"

"Don't worry," she said. But she didn't explain.

We tied our horses to the empty hitching post outside the gate. Behind us, only our tracks disturbed the sand. I couldn't imagine they got many visitors. A guard in leather armor watched us through the gate's thick iron bars.

"Hey, Louie," Jane said as she shook dirt and sand from her cape. "How's tricks?"

"Same as always, Captain Argo," Louie the guard said. He spoke to her but kept his eyes on me.

"I'm not a captain anymore, Louie, just a plain Jane. But we *are* here to see the Hawk."

Louie pondered this. "I'll have to get the warden."

"You do that," she said.

The whole area was silent, except for a lone crow cawing somewhere in the mist overhead. Given the absence of trees, it must nest somewhere on the grounds. I asked quietly, "You ever been in prison?"

"Nope. If I get arrested, I try not to stick around for the trial."

"Me, neither." I'd been in jail on occasion, but never served a real sentence. Standing here in this ghostly silence, I suddenly wondered if I'd be man enough to handle it. I hoped never to find out.

Louie returned with another man, this one in an official uniform. "Good morning, Captain Argo," the newcomer said. "I hadn't heard you were coming."

"There wasn't time to send a message ahead. Hope that's okay."

"Well, we do have protocols for visiting the prisoners, especially *him.*"

"I know. I came up with them, remember?"

"I do, but it puts me in an awkward position."

Jane leaned casually on the iron bars. "Warden, really. You think I'm here to bust him out?"

"I think we have rules for a reason, Captain."

"She's not a captain anymore, sir," Louie said helpfully.

"That's true," Jane agreed. "I'm just here to visit a friend."

The warden smiled a little. "So he's your friend now, is he?"

Jane laughed. "Warden, in some ways I'm closer to Rody Hawk than to just about anybody else in the world."

The warden nodded at me. "Including him?"

I stepped forward. "Eddie LaCrosse. I'm a business associate of ex-Captain Argo."

"Warden Jim Delvie," he said as we shook hands through the bars. It was firm enough, but the skin was smooth. The warden had been pushing a quill so long that any sword calluses had faded.

"Warden, either let us in or send us on our way," Jane said impatiently. "Which in my case will be straight to the court of

Queen Remy to get permission to visit the Hawk. You know she'll give it to me. And you know what she'll say when I explain why I have to bother her with it."

The warden thought this over, then turned to Louie. "Open up."

"Yes, sir," Louie said.

Through the gate there was nothing but more open space around the main jail building and celebrity tower. The ground was hard and cracked, with no grass anywhere. The building rose only one floor above the ground, well below the top edge of the outer walls. Most of its cells were deep under the hardpacked earth.

Jane turned to me. "So who talks to him, me or you?"

"We can't both do it?"

"No. Only one of us. Less risk that way."

"Risk of what?"

"He has this knack of turning people against each other."

I looked up at the tower, or at least the part of it not hidden in the mist. "I suppose I should do it. It's my case, after all."

"Are you sure? I know him."

"I'm sure."

She grinned. "You want to be able to tell Liz that you met Rody Hawk, is that it?"

I ignored the dig and looked at Delvie. The warden asked, "So who's it going to be?"

"Me," I said.

Delvie and Jane exchanged a look I couldn't interpret. He asked her, "Are you all right with this?"

She shrugged. "He's paying me, so he's the boss."

The warden turned to me. "Have you had any prior dealings with Captain Hawk?"

"No."

That seemed to satisfy him, if barely. "Follow me, please."

He led us to the base of the tower. As we crossed the courtyard, a door opened in the main building and six pale, grimy men chained together at the neck were marched out by an equal number of guards. The prisoners were naked, but their bodies were so filthy, I first thought they wore black pajamas. Their smell stayed behind long after they'd disappeared around the corner.

"Monthly cell-block washdown," the warden explained. "They get rinsed off, then they clean their own cells."

One of the prisoners turned and looked at us. His face was long and thin, and one eye socket was puckered shut. There seemed very little humanity left in his gaze, just the numb survival instinct of a clever animal.

When we reached the base of the tower, Delvie gestured at something on the ground. "Well, here we are. Your chariot to the clouds."

A wooden basket about three feet across rested there, attached by a rope to a pulley mounted, I assumed, at the edge of the tower's roof. I looked at it, then at the warden, then at Jane. She bit her lip and looked down to keep from laughing.

"This is how we get his food up to him," the warden said. "If you want to talk to him, it's the only way up." He turned to Louie. "Go get some men to help lift this. A dozen would be good. Check the break room."

"Yes, sir," Louie said, and went into the main building.

I continued to look at Jane. "You've got to be kidding. It's a picnic basket."

With mock camaraderie, Jane punched me in the arm and said, "Come on, Eddie, you're not afraid of heights, are you?"

"No, but I'm a lot bigger than a loaf of bread."

"It'll hold you."

"Says you."

"No, she's right," Delvie assured me. "The balance is a little tricky, but it should bear your weight just fine."

"Do I sit in it?"

"You're better off standing."

"Fine," I said, making no effort to hide my annoyance. Jane could've mentioned this earlier.

"You sure you don't want me to do it?" she said.

"No, damn it," I muttered.

"I'll need your sword," the warden said. "And all your other weapons. And anything that might remotely be used as a weapon."

"I'm not going to hurt him," I said.

Delvie stepped close. I could smell his morning tea on his breath. He said, "We used to send a guard up with the food, in case he cracked and started blabbering. This was back when we seriously thought he might tell us where his treasure was hidden. For a year, nothing happened. Then one day Hawk yanked him out of the basket and held him against the window bars. He threw the guard's sword down, impaling another guard, then killed another with the first guard's crossbow. One-handed, mind you, while still supporting the guard's weight with the other arm. Then he dropped the man to his death." He pointed at a spot on the hard-packed ground that was darker than the surrounding dirt. "He landed right there. You can see that the stain still hasn't worn off."

"The point is, he could've done it at any time," Jane added. "He just picked that day, and that guard. He never said why. So now no one ever sees him. They just send up his food."

"Then how do you know he's even still up there?"

"The basket always comes down empty." He paused, stepped even closer to me, and said in a grim whisper, "Hawk's been called many things over the years, but you know what captures him best, in my opinion? That he's simply a shiver looking for a spine to run up. If you still wish to see him, then I won't stop you."

I looked into the mist. I wondered if Hawk could hear us discussing his exploits. More important, how would I convince him to help me if he didn't want to? What could I possibly offer him? I hadn't put any thought into that.

"You could keep a bigger basket around, you know," I pointed out as I unbuckled my sword belt. "For special occasions."

"I'll mention that at the next budget meeting," the warden said. Louie returned with the requested men, all of whom looked at me with a mix of respect and suspicion. They were big men, with the scars of former battles on their bare arms and faces. I suspected they were also one moral slip away from becoming inmates themselves. Luckily, all I needed them to do was have firm grips and strong backs.

"Yank the rope twice when you're ready to come down," the warden said.

As I started to step into the basket, Jane said, "The knife in your boot, too."

I glared at her. That knife had saved my life more than any other weapon I owned. But as I withdrew it, I suddenly knew what I could offer Hawk that might make him cooperate.

"Ow!" Jane cried. "What was that for?"

"Something to keep my courage up," I said. She took my knife and tucked it into her belt. I enjoyed her annoyed scowl.

I put one foot in the basket, then the other. The ropes from each corner joined at a waist-high iron ring, and above that a single rope led to the top of the tower. I grabbed that rope for dear life, the guards pulled, and I began to rise.

Immediately, I nearly fell back and the whole contraption spun as I fought to regain my balance. Jane laughed uproariously.

I rose into the mist. Jane and the guards disappeared below me, and for a few moments I was isolated in the haze, nothing visible above or below. There was absolutely no wind, and the faceless side of the tower made it hard to mark my progress. Only the squeak of the pulley above me, growing louder, assured me I was rising.

I passed a chink in the stonework where a huge black crow, the one I must've heard earlier, sat preening her feathers. She cawed once and regarded me with the same vague suspicion as the guard below. Even the wildlife knew I was doing something stupid.

Eventually the pulley stopped, and I hung in place outside a wide rectangular window. Vertical bars blocked it, and a heavy fishing net hung just inside them, making a double barrier. The room was painted bright white, even down to the window bars. Nothing moved, and of course in a round room, there were no corners to hide in. The combined net and mist made it difficult to see the dim interior, but I stared until I made out a cot, a chamber pot, and something on the floor.

I risked one hand on the bars to steady myself and called out, "Hey! Rody Hawk!"

There was no reply.

I pulled myself closer to the bars. The basket creaked and tilted as my weight shifted.

The sun chose that moment to flicker through the mist and momentarily flood the cell with light. The shape on the floor instantly resolved itself.

It was a body.

The man sprawled on his back. He was tall and slender, with long dark hair, a long beard, and a black eyepatch. He wore white trousers and a loose tunic, with no shoes.

The sun glinted off his exposed eye. It was wide open, and stared at nothing. I'd seen enough lifeless eyes to recognize this one at once.

"Son of a bitch," I muttered. Rody Hawk was dead.

Then a sepulchral voice commanded, "Don't talk about my mother."

Murder, betrayal, and magic—
just another day on the job for
sword jockey Eddie LaCrosse

Dark Jenny
Burn Me Deadly
The
Sword-Edged Blonde

Alex Bledsoe

"Bledsoe has written a compelling story with fascinating
characters—who are so witty and whose attitude is so
wry that I laughed *and* cared."
—Orson Scott Card on *The Sword-Edged Blonde*

★"Bledsoe effortlessly draws readers into his created world and
manages to stay true to both fantasy and mystery traditions."
—*Publishers Weekly* (starred review) on *Burn Me Deadly*

★"Bledsoe's clever combination of noir and myth makes for an
engaging story, and placing investigator Eddie at the center offers
a fresh twist.... Fans of Bledsoe's other blends of fantasy and noir
will love his latest, and new readers will be able to jump right in."
—*Booklist* (starred review) on *Dark Jenny*

Paperback / eBook   tor-forge.com TOR

In the valley of the Tufa, songs live...and kill.

THE
HUM
AND THE
SHIVER

Alex Bledsoe

"Haunting." —*The Wall Street Journal*

"A fascinating and absorbing
masterpiece of world-building."
—*Publishers Weekly*

★"Elegantly told." —*Library Journal* (starred review)

NO ONE KNOWS WHERE the Tufa came from, or how they ended up in the
mountains of East Tennessee. But there are clues in their music, hidden in
the songs they have passed down for generations. Private Bronwyn Hyatt,
a true daughter of the Tufa, has returned from Iraq, wounded in body and
spirit, and a restless "haint" has followed her home from the war. Worse
yet, Bronwyn has lost touch with herself and with the music that was
once a part of her. With death stalking her family, will she ever again join
in the song of her people, and let it lift her onto the night winds?

Trade Paperback / eBook   tor-forge.com